P9-CRQ-682

# The
# CHARMED RETURN

Also by Frewin Jones

The Faerie Path
The Lost Queen
The Seventh Daughter
(also published as The Sorcerer King)
The Immortal Realm
The Enchanted Quest
Warrior Princess
Destiny's Path
The Emerald Flame

# The
# CHARMED
# RETURN

Book Six *of The* FAERIE PATH

# FREWIN JONES

HARPER TEEN
An Imprint of HarperCollinsPublishers

HarperTeen is an imprint of HarperCollins Publishers.

The Charmed Return
Copyright © 2011 by Working Partners Limited
Series created by Working Partners Limited
All rights reserved. Printed in the United States of America.

Library of Congress Cataloging-in-Publication Data
Jones, Frewin.
The charmed return / Frewin Jones. — 1st ed.
p. cm. — (Faerie path; bk. 6)
Summary: Tania must appempt to return to the Faerie Realm in order to save her people
from a deadly menace.
ISBN 978-0-06-087161-1
[1. Fairies—Fiction. 2. Princess—Fiction. 3. Fantasy.] I. Title.
PZ7.J71Ch 2011                                                      2010019301
[Fic]—dc22                                                                 CIP
                                                                            AC

Typography by Al Cetta
11  12  13  14  15    CG/RRDB    10  9  8  7  6  5  4  3  2  1
❖
First Edition

*For Deena Omar*
*and Adrian Whittaker*

*Faeries tread the Faerie Path*
*A mind astray, a sundered soul that sleeps*
*A human heart to show the way*
*A Faerie love that faith and fealty keeps*

*An ancient foe holds deadly thrall*
*A word that's left unspoken on enchanted lips*
*The Family Royal heeds the faint and far-off call*
*All paths converge upon the Pure Eclipse*

# _The Story So Far . . ._

A savage plague is sweeping through Faerie, the Immortal Realm that has for thousands of years been free of illness. Suspicion over the cause of the outbreak falls on Tania's mortal parents, Clive and Mary Palmer. It's believed that they brought the deadly illness through from the Mortal World. Clive and Mary Palmer are banished, and half-Mortal Tania is put under close guard. The Conclave of Earls commands that the ways between the worlds be closed forever.

Before that can happen, and against the wishes of the King, Tania steps secretly into the Mortal World with her sister Rathina at her side. Tania's intention is to bring family friend Connor Estabrook, who is studying to be a doctor, back into Faerie in the hope that he can help her defeat the disease with his knowledge of modern medicine.

Upon her return, Lord Aldritch of Weir accuses Tania of bringing doom to Faerie. When Princess Eden learns that the sickness comes from Faerie itself, suspicions toward the Mortal World ease and Tania is free to find a cure.

But her relationship with her beloved Edric is under severe strain. He is meddling with the Dark Arts, and when she rejects his unexpected proposal of marriage, he tells Tania that he intends to return to his childhood home of Weir as a captain of Lord Aldritch's court.

Brokenhearted, Tania begins her quest without him, and she, Connor, and Rathina seek the submerged Lost Caer, a sunken fortress off the coast of Weir, where they hope to find word of a cure for the plague. Here, Tania and her companions learn that in the long-ago times, the people of Faerie were Mortal and winged. They also discover that this is not the first time the plague has fallen upon them.

A mysterious entity calling herself the Dream Weaver tells them of a time when Oberon traveled to Tirnanog and made a covenant with the Divine Harper that gave the folk of Faerie the gift of Immortality in exchange for their wings. This covenant was broken when the Sorcerer King of Lyonesse temporarily took the throne of Faerie from Oberon. The breaking of the covenant has allowed an ancient enemy known only by the name Nargostrond to return. Nargostrond is working his evil again in the land, and now Tania, Rathina, and Connor must travel across the Western Ocean and seek the mythical land of Tirnanog to renew the covenant of Immortality and to bring Nargostrond's plague to an end.

Tania communicates with Queen Titania through a water-mirror and learns that a Great Spell is being cast that will cover all of Faerie in a shield of Gildensleep. Faerie will slumber while Tania quests for the Divine Harper, and the plague will not prevail while the Royal Family can keep the mystic shield active.

The travelers take a boat across the Western Ocean. The Dream Weaver speaks through Rathina again, telling Tania that now that she is beyond the shores of Faerie, her power to walk between the worlds has returned to her. They sail on, but before they make landfall in Alba, they are accosted by the pirate Lord Balor. Tania and Rathina make their escape when Tania sidesteps into the Mortal World, but Connor is left behind, a captive of the pirates.

In the Mortal World Tania and Rathina meet a strange man and woman who seem to have some sense of who they are and what they mean to do, and who offer them help. Tania sidesteps back into Alba, and the sisters manage to penetrate the dark castle of Lord Balor. Connor is in a dungeon, being threatened by Lord Balor, who is accompanied by a great white salamander. The sisters overhear Connor agree to betray them and help Lord Balor discover the secret of Immortality, but they are sure he does this only to stave off torture.

They rescue Connor from the dark castle and flee across Alba to a safe haven: the palace of Caiseal an Fenodree, the home of Queen Titania's ancient Mortal family. Here they are shocked to encounter Edric, who has tracked Tania by the use of the Dark Arts. He tells her he knows how to make her whole again: either entirely Mortal or entirely Faerie. But Tania cannot accept this offer; she needs both of her sundered selves to do her duty and finish the quest.

Learning that Lord Balor is in close pursuit, the travelers flee the castle of Fenodree, accompanied by Edric, who has promised Tania never to use the Dark Arts again. There is distrust between Connor and Edric, and Tania is stretched to prevent conflict from erupting as they enter the enchanted realm of Erin.

They find that Erin is a land without rhyme or reason. Insane sorceries swirl around them, and they can find no way out of the realm until Edric seeks a path by using the deadly Dark Arts once more. But his Arts draw the Green Lady to them: the Enchantress who holds this entire realm in thrall. Edric is stolen away by the Green Lady, and it is up to Tania to find and rescue him.

Tania survives the trials and magicks of the Green Lady, and upon mystical horses the travelers make their way across dragon-haunted Hy Brassail to the far coast, where they expect to find the land of Tirnanog.

Instead, they are ambushed by Lord Balor. Tania learns that Connor has been working for the sinister lord all along—keeping in contact with him and guiding him to them in exchange for a promise of wealth and fame in the Mortal World.

Tania overpowers Lord Balor and the Great Salamander is set free. The liberated Salamander tears Tania's back open. Wings grow from her wounds, and she flies to Tirnanog. She meets the man and woman who befriended her in the Mortal World, and they take her to the Divine Harper.

But the Divine Harper asks a great price for the information Tania seeks: She must give up the deepest wish of her heart. Tania agrees, although she is sure this will mean the loss of Edric's love. Now she learns some of the truth. Nargostrond, the plague-bringer, is King Oberon's older brother, Prince Lear, banished thousands of years ago for his evil ways and his desires of conquest, both of Faerie and the Mortal World.

But even while Tania is trying to grasp the full dread of this revelation, the Divine Harper exacts the price for her enlightenment and Tania falls into deep unconsciousness.

# Part One:

## Just Another Girl from Camden Town

# *I*

Anita Palmer sat up on her bed, blinking and disoriented.

She felt drowsy and woozy, but outside the open curtains she could see that it was still daylight.

And on top of that, she was fully dressed.

What had she been thinking, napping in the middle of the day? What was she, a doddering old granny or something?

She got up, dizzy for a moment. "I've got to tell Jade about that dream!" she said, grinning and heading for the computer. "She'll freak out."

She sat down, still rubbing the sleep out of her eyes as she turned on the computer and connected to the internet. And Evan—she'd have to tell him, too. He'd be well impressed; he was totally up for freaky things like that: legends and mythology and all that kind of . . . strange . . . old . . .

"Now that's bizarre," she said, the chat room open, her fingers poised over the keyboard.

The dream had gone. It had been so vivid—but now she couldn't remember a single thing about it.

*Weird!*

She yawned and stretched, her head still foggy. She looked at the time display at the bottom of the screen: 11:09.

Midmorning. But what day was it? Saturday or Sunday?

"Oh, great," she said. "Now I don't even know what day of the week I'm in! Losing my marbles or what?"

She got up and wandered out of her room, still feeling odd. She clattered down the stairs and turned in the hall, heading for the kitchen.

Her mum was there, at the table, packing her handbag.

Yawning still, Anita strolled in. "Hi, Mum," she said. "What's up?"

Her mother jumped—then stared at her—a huge smile breaking out across her face. "Tania!" She gasped, running and throwing her arms around her. "Oh, sweetheart, it's so wonderful to see you! And your dad will be so pleased. We thought we might never see you again!"

Anita stared at her, taken completely aback—half stifled by her mother's frantic embrace.

"What are you talking about, Mum?" she asked. "I was only upstairs." She stared at her mother, completely baffled by this sudden display of affection. "And who on earth is *Tania*?"

Her mother took a half step back, her hands still

gripping Anita's shoulders, her face still showing relief
and joy. But why? Why the *relief*? Why the big deal?
What was going on?

Anita let out a breath of bewildered laughter.

"Mum, what's with you?" She frowned. "Has someone died or something?"

"Tania! That's not funny."

"It wasn't meant to be."

"How are things in Faerie?"

"*What?*"

"The plague, sweetheart. Is it still spreading?"
Anxiety creased her mother's brow. "Oh dear god, tell
me it isn't. Tell me they've found a cure."

Anita stepped back, her hands up as if to ward
her mother off. "I've only just woken up, Mum—my
brain's too fuzzy for this kind of thing. How long was
I asleep?"

"You were sleeping?"

"Yes. I was flat out on my bed."

"You came through from Faerie in your sleep?"
Mary Palmer shook her head. "I didn't know you could
do that."

"Okay, now. Stop this. I feel weird enough already,
thanks. But if you're trying to freak me out for some
reason, well done: mission accomplished."

"Tania . . . ?"

"Stop it!" Anita snapped. "Stop *calling* me that!"

Confusion filled her mother's face. "Anita?" she
murmured.

"Yes! Yes, Anita." Her voice dripped sarcasm. "Your

daughter, Anita. I live here, remember?" She peered into her mother's eyes. "Hey, you're not going batty on me, are you, Mum?" She gave her mother a crooked half-smile, hoping a joke might click things back into place.

"Anita . . ." Her mother's voice was only just above a whisper. "Not Tania anymore . . ."

A sick, heavy feeling began to grow in Anita's stomach. Was her mother ill? Was there actually something wrong with her inside her head?

Her mother sat down heavily, her face pale and blank, her fingers gripping the edge of the table.

Not funny. Not even remotely funny.

"I'll get you a drink." Anita snatched up a glass from the draining board and reached for the water tap.

"No!" Her mother surged up, dragging at Anita's arm as she turned on the chrome tap. "You'll hurt yourself!"

Anita dropped the glass and it shattered in the sink. The water splashed over her arm.

"Mum!"

"The metal will burn your hand!"

"Mum, please stop saying these things. You're frightening me."

Her mother wrenched Anita's hand off the tap and twisted it palm upward. She stared at it for a second before Anita pulled free, the edge of the sink unit sharp in the small of her back, her mother pressed against her.

"Your hand didn't burn."

"No, of course not." Anita forced some calm into her voice. If there was really something wrong with her mother, Anita needed to keep a level head until she could get help. "I'm fine." She held her palm up to her mother's face. "See? No burns. Everything the way it should be." *Get help!* "Uh. Where's Dad?"

Her mother raised her hands to her face. "Oh! You don't know, do you? He's in hospital. But don't worry—he's fine."

"In *hospital*?"

"Yes. He's been in there for a few days. Under observation and getting fluids and so on. But he's fine, really. Completely on the mend. It was a touch of pneumonia, but he's over it. I was just getting ready to go and pick him up when you . . . when you arrived . . ."

Panicking was not an option. Anita locked the fear away. She needed to be practical now.

"Mum, listen to me carefully, please," she said. "You're remembering stuff that isn't true. Dad hasn't been in hospital. Last time I saw him he was in the garden, mowing the lawn. That was this morning."

Anita wished Evan were here. He'd know what to do. Nothing ever rattled him.

Her mother looked into her eyes, the confusion suddenly gone. "What date do you think it is?" she asked.

"What date do I *think* it is?"

The familiar no-nonsense voice. "What's the *date*?"

"June tenth. Two days before my birthday."

There was a strange pause.

"Look at the calendar, sweetheart."

"Excuse me?"

Her mother pointed across the room to where the calendar hung on the wall. Anita looked over expecting to see scenes of the Cornish countryside. *Oh! Weird.* Not the picture she remembered from breakfast that morning. A new one. Some standing stones on green moorland.

Her eyes dropped to the grid of days.

August.

*August?*

"You've changed the calendar," Anita said. "Why did you do that?"

"It's not the tenth of June, sweetheart. It's August the fourteenth."

"No, it isn't. You're confused, Mum. Listen, sit down. I'll make you a nice cup of tea; how does that sound?"

Her mother seemed in control now. Confused but in control. "Do you remember the accident?" she asked.

"What accident?"

"On the river. With Edric."

"Who's Edric? Is that even a real name?"

A deep line formed between her mother's eyes. "With Evan, I meant."

"What about Evan? What *accident*?"

"Tania . . ."

"No, Mum. *Anita* . . ."

"Yes, sorry. Anita, of course." This was so weird.

Apart from the things she was saying, her mum seemed perfectly okay now—perfectly rational. "What's the last thing you remember?"

*Humor her. While she's calm, just go along with things till you can get help.*

"The last thing?" Anita cast her mind back. Waking up on her bed a few minutes ago. But before that? A kaleidoscope of images wheeled across her mind. Most of them contained images of Evan Thomas.

Rehearsals for the school play, *Romeo and Juliet.* Evan as Romeo and she as his Juliet. So romantic! Except that in the play the two lovers wound up dead. That wasn't quite so cool. What else? Oh, chatting to Jade about the computer Anita hoped her folks were going to get her for her sixteenth. Googling the words "investigative journalist" as a possible career path. The trip to Hampton Court where she'd met Evan. Their first kiss. That had been when he had told her she had gold dust in her eyes. Then there was the second kiss. His brown eyes closing. The touch of his fingers in her hair.

His big secret! Yesterday he had told her he'd arranged something exciting for her birthday, but he wouldn't tell her what. She wondered if he was planning on taking her somewhere special—somewhere where he would tell her he loved her . . .

. . . and *that* idea still made her tingle from head to toe.

"Anita?"

Her mother's voice snapped her back into reality.

"I don't know what I remember last," Anita said. "Being in my room, I guess." Except she didn't remember being in her room . . . not before waking up. There was a white void in her head where that memory should be.

Her mother took her hand. "You've forgotten," she said. "You've forgotten it all. The accident. Everything."

"I don't like this," Anita said, uneasy now. "What accident?"

"Sit down, Anita."

She tried to pull away, but her mother's hand held her tight. "I don't want to sit down. It's June tenth. Why are you saying these things?"

She could feel the ground sliding away from under her feet. *Get a grip! It's the tenth of June. Hold on to that idea.*

"You poor girl," said her mother. "How did this happen?"

"Nothing's happened to me!" Anita shouted, tears stinging her eyes. "Mum, what's wrong with you? Why are you behaving like this?"

Her mother's eyes were compassionate but determined. She reached into her handbag and drew out her mobile phone. She flipped it open and held it up toward Anita's face. "Read the date, sweetheart," she said.

Anita looked at the illuminated screen. 14—AUG.

"That's not right . . ."

Her mother stood up, gripping Anita's arms, staring

hard into her face. "I know this must be very confusing for you, Anita, but you have to keep calm."

"I'm calm. I'm totally calm." Calm like high explosives. Was it really August? Had she lost nine weeks of her life because of an accident? It seemed impossible but . . .

"Good. Now stay with me, Anita. There are things I need to tell you."

"I had an accident?"

The world was turning itself inside out in front of her eyes.

"Yes. It *started* with the accident."

"I don't remember it."

"No. I get that. Sit down. Edric . . . *Evan*, I mean. Evan took you on a boat trip on the Thames. For your birthday—a birthday surprise. Do you remember that?"

"No, but . . ."

It fit. A boat trip. That made sense. Evan's big birthday surprise.

"The boat crashed into a bridge."

Coldness like death drained through Anita. "Was he killed?"

"No," said her mother. "No, he *wasn't*. But you were both taken to hospital. And then . . ." Her voice faded.

"And *then*?"

"There was the book. The blank book. And then you both disappeared. You were gone for three days, and when you came back, everything was different. It turned our whole world upside down." She laughed softly. "*Our* world—listen to me. As if it was just about *our* world after that . . ."

Her mother began the tale of the lost nine weeks.

# *II*

Anita stood at the door that led to the garden. She was shaking so much she could hardly keep upright. Her mother's voice was like white noise in her head.

Saying things that were unbelievable.

". . . and Oberon took us to the Brown Tower on the downs above the Faerie Palace. You went inside with us and up the stairs. Then you took our hands and stepped through from Faerie with us—and the last thing you said was 'I'll be back soon. I'll see you soon.' Then you were gone. That's the last we heard from you till the phone calls."

*Insane! Totally insane!*

And yet, what Anita saw in the garden fit with her mother's impossible fairy tales.

The back fence was broken, the cracked and ruptured wooden panels stacked together by the tree. Deep brown grooves clawed their way over the flower bed and up the lawn. Parallel tire marks. The flagstones of the patio were scratched and cracked. New scratches.

New cracks, white edged and sharp. And the garden door was scored with long narrow wounds, pale wood showing through the white paintwork.

The fence had been broken by Queen Titania of Faerie crashing through in her BMW.

Of course it had! How else?

According to her mother, Anita had been in the car with her. Oh, and with some of her Faerie princess sisters, and with Evan—except that Evan wasn't Evan. He was Edric Chanticleer, a lord of the Faerie court. And she wasn't Anita. She was Princess Tania Aurealis—half-Faerie, half-human. Able to walk between the worlds.

They had fought the Gray Knights of Lyonesse, with swords and spears. Then they'd gone up to her bedroom and stepped through into the Immortal Realm of Faerie. Yes, of course . . . in some kind of insane nightmare they had!

"What phone calls?" Anita asked, trying to latch on to something real.

"You left two voice mail messages on my mobile," said her mother. She pressed some buttons on her phone and held it out toward Anita. "I saved them so I could hear your voice whenever I needed to. Listen, Anita. Just listen."

Anita took the phone from her mother's hand and pressed it to her ear. She heard her own breathless voice.

*Mum, it's me. I'm just phoning to say I'm okay. I can't get home right now, but I'm fine. I'll call again when I have a chance. And . . . and . . . you and Dad had nothing to*

*do with the illness. You know what I'm talking about. It was*
*something else. Not you.* Her voice sped up, becoming
even more urgent. *I love you. I hope Dad is okay. Tell him
I love him so much. I'll call again when I can.*

She handed the phone back to her mother. Her
head filled with rushing air. Clutching the doorframe,
she began to laugh. She couldn't help herself. The
laughter filled her like a tempest.

"Anita!"

She could hardly catch her breath. She was drowning
in laughter. Her legs gave under her and she slid down
the doorframe, dying of laughter.

She felt hands shaking her.

*"Anita!"*

A sudden slap snapped her head to one side. Anita
gasped, fighting for air, red lights flashing in front of
her eyes.

She pushed her mother away and fought to get
back on her feet. One thought emerged clearly from
the debris of her brain.

*Call Evan.* The sound of his voice would anchor
her. She needed to hear his voice.

She saw her mother's face swimming in front
of her. She could hear her speaking, but the words
boomed and echoed. She stumbled across the kitchen
and out to the foot of the stairs, locking her fingers
around the banister.

Somehow she arrived at her bedroom door. She
slammed the door and, fumbling with clumsy fingers,
she turned the key.

Safe now.

She was trembling violently.

*Is this what it's like to be insane?*

"Anita? Let me in, please."

"No."

"I know how you must be feeling. . . ."

"Do you?"

A pause.

"No. No, I don't . . . not exactly, but I had to go through the same thing. We both did. Your dad and I. But something must have happened to you in Faerie . . . something to make you lose your memory."

*Shut up about Faerie!*

Anita took a breath. "I'm going to call Evan now."

"He won't be there, sweetheart."

"Yes. He. *Will.*" He *had* to be.

She saw that her computer was brand new. How come she hadn't noticed that before? Her mobile phone was lying by the computer. Plugged in. Recharging. Next to a neat pile of sixteenth birthday cards and some gift vouchers that hadn't registered with her before. There were other things in her room that she didn't recognize. A red scarf draped over the chair. A new backpack. A chrome tin with CHIK KIT stamped on it. An empty photo frame in Day-Glo colors. Things she had been too out of it to notice before. The spoils of a recent birthday . . .

Forcing herself to breathe steadily, she walked across the room and unplugged the wire connecting her phone to the socket. She pressed the button to switch the phone on. It beeped, showing twenty-five missed calls. Eleven messages. A whole bunch of texts.

The most recent texts were from Connor Estabrook. She'd known Connor all her life. He was the son of family friends, a med student. They met up maybe twice a year these days. He'd sent three texts that morning.

CALL ME IMMEDIATELY.

And the next one. SOMETHING CRAZY IS GOING ON. CALL ME WHEN YOU GET THIS.

And the third. IT'S YOUR FAULT. YOU DID THIS TO ME. CALL ME. WE HAVE TO MEET UP.

Her hands shaking, she accessed the voice messages. They were mostly from friends asking her how she was enjoying her holiday and when she'd be back. Invitations to parties. Natalie: *We're going up the Market Sunday. If you're back by then, meet up in the Stable Block at eleven. t.t.y.l.* Rosa: *OMG! Saw some amazing shoes in Fantasy in the High Street. You'd love 'em.*

None of the missed calls were from Evan's phone. She speed-dialed his number, but the phone diverted her to voice mail.

"Evan?" She sounded terrible! Like she'd been half strangled or something. "Evan? When you get this—the *second* you get this—call me back. It's really important." A brief pause. "Get back to me. Please."

"Anita? Let me in, please."

She glanced over to the door.

"No. I can't do that right now." She couldn't listen to anything else her mother had to say. She needed a different voice. A different version of what had happened to her. Her mother's version was no good. It was way, way beyond no good. It was totally unacceptable.

"Please, Anita."

"Go away, Mum. I need to think." That wasn't true. The last thing she wanted to do was *think*. Maybe talking with Evan would make things right?

"Listen, sweetheart." There was a soothing tone in her mother's muffled voice. "I know this must be hard for you. . . ." *No, actually it's really simple. Nothing you've told me is true.*

*But the nine lost weeks?*

*Evan will know what really happened.*

The words of Connor's last text echoed through her mind. IT'S YOUR FAULT. YOU DID THIS TO ME. CALL ME. WE HAVE TO MEET UP.

She walked over to the door. "Mum? Have you heard from Connor recently?"

"Yes. Last week. Why?"

"How did he sound to you?"

"The same as usual. Anita? Why is this important?"

"It isn't. I just wondered."

"You must have asked for a reason. What do you remember about Connor?"

"I don't remember anything."

"Anita, if you won't tell me the truth, how am I supposed to help you?"

The melodic bleat of the phone echoed up from the hall. Anita heard her mother give an annoyed snort. There was the patter of feet along the hallway and down the stairs.

Anita rang Evan's number again. He'd answer this time. For sure.

Straight to voice mail.

"Evan. Call me, please."

She realized that there were no recent messages or texts from Jade. That wasn't like her. That girl texted like thirty times a day. Anita scrolled down the screen, looking for something from her best friend.

There it was. Weeks ago.

A single word. WHATEVER!

It had been sent in response to a text from Anita: SORRY. I HAD NO CHOICE.

That was a *weird* message; it had been a reply to Jade texting, I DON'T BELIEVE YOU!

Anita had no memory of what had provoked that abrupt exchange. What didn't Jade believe? What was it that Anita had no choice about?

The answers were lost in the white fog of the nine missing weeks.

But at least a quarrel with Jade was *normal*.

She called Evan again.

"Evan. It's me. Things are . . ." Things were *what*, exactly? "Call the moment you get this." She gripped the phone till her fingers hurt. "I really have to talk to you. I . . . I *love* you."

*Oh god, I shouldn't have said that. I sound so needy.*

"Anita, honey?"

She leaned into the door. "What?"

"I have your dad on the line. He'd like to talk to you."

Anita licked her lips. "Will he tell me the same stuff you've been telling me?"

A pause. "Just speak to him, sweetheart."

"No. I don't think I will."

The last thing she needed was to hear her rational, scientific, logical father telling her that she was a fairy princess. She'd crack up completely if that happened.

She heard her mother move away from the door. There was a brief, one-sided conversation that Anita couldn't make out, then her mother was back.

"Anita?"

"I'm not going to talk to him."

"No. Fine. I understand. But I need to go to the hospital. Your dad's waiting there for me to come get him and bring him home. Why don't you ride along with me? He's really looking forward to seeing you. Please open the door."

"No. You go. Go pick Dad up." That's it. Get that voice to go away. Then she could think straight. Then she could work out what was really happening.

"I don't want to leave you like this. . . ."

Anita took a slow breath. She needed to convince her mother it was all right to leave her on her own, and she had to look her mother in the eyes to do that. She unlocked the door and opened it a crack. Her mother was standing there, pale but smiling.

"Come with me to the hospital? Your dad will be so happy to see you."

"No. You go. I'll stay here." A single tear crawled

down her cheek. "I'm fine, Mum. I just need some time to adjust."

Her mother reached out, but Anita drew back and closed the crack of the door to the width of an eye.

"Go get Dad."

Her mother hesitated. "Okay. But if I go, you have to promise you'll stay here."

"I promise."

"I won't be long. We'll be back as quick as we can. Stay here, sweetheart, and don't worry about anything."

"I'll be fine."

Still her mother hesitated. "Forty-five minutes there and back, okay?"

Anita nodded and smiled, and finally her mother dragged herself away and pattered down the stairs.

Anita closed the bedroom door and heard the front door bang shut. She felt a rush of relief.

She called Evan but this time she didn't bother to leave a message.

Why were there no messages or texts from him during the lost weeks? Then a gut-wrenching thought smacked into her brain.

He was dead. Evan was dead. He had died in the accident. Her mother had made up all that crazy stuff about other worlds to cover for the fact that Evan was dead.

"I have to know." Now that her mother was gone, she could make her escape from this madhouse. She snatched a handful of cash from the emergency fund in her bedside table, then she ran out of her bedroom and stumbled down the stairs.

She had to know whether Evan was alive or dead.

She burst out of the house and went running along the street.

# III

Anita ran all the way to the hostel where Evan lived.

It had seemed odd when Anita first met him that a boy his age should be living in a hostel; but his home was in Wales, hundreds of miles away, and apparently his parents had made some kind of arrangement with the people who ran the hostel so that Evan could take a room there during the school term.

Of course, if her mum was right and Evan was a Faerie lord, then he'd probably fixed the whole thing with magic!

The manager was in her small office, off the main hall. She seemed surprised to see Anita, although she'd been there several times with Evan. Her desk was awash with forms and papers.

"Evan Thomas? No. He's not been here since the school term ended. We're full of foreign students doing a summer language course. It's total mayhem."

"Do you know about the accident? On the river?"

"Yes, of course."

"Evan wasn't killed?"

The woman looked taken aback. "No, he wasn't killed. What kind of a question is that? You know he wasn't killed. You were here with him at least twice after you both came out of hospital."

A flood of relief. But the woman was looking at her suspiciously now.

"Are you okay?"

*No, actually I'm a million miles from okay.*

"I'm fine. Where did he go?"

"Home, I guess. His folks live in Wales, don't they?" A raised eyebrow asked the question: *How come you don't know where he is?* "Have you tried his mobile?"

"Yes. I've left messages."

Understanding filled the young woman's face. Anita knew what she must be thinking: Anita's boyfriend had skipped town without telling her, and now he wasn't taking her messages. Just another ruined teen romance.

"No!" exploded Anita, although the woman hadn't said a word. "It's not like that!"

The woman dropped her glance. "Sorry, I can't help you. I'm sure he'll call as soon as he gets your messages."

Anita walked out of the office. She found herself out on the street again, sucking in air, feeling dizzy. She speed-dialed Evan's number.

This time he would answer. She could hear his voice already.

*Hey, sorry—I was in the shower. Yes, a really lo-o-ong*

*shower. I'm fine. . . . Sure we can meet up. Yes, I love you, too.*

She was diverted to voice mail.

She wandered the streets with nowhere to go. Home? No! That was an insane place now. Jade's house? She looked around, orientating herself. Yes, she could go to Jade's.

Her phone beeped.

A new text from Connor. I HATE THIS! WHAT DID YOU DO TO ME! IF YOU DON'T GET BACK TO ME THIS TIME, I'M GOING TO CALL YOUR FOLKS!

She took a long, slow breath then searched out his number and pressed Call.

Anita sat in the train carriage, watching the houses flit by under a blue sky. Houses full of people living normal lives.

Connor had been wired when she'd called him. *No. I'm not talking to you on the phone. You have to meet me.*

He had given her brief instructions about where he would be, then he'd hung up before she'd even agreed to go all the way across London.

Odd thing, one more odd thing in a whole blizzard of odd things: When she got off the train at Denmark Hill station, she had the weirdest feeling she'd been here before although she knew she hadn't. She was a North London girl, a Camden girl. South of the Thames was just one big sprawling suburban blur to her.

She followed Connor's instructions and walked into Ruskin Park. What had he said? A bandstand by a pond. She walked the narrow, gray tarmac paths between huge rhododendron bushes filled with deep pink blossom.

The path led to a small oval pond where ducks swam and waddled, swarming noisily when mums with kids threw bread crumbs over the low black iron rail.

The bandstand looked as if it hadn't been used for a long time. Chain-link barriers blocked the entrances. There were notices. KEEP AWAY. DANGEROUS BUILDING.

Anita walked twice around the pond before sitting on one of the benches to wait.

A middle-aged man in a suit sat at the other end of the bench, eating sandwiches and reading a magazine.

Where was Connor? He said he'd be here.

Anita had given herself a target. Get to the park without losing it. She'd held on to that. But deep inside her she could feel a big scream brewing—one that would shatter the sky like thin glass and crack the world open.

Where was Connor?

She glanced at the man's magazine, needing to distract herself.

It was some kind of science mag. He was reading an article with the headline *Longest Solar Eclipse of the Century to Pass over Europe.* There was a photo: a ring of white fire with a black heart.

The opening paragraph of the article had large bold writing that she was able to read.

*August 19. The longest solar eclipse of this century, last-ing 6 minutes and 45 seconds in some areas, will plunge cities, including London, into darkness as it passes over Europe this Friday.*

A shadow crossed the sun and she looked up.

Connor was standing over her.

His hair was wild, his eyes red-rimmed as if he hadn't slept for a week. There was a look on his face of pure desperation.

What had she done to him to make him look at her like that?

She stood up without speaking. The man with the magazine threw them a quick glance, then went back to his reading. Connor turned and walked away, and Anita walked after him.

They came to the far side of the bandstand. There were no people nearby. There was a wooden fence, then a row of trees that bordered a long sloping field of grass where dogs ran for sticks and families picnicked while rooks strutted and flapped. Connor turned to her. "What did you do to me?"

She swallowed, disturbed by the anger in his eyes. "I don't know what you mean."

His voice was shrill, like a valve releasing pent-up steam. "I lost two weeks, Anita. I want to know what happened. I want you to tell me what you and that other girl did to me."

"You think two weeks is bad?" she said bitterly. "Try two months, Connor."

"What are you talking about?"

"I've lost *nine* weeks, Connor. The last thing I remember, it was June tenth. You've got seven weeks on me, so how about you tell me what *you* know?"

As she looked steadily into his eyes, his disbelief gave way to a crumbling despair. "Nine weeks?"

"Yes. Why do you think I did something to you?"

"The last thing I remember is meeting you and that dark-haired girl at my flat," Connor said, spitting words like shards of stone. "After that, nothing. Then waking up this morning in the back garden of the house where I live, wearing the same clothes and with two weeks of my life missing."

"What dark-haired girl?"

"You said she was a school friend," he said. "Her name began with R. It was a strange name like Rachel but not. Ruth? No, a longer name than Ruth."

"I don't know anyone called Ruth or Rachel. What did she look like?"

"Long black hair. Drop-dead gorgeous. She spoke funny. I can't remember exactly. Like she was a foreigner."

Anita shook her head. "I don't know anyone like that. Why were we there?"

"You said you needed me to help you with medical stuff for a project you were working on over the summer."

"No, that's not right." Then something her mother had told her stabbed into her mind like a poisoned dart. "Was the girl's name Rathina?"

Connor's eyes widened. "Yes! That was it. *Rathina.* What is that? Spanish or South American or something?"

"Not according to my mum."

*Princess Rathina Aurealis, the sixth daughter of Oberon and Titania, King and Queen of Faerie.*

"Your mother knows her?"

Anita felt the hysteria bubbling to the boil in her head. But this time she was able to keep it under control. "According to Mum, she's my sister."

Connor gaped at her. "You have a *sister*? Since when? Was she adopted at birth by another family or what?"

"You wouldn't believe me if I told you." She gripped his arm. "What else do you remember from that night when I came to your place with Rathina?"

"Nothing."

"You have to remember more."

"No! You're supposed to be filling in the blanks for me."

But it wasn't the empty spaces that drew Anita's thoughts; it was another aspect of her mother's lunatic story. Connor was a med student—he knew about illnesses and cures. "Did we say anything about a plague?"

Connor gave a choking gasp. "The plague," he said breathlessly. "Yes. There was something. . . ." His face screwed tight. "People were ill . . . people who shouldn't be ill. But no, I don't remember anything else."

"Try!"

He glared at her. "You think I'm not trying? You think I don't want to know what happened to me?"

*Be careful what you wish for, Connor—you might not be able to handle the results.* It was clear he wasn't going to be able to help her. He had seen her during the lost nine weeks—he had seen her with a dark-haired girl from her mother's fantasy stories. They had spoken to him about the plague, the sickness that had come to the Immortal Realm of Faerie.

He was leading her down that same insane road.

She let go of his arm. "I'm sorry, Connor. I can't help you. I have to go now."

"No. Don't go. You can't go." His voice was desperate. "I have to know what happened. What was that stuff about a sister . . . ? What *sister*?"

Anita shook her head, stepping back to put distance between them. "Don't go there, Connor. You won't like it. Trust me on this; you're way better off not being told what I've been told."

"You can't leave me like this. I won't let you!" He lunged forward and grabbed at her. "You *stay* here! You *explain*!"

She hardly knew what happened next. Some kind of fighting instinct took over. She twisted in his grip, loosening his fingers, and jerked her elbow into his midriff. He doubled up with a gasp and dropped to his knees, clutching his stomach.

"Oh god! I'm sorry!" Where had that come from? She'd never taken any self-defense courses, but she'd put him down like it was the most natural thing in the world.

She crouched at his side.

"Are you okay?"

"I'm fine. Winded is all." He looked at her. "I have to know what happened to me."

She helped him to his feet. "So do I."

His eyes were haunted. "I'm so messed up, Anita! Everything is so messed up!"

"I know." She looked into his face. "I'm going to find out what happened to us, and when I do—the moment I do—I'll call you." She held his gaze. "Trust me, please?"

"Like I have a choice . . ."

"And if you remember anything—*anything*—call me, yes?"

He nodded.

"I'm going now."

She turned and walked quickly away. Connor called after her. "Anita? Have we both gone crazy?"

She didn't look around. She didn't answer. She began to run.

Her brain on fire, she ran wildly across the long sloping green field of Ruskin Park.

# *IV*

Anita was leaning over a concrete wall and staring into the gray-brown foamy swirl of the River Thames. It was high tide and the water was as thick as molten metal. She was north of the river again, in a quiet place under Blackfriars Bridge. The great black-iron structure hung above her, making the river noises echo and reverberate. She could hear traffic roaring overhead. A few people were walking to and fro. A young couple passed by her—the girl's arm draped over the boy's shoulder, his hand tucked into the back pocket of her jeans—stopping every now and then to kiss as they strolled along the Embankment.

*Aren't you the lucky ones?*

Her phone rang. She scooped it out of her pocket.

It was her mother's mobile number. Not too hard to guess what had happened. She'd got back home and found Anita missing.

Anita didn't answer the call. "Sorry, Mum. No can do right now."

She waited till the beeping stopped then opened the screen to send a text. DON'T WORRY. I'M FINE. I'M CHECKING A FEW THINGS OUT. BACK SOON. XXX.

She sent it to her mother's phone.

Without any hope she dialed Evan.

*The number you are calling is not available right now. Please leave your message after the tone.*

"It's me. I know you're alive; the woman at the hostel told me so. Call me back, please. Unless this is all a dream, in which case . . . Well, call me anyway."

The phone beeped once. A text from her mother. She didn't read it.

*What I need is someone to snap me out of this.*

Jade was the perfect person to do that. And she'd been planning on going to Jade's house before the text had come from Connor. She speed-dialed her number.

The phone purred a few times. One of three things was happening: Jade was screening her calls and didn't want to talk to her, she was out of earshot of her phone, or her phone was turned off.

That final choice wasn't even possible, knowing Jade, and the second one was pretty unlikely.

There was a soft click, followed by Jade's voice in full-on scornful mode. "Hey, thanks for the call. Nice of you to get in touch. I've missed you *soooo* much." Anita felt a rush of affection for the familiar, and oh-so-*normal* voice—no one did sarcasm as well as Jade Anderson.

"Jade? I need to see you. It's really important. Can I come over?"

"Let me check my diary. Aww, sorry, Tania, it says here I have an appointment this afternoon to totally screw with my best friend. Maybe you should try again later. *Way* later!"

"I get that you're mad at me," Anita said. "That's fine. Mad is fine." And then something truly appalling clicked. "You called me Tania."

"Oh, changed the name *again*, have we? What is it this time? Tallulah? Betty? Harriet Head-case? Madeleine with the emphasis on the *mad*?"

"Changed my name . . . ?"

"Oh, don't bother explaining. I really don't want to know what you've been doing all summer. Some people with new boyfriends get so obsessed by them that they forget all about their other friends."

"Why did I want you to call me Tania?"

"Don't ask me, crazy girl. You've been way off the chart since before you bailed on me with that trip to Florida. But you know what? I couldn't care less. Do what you like; this girl officially doesn't care anymore."

"Are you at home? Can I come over?"

"Yes, I'm home, but there's no way I want you here. I'm busy. Try again in a lifetime or two."

"Please, Jade. I really need you."

"What*ever.*"

"I'm coming over. Please stay put."

"I'm not going anywhere. I'm catching some rays in the garden. Topping up the Florida tan. There's no one else in, so if you *have* to drop by, come around the side entrance."

Anita began to walk rapidly toward the nearest tube station. "Thanks. Jade? My life is so weird right now. I think I'm going crazy."

"Oh, get over yourself!"

The two patches of grass on either side of the path to the front door of Jade's house were churned up. That was strange. Jade's mother was one of those people who spend all their spare time in their gardens, front and back of the house: pruning, deadheading, planting, and weeding. She didn't have just green thumbs; her arms were green all the way up to the shoulder. Last time Anita had been there, the lawns had been as smooth as a pool table. Now they looked as if a herd of cattle had stampeded across them.

Anita went to the side of the house. The wooden door was unlatched. She pushed through and walked down the path to the garden. It was a big garden, shielded by tall laurels, the sculpted lawns weaving in among elaborate and colorful flower beds. There was a water feature at the far end, a low wall of white stones over which clear water washed into a small pond. The water rippled as it poured down as smooth as silk, making the wide, pale green lily pads waver and the spiked pink blossoms of the lily flowers bob and weave.

Jade lay stretched out on a sun lounger alongside the pond, berry brown from Florida, wearing a tiny yellow bikini and sunglasses. Her mobile phone was within hand's reach. The lounger was angled so the high afternoon sun beat down on her.

Jade was listening to the radio. Some talk show or other. An overexcited voice was babbling at full speed.

"Hey, did you realize that there's not going to be another eclipse like the one that's coming this Friday until July 2132! That's over a hundred years, people! You don't want to miss this one—this is the biggie. . . ."

Jade didn't seem to hear Anita approaching her.

Anita stood looking down at her best friend. She hesitated. One of two things could happen now: Either Jade would be part of the weirdness or she'd say something to make it all go away.

Anita dreaded one and hoped for the other. The longer she waited before making her presence known, the longer she could hope that Jade would rescue her.

"Hi there," Jade said in a slow drawl. "How are things in Freakville?"

"Hello."

Jade slapped her hand down on the radio, silencing the voice. She flicked her sunglasses onto her forehead with one red-nailed finger. She looked at Anita with raised eyebrows.

"So? What happened?" There was a mocking poutiness in her voice. "The bad Mr. Thomas go home without you, did he? Are you bereft and all alone now, Tania? Need some of your old friends again?"

"It's not like that."

"Oh, please!" Jade stormed up off the lounger, her arms folded. "It is *so* like that. Jeez, Tania, I know love can drive you crazy and stuff, but you're just plain unbelievable!"

"Is that what you think? That I've been off having high jinks with Evan?"

"I know you were reasonably normal before you hooked up with him and that you've been loony-tunes ever since. I know *that*, Tania."

"Can you call me Anita?"

"I don't especially want to call you at all."

"Don't be like that. I'm having a bad day, Jade." Her voice cracked. She felt close to tears. Again. "The worst day ever." Anita's legs gave out and she folded up to sit on the lawn.

Jade peered down at her. "He broke up with you, huh?" She made a sharp *tik* noise in her mouth. "Typical boy! Create a need then refuse to fill it! You know, I never liked him. Too cute. Too smart. Know what I mean? You're better off without him."

Anita shook her head. "Don't say that."

Jade stared down at her for a few moments, as though weighing up her next move. Angry or forgiving? Then she gave a small crooked smile. "Sorry, it's in the rules. The best friend trashes the ex. That's the way these things work." She sat down at Anita's side. "Then I take your mind off things. I mean, have I got stuff to tell you!"

"Jade? There's stuff I need to tell you first. . . ."

"Hush! This is therapy. Listen up and forget all about what's-his-name. I've got major news. For a start, did you know we had a bunch of squatters invade our house while we were in Florida? We got home and the front garden was all messed up and ruined. And they'd been in all our rooms. It's totally disgusting! Someone had actually slept in my bed. Isn't that foul? I told Mum to burn the sheets. And they messed with my dad's stuff in the basement. We think they got in through the back door—the glass was all broken and stuff was smashed and wrecked."

Odd. Anita had the feeling she knew something about this already. But before she could get a handle on it, Jade went on, unstoppable as a wrecking ball.

"And then Dan came back early from his adventure holiday in India. He got mugged first day out there and had all his gear and his money stolen. Mum had told him to take traveler's checks, but you know my brain-box big brother! He said traveler's checks aren't *cool*. So we had to wire him money for a flight home, and now he's in residence again like a total pain. And he's got no money and no job and he spends all his time hanging around and mooching off Mum and Dad and making my life miserable."

"Jade—"

"And then there's Anthea at my tai chi martial arts class—if she gets to be any more of a pain in my butt, I'm going to add an extra number to the thirty-two sword forms and cut her weaselly little heart out."

"Jade! Shut up and listen to me!" Anita shouted.

Jade blinked at her. *"What?"*

"I've lost my memory."

A pause and then: "You've *what* now?"

"I don't remember anything that happened to me over the past nine weeks."

A wide grin spread across Jade's face. "Funny girl. Let me fill you in, then. Uh . . . it went like this. You talked about Evan. *All the time.* You mooned over Evan. You skipped town with Evan for three days. You didn't call me. You didn't explain properly when you got back. You drooled over Evan. You changed your name to please Evan. You totally abandoned me although you were meant to go on holiday with me. You vanished without a word, probably because of Evan. Get the picture?"

"You think I'm joking?"

"I think you're cracking up, that's for sure."

Anita took a deep breath. "I woke up on my bed at half-eleven this morning thinking it was the tenth of June." She looked into her friend's bright, cynical eyes. "I've lost nine whole weeks of my life, Jade." She was aware of a hot feeling behind her eyes and then there were tears. "I'm so lost, Jade. I'm all alone, and I can't get in contact with Evan, and my mum is telling me crazy things, and I just want it all to stop! I want it to stop right now!" She dropped her face into her hands.

She'd been holding herself together for hours now. It was too much. Now that she'd let go, there was no way for her to stop the crying.

A moment later Jade was at her side in the grass.

"Hey, nothing's that bad!" Jade's sun-warmed arms enfolded her, smelling of suntan oil. Anita pressed her face into her friend's neck, clinging on to her for dear life.

*V*

"Feeling better?"

"No."

"You've stopped bawling, though. Drink some of this. It's nice. Cranberry juice with just a smidge of cola. It's my own invention. Come on, Anita—try it."

Anita took the frosted glass from Jade's hand. Ice rattled. The rim was cold against her lips.

Anita wasn't sure how long she'd been crying. Ten minutes? Half an hour? They were sitting together on the lawn, except that Jade had dashed indoors and had come back with a box of tissues and some fresh, iced drinks. She had also covered up with a bright yellow top.

Anita swallowed, the ice tinkling against her teeth. "Like it?" Jade asked, nodding toward the glass.

"No. Not much."

"Me neither. Some beverage-based experiments are just doomed to failure." She grinned and lifted a lock of Anita's hair off her face, tucking it behind her ear.

Jade looked thoughtfully at her. "So. Do you know *why* you lost your memory? Did you get a whack on the head or something?"

"You know about the accident—on the river?"

"Sure—everyone does. But you were fine after that." Jade's eyes widened. "At least, you were walking and talking. But is that what did it? Was it some kind of delayed reaction to the accident? Oh, wow! That would make so much sense. Now I think about it, that's when you started acting crazy. Jeez, Anita—you've got to get to a hospital. You have to be checked out. You probably need a CAT scan or something."

Anita looked at her friend. *Tell her? Don't tell her?* "Maybe so—but Mum has told me the weirdest stuff," she said in a rush.

"You've spoken to your mum since you woke up?"

"Yes. She was there."

"And she let you out without getting you examined?" Jade sounded incredulous. "What's *that* all about?"

"According to Mum, there's nothing wrong with my head."

"Ooh-kay. And she knows this how?"

"Because she says she knows what I've been doing for the past two months."

"Go on. . . ."

Anita took a long, slow breath. "Okay, you need to let me tell you the whole thing, right? And you need to not interrupt."

Jade made the padlocked-lips-and-thrown-away-key gesture.

Another breath before the plunge.

"Well, according to my mum . . ."

Jade stood up, turning in a slow circle, smiling and waving and calling. "Hello, guys! Nice try!"

Anita stared at her. "What are you doing?"

"Waving at the cameras," said Jade. "I figure they're out there somewhere, because that story has to be part of one of those reality TV shows where they check out a person's gullibility factor."

Anita stood up, wanting to rush at her friend and shake her. "You think I'm making all this up?"

Jade rested her hands on her hips. "Do I think that was all crazy talk, or do I think you're a fairy princess? Well, let me see. . . . Hmmm, which is more likely? Crazy or a princess? Fairy princess or crazy? It's so hard to choose!"

"Stop it!" Anita shouted, stumbling forward. "Just stop!"

Jade backed off a couple of paces. "Oh. My. God. You're serious, aren't you? Your mum really told you all that stuff? And she expected you to believe it?"

"Yes."

"And you're sure she wasn't teasing you? Come on, Anita—she had to be kidding with you."

"She wasn't. I swear she wasn't."

"Jeez louise!"

"Exactly! Now you know how I've been feeling all day!" She looked hard into Jade's face. "And there's something else. Something that's only just clicked.

Mum told me that when we were hiding from the Gray Knights, we were in someone else's house. A friend's house. She didn't say which house—which friend. But I've just figured it out."

Understanding crept over Jade's face. "No . . . way . . ."

"I think so," Anita said. "I think I was here. I think all that mess you found when you got back here from your holiday—I think that was me."

Jade lifted her hands, palms out, fingers spread. "No! This is insane. *You're* insane." She ran for the lounger. "I've had enough of this. I'm calling your mum right now." She picked up her mobile and pressed buttons.

"I can't let you do that!" Anita said, moving toward her.

Jade stepped backward over the lounger, the mobile held to her ear, her other hand stretched out, fingers pointing. "Keep back, Anita. I'm going to make this call, whether you like it or not."

Anita took a half step forward.

She paused as a sudden muted sound rang in her ears. It was like discordant music sounding from far, far away. At the same moment the air behind Jade—the air over the wall of water-slicked white stones—began to shimmer and darken.

"What the . . . ?" Jade frowned, shaking her head. "What's that noise?"

The air behind her was crackling now, sparks striking up off the stones, and a heart of deep, grainy blue was forming like a bruise over the trembling pond.

The sound intensified in Anita's head. Now it was like an orchestra tuning up, like strands and fragments of disparate music weaving together—growing louder, making the air vibrate.

The stain of deep blue light over the water feature seemed to be taking on definite shapes. There were two human figures hanging over the stones.

Anita was about to yell to Jade to turn and look when the music faded and the ultramarine blemish in the air over the stones dissolved.

"That was a weird noise," said Jade. "What was it?" She looked at her arms. "Check this out! It made the hairs stand up all over me."

Anita gasped. "Did you see that?"

"See what?"

"Jade." Anita tried to keep her voice steady, to keep from sounding crazy. "Something nearly happened. Something"—she licked dry lips—"behind you."

Jade glanced over her shoulder. There was nothing to see now. "What kind of something?"

"I'm not sure."

There was a taste in Anita's mouth that seemed familiar. Unpleasant but familiar. She associated it with pain or discomfort.

"Oh! Hi, Mrs. P. It's Jade." The phone was still to her ear. "Yeah—fine, thanks." She stared hard at Anita, one arm extended toward her, warning her to stay back. Between her Sunday morning tai chi classes and her karate night school lessons, Jade was not a person to mess with.

"Thing is—I've had a strange call from Anita," Jade continued.

That was something—at least Jade hadn't told her mother she was here.

"Huh?" Jade's eyes were wary as she looked at Anita. "No. I have no idea where she is. Why?"

Jade listened for a few moments. Anita watched her distractedly, her brain still tingling from the outlandish music. The charged air prickled on her skin. And she had that bad taste in her mouth. A taste like rusty iron.

"Really?" said Jade. "That explains the strange stuff she was coming out with. Listen, I'll give her a call back, okay? I'll try to talk her down—see if I can persuade her to go home or to meet up with me so I can bring her home. I'll let you know how it goes. Yeah. Fine. Okay. Bye."

"Thanks for not saying I'm here," said Anita. "What did she tell you?"

"She said you hit your head," Jade said, her voice cautious now. "She said you ran out of the house before she could get you to a doctor. She said that you're probably not too coherent right now."

Anita felt a chill in her heart. Her mother had lied. It felt like a betrayal. "She *would* say something like that," she insisted. "Of course she would. She's not going to tell you that other stuff over the phone. Even if *she* believes it, she'd know you wouldn't."

"You got that right."

"How did I hit my head? Did she tell you that?"

"No."

"But she made out it was recent, yes?"

"I guess so."

"Feel my head, Jade!"

"Excuse me?"

"Feel my head—if I hit my head there'll be a cut or a bump or something. If I hit it hard enough to scramble my brains, there'd be some sign of it, surely?"

"Okay." Jade pointed to the grass. "Sit down with your hands in your lap. Make any sudden moves and I'll swat you like a fly. Okay?"

"Okay." Anita folded her legs under her and knelt on her heels in the grass, her fingers linked together in her lap.

"If I find a bump or whatever, you're going to let me take you home, right?" Jade said as she padded across the grass.

"Yes."

Jade stood behind her. Anita felt her hand moving slowly over her head, feeling for anything unusual.

"Well?" Anita asked, staring straight ahead.

"No bumps. No lumps." Jade sounded puzzled. "This just keeps getting weirder by the second. Why would your mum tell me you've had a bash on the head if you haven't?"

"To cover up for something too weird to tell you about?" Anita suggested, craning around to look up at her friend. "Are you freaked out yet?"

Jade shook her head. "I don't freak out that easily. Let's just say I'm intrigued with a side order of slightly spooked."

Anita got up. "I need something else to drink. I have the foulest taste in my mouth." She was halfway to her feet when the jangling music came crashing into her head again. Louder this time, dissonant, grating—clashing and strident. She staggered at the shock of it. Through the cacophony she could just about hear Jade's voice shouting words she couldn't make out.

The air thrummed, the laurel trees rippling as if they were reflections in troubled water. The grass seethed under her feet. The flowers in the beds bled into one another till all the different colors became a single rainbow swirl. Shards of silvery blue light skidded on the stones over the pond. The wound of dark blue light appeared again, throbbing in the air, pulsing and darkening and becoming more solid.

The terrible music grew even louder, coming to a crescendo of screaming strings and clashing cymbals and blaring trumpets. A silvery line cut down through the heart of the dark blue blemish that hung over the stones. A thin line that sparked and flared and opened.

Through the widening gap Anita caught the briefest possible glimpse of a shingled shoreline and a cobalt sea that stretched away to the horizon. There was a galleon—an old-fashioned, fully rigged galleon! A huge, white lizard reached forward with raking claws.

Two figures blocked the light: one male, the other

female. They came tumbling through the gaping silver-lipped portal, plunging headlong into the pond, sending up a fountain of greenish water.

The fire-rimmed mouth closed. The dark blue stain winked out of existence, and the music stopped abruptly, as though someone had thrown a switch.

"No . . ." It was Jade's voice, strangely loud in the sudden silence. "No . . . this isn't happening, this isn't happening. . . ."

The two figures scrambled to their feet, water flooding off their clothes as they stared wildly around themselves.

One was a girl, a dark-haired beauty in an old-fashioned olive green dress. The other was . . .

The other was *Evan*!

But he was wearing the weirdest clothes: a strange black tunic and leather boots, like someone in a Shakespeare play. Like *Romeo*.

"Forsooth!" gasped the girl, floundering to the edge of the pool. "Your powers are formidable indeed, Master Chanticleer! But I'd fain travel a less hectic path in the future and mayhap arrive dry-shod!"

"No. Way. No. Way. No. Way." Jade backed away, shaking her head.

Anita took a stumbling step forward. "Evan?"

Evan Thomas was knee-deep in the pond, gazing at her, his fair hair hanging wet in his silvery eyes.

Silvery eyes? No! Evan's eyes were brown! But . . .

The girl stepped out of the water, a slow grin spreading across her face as she opened her arms.

"Come, Tania!" she cried, her eyes shining. "Look not so moonstruck! We are neither apparitions nor flibbertigibbets! By Master Chanticleer's Arts we have come across entire worlds for you! Come, my sweet, darling sister—embrace me and tell me all that you learned in the airy realm of Tirnanog!"

# VI

"Get away from me!" Anita's terrified shout cut the air like a blade.

The dark-haired girl stumbled to a halt, astonished. "Tania? Do you not know me?"

Anita stood her ground, but she was trembling from head to foot.

*This isn't real. It's all in your head. Refuse to buy into the hallucinations and they'll go away. They will. They have to. . . .*

The girl moved warily forward, her face concerned.

"Tania, sweet sister, why so distressed? There is nothing to fear here. All is good."

*Confront the nightmare. Break it down.*

Anita looked into the girl's anxious face.

"I'm Anita Palmer," she said, slowly and deliberately. "And *you* don't exist!"

"By all the spirits of love and devotion, I do!" said the girl. "I am your sister Rathina. Why do you not know me? What dread blight has the Divine Harper put upon you that you know me not?" She turned her head. "Master Chanticleer! I fear her wits are addled. Is there aught you can do to amend her sorry state?"

Anita turned to look at Jade; she needed to make sure the whole world hadn't gone crazy. Jade was staring from Rathina to Evan with a look of absolute disbelief on her face.

*If these are my hallucinations, how come Jade can see them?*

Evan waded to the stone rim of the pool. His face was empty, his eyes still filmed with silver. He lifted a leg, awkward, unsteady. His foot slipped on the stones, and he pitched forward into the grass.

"Evan!" His heavy fall jolted Anita out of her unbelief. She pushed past the dark-haired girl and ran headlong toward where Evan lay as still as death in the clipped grass.

She crashed onto her knees, leaning over him, using both hands to turn him onto his back. His face was pale, wasted, the silvery eyes staring up at nothing.

Rathina stood over her. "The summoning of the spirits was hard," she said. "It has taken much of his strength. His first charm failed, and it was not until the Great Salamander used his claws to tear asunder the fabric that divides the worlds that we were able to break through." Anita felt Rathina's hand on her shoulder. "But he would have spent his last breath to be by your side, Tania." Her voice trembled. "He would have done this thing, even if the Dark Arts had devoured him."

Anita peeled Evan's hair off his face, stroking his damp skin, leaning in close.

"Evan?"

The eyes were frightening. Like balls of molten quicksilver.

She held his face between her hands, her forehead touching his. "Wake up! Please wake up! I need you."

The silver slithered over his eyes.

"Tania?" His voice was faint and far away.

Jade's voice came from somewhere close. "Is he okay? Should I call an ambulance? I'll call an ambulance. Is that the thing to do?"

The silvery sheen faded away like dissolving mist, and Anita found herself looking into Evan's chestnut brown eyes.

His hand came up to cradle her cheek. "Tania," he breathed. "It worked. I found you." He let out a gasp of exhaustion. "That was hard!" he said, smiling wearily. "That was really hard."

As Evan sat up, Anita drew away from him, resting back on her heels, gazing into his face.

Rathina's voice drifted through the white fog that filled Anita's mind. "She knows not your true name. And she does not remember me. What bane came upon her in Tirnanog? And how did she come here?" She looked around, seeming to notice Jade for the first time. "You! Maiden! What place is this?"

"This is my house—my garden," Jade replied, looking dazed. "How did you do that . . . that appearing-out-of-nowhere thing?"

"This is the Mortal World," Rathina said, lifting her head and sniffing the air. "I smell it well enough. Unclean is the air, but I have endured it before, and I'll endure it again till we can escape and return to Faerie."

"Oh my god!" Jade gasped. "Oh! My! God!"

"And what are you, maiden?" asked Rathina, eyeing Jade up and down with disapproval in her eyes. "Are you human, or are you some feckless water nymph that you disport yourself with hardly a stitch on your body?"

"I'm a person!" Jade said. "What are *you*?"

"I am Rathina Aurealis, princess of Faerie."

Jade let out a long, low breath. Lost for words.

Evan reached out and touched Anita's cheek. "Are you okay?"

"I don't know," said Anita breathlessly. "Am I?"

"You will be," he murmured, "now we're together."

She sighed, not knowing what to say.

"We waited on the shore for you to come back," said Evan. "The Great Salamander was with us. He told us what had happened. But . . . but you never returned. You never came back from the land in the sky." He smiled reassuringly. "Didn't I tell you that I'd find you wherever you went? Remember? You're in my blood, Tania, and I'm in yours. Love never dies in Faerie. Nothing can keep us apart."

"I'm not Tania."

"Yes. You are." His brow furrowed. "Something happened to you in Tirnanog." His fingers touched cool against her forehead. "Your Faerie soul sleeps," he whispered. "Deep within, behind locked doors, in a dark and silent place."

Anita swallowed hard. "Who are you, really?"

"My name's Edric, and I'm in love with you."

Anita gasped. "You never told me you loved me before."

"Yes. I did. Plenty of times. You don't remember is all."

"Truly?"

Edric nodded. "Truly."

"I'm not crazy?"

"No, you're not crazy. Your memory has been taken away from you."

"We cannot tarry in this benighted place, Master Chanticleer," Rathina declared. "We have found Tania—let us be on our way! The people of Faerie need us! The balm of Gildensleep cannot last forever. Even now the sickness may be spreading."

"I don't have the power to get through to Faerie," said Edric.

Anita gazed into Evan's face.

Edric's face.

*Am I Anita Palmer? Or am I Tania Aurealis?*

"This is crazy weird." Jade sounded almost as stunned as Anita felt. "Evan Thomas from our school is really a guy called Edric from another world?" She shook her head. "I *always* thought there was something freaky about you!"

The shimmering sound of bells brightened the air.

"Hist! What is that?" said Rathina, staring around herself.

"Something is coming," murmured Edric, getting to his feet.

As Anita stood up she saw that Rathina's hand moved to her waist, as though she expected to find a weapon there. But her fingers closed on empty air.

The chime and chink of the bells grew louder and deeper until it was no longer the shimmering sound of tiny bells, but now also a plangent ringing, and finally the toll of great booming bells that shook the ground under their feet. Sweet voices mingled with the bells, adding harmonies and descant to the rising music.

A wheel of blue fire blossomed in the air, warping everything around it. It was like and yet unlike Edric's portal—deeply blue but without the white lightning.

"Something has followed in our wake!" shouted Edric. "It's using the trail of my charm to get into the Mortal World!"

From the heart of the wheel stepped a female figure.

The hoop of blue fire vanished, and the pealing of the bells and the singing of the voices were blotted out.

Joy filled Anita's heart as she stared at the girl, although she had no idea why.

The girl seemed dazed. She was small and slender, clad in a gown of vibrant sky blue that echoed the light in her eyes. Her long golden hair cascaded over her shoulders, her features fine and delicate. Her chest rose and fell as she gulped in breath.

There was something so deeply familiar about her

that Anita was drawn toward her. *I know her. Who is she?*

Rathina stumbled toward the swaying girl. She let out a cry, her voice filled with wonder and disbelief.

"Zara!"

The golden-haired girl smiled. She held her arms out. "Rathina! Sister! And Tania! I . . ."

But then her eyes glazed over and she fainted into the grass.

# Part Two:

# The Seekings of the Sundered Soul

# VII

Jade's voice was the first to break the uncanny stillness. "I can't take much more of this!"

Anita had an ache in her heart that made it hard to breathe. Rathina was on the ground, cradling the girl in her arms and weeping silently. Edric was staring at the girl, dumbfounded.

Anita tore her gaze away from the two girls and glanced at Edric. "I think I know her," she murmured.

"She's your sister Zara," Edric said blankly. "But she died in battle against the Sorcerer King." He looked as if he was about to pass out himself. "She shouldn't be here. We held the Ceremony of Leavetaking. . . . Her body was sent to Albion." He took a gasping breath. "None that pass through the gates of the Blessèd Realm ever return," he said. "Never."

Rathina turned her tear-streaked face to them. "She is alive!" she cried. "Her body is warm. There is breath in her lungs. She is neither spirit nor phantom.

But how can this be? How, by all the fragrant stars of heaven?"

"I don't know," began Edric. "I've never . . ." A bouncing, electronic melody cut him short.

"Phone!" breathed Jade, walking unsteadily over to the lounger and stooping to pick up her trilling mobile. "Excuse me—it's my mum—I need to answer."

Anita looked at her friend. A phone call! In the middle of all this insanity—an honest-to-goodness everyday phone call! She didn't know whether to be comforted by the normality of it or annoyed by the intrusion.

She snatched hold of Edric's hand. "This is all real, isn't it?"

"Yes. It is. The thing is—"

"No!" She stopped him. "Don't tell me any more right now. I can't handle any more. I feel like my head's going to explode as it is."

Edric smiled faintly. "That's understandable." He leaned forward and gave her a gentle kiss on the cheek.

She stared at him, emotions tangling like barbed wire in her head.

"Yeah. Hi, Mum." Jade's voice wavered a little. "No. I'm fine. Why? Do I? No, everything's cool here." She was staring at Rathina and Zara as if her eyes were about to bug out of her head. "Oh, just sitting in the sun. Yeah. I'll get the parasol out. Yes, I know you told me to be careful. Yes. SPF twenty and the parasol. I'll do it right now. Quit fussing, Mum."

Anita smiled. This was so wonderfully ordinary

that she could have run and hugged Jade till her ribs creaked.

"You want I should do what? Yeah, fine. I'll do it right now." Her eyes widened. "You'll be home in half an hour? Okay. Yes. Okay. Will do. Bye, Mum."

She dropped her arm to her side. "My folks are on their way back here," she said, speaking to no one in particular. "They want me to take the meat out of the freezer and defrost it in the microwave." She gave a huge, vacant smile. "Apparently we're having a barbecue this evening!" An edge of bleak sarcasm came into her voice. "Won't that be fun?" She looked from Edric to Rathina. "Do you guys like barbecues at all? My dad does an amazing Chimichurri marinade and I can rustle up a great chili sauce. . . ." Her voice faded and she closed her eyes. "Would one of you do me a big favor and beat me over the head with a rock till I'm unconscious, please?"

"Master Chanticleer!" Rathina's voice cut the air. "We must return to Faerie! Use your Arts. Remove us from this place!"

"I can't take us through to Faerie," said Edric. "I don't have that kind of power. I wouldn't be able to do it even if the earls of Faerie hadn't closed the ways between the worlds." He looked urgently at Anita. "Have you tried to step into Faerie?" His face clouded. "No! Of course you haven't—you don't remember anything about that, do you?"

Anita looked at him. "I want to remember," she said forlornly. "Help me to remember."

He put his hands to her face. "I don't know how."

"We cannot stay here!" declared Rathina. "We must seek some place where Zara can come to herself in safety—away from the prying eyes of ignorant Mortals." She got to her feet, Zara's limp form cradled in her strong arms. "We have little time, Master Chanticleer. Find us sanctuary, and find it swift."

"I know where you can go!" Jade exclaimed. "Anita's mum knows all about you guys! She knows about the place you come from and everything. You should go to her."

"Is this wisdom?" asked Rathina. "To seek the dwelling of Master Clive and Mistress Mary?"

"I think it might be," said Edric. He looked at Anita. "Is it true that your parents still remember everything about Faerie?"

Anita nodded. "Mum does, for sure. I don't know about Dad. Jade's right, we should go there."

"Is it far?" asked Rathina.

"Not by cab it isn't," said Jade, pressing buttons on her mobile. "I'll call a cab right now. You'll be there in ten minutes." She put the phone to her ear. "Yes? Oh, hi there. I need a cab. As soon as you can, please. In fact, right now would be totally excellent!"

She gave pick-up instructions then ended the call. She looked Rathina and Edric up and down. "There's no way the driver will let you in the cab in those wet clothes. Those wet, *weird* clothes." She gestured toward Edric. "Evan—whatever your real name is— you're pretty much the same size as my brother. I'll find something of his for you to wear." She turned to Rathina. "And I can probably find some loose stuff of mine that you'll be able to squeeze into."

She strode down the lawn toward the house. "Anita? Come on, help me out here. Do I have to do *everything*?"

Anita quickly caught up with her friend. "Thank you," she said softly.

"For what?"

"For not freaking out."

Jade gave her an incredulous look. "Don't kid yourself, Anita. I am so freaking out here; it's not true." She linked her arm with Anita's as they walked in through the open patio doors. "Thing is," she said, "crazy as all this is—it totally explains the way you've been acting for the past couple of months. It's insane, you know? But it also makes perfect sense." She laughed breathlessly. "You're a fairy princess. A total and utter fairy princess! That is *so* cool!"

"You didn't need to come with us, Jade," said Anita. "You should've stayed home."

"What? And get chewed out for letting the lily pond get mashed? I don't think so." Jade retorted. She looked at Anita, lowering her voice so that the taxi driver couldn't hear her over the piped pop music that filled the cab. "Besides, if you think you can just turn up and dump all this crazy stuff in my lap, then stroll off without any explanation, you can think again."

They were in a taxi, heading for Anita's home. Edric was sitting in the front passenger seat wearing a borrowed T-shirt and jeans. The four girls were crammed in the back. Rathina was in a halter top and a light cotton skirt, holding Zara's hand, nestling the drowsy girl's head against her shoulder. Zara's Faerie gown was hidden under a tan suede coat. She was awake and she was able to sit up on her own, but she had a faraway look in her blue-diamond eyes and she didn't respond when she was spoken to.

"So, what do you think about this eclipse we're due to get on Friday?" said the driver, who had been talking nonstop since they'd gotten into the cab. "Odds are it'll be a cloudy day and we won't see a thing."

"I don't know anything about it." Edric just managed to wedge the words in.

"You're kidding?" replied the cabbie. "It's been all over the news for days, mate. Longest eclipse this century, it said on the radio."

"Really?" said Edric. "I must have missed it."

"Where have you been? Mars?" The cabbie chuckled. "My kids can't wait. They've already got their bits of cardboard with pinholes in them. That's the safest way to look at it, apparently. What you do is . . ."

Anita tuned the cabbie out. Zara was gazing out of the window, her eyes glassy, as if she was far, far away inside her head. Anita had noticed that Zara's lips were moving. She leaned in close to try to catch what this girl—this dead sister of hers—was saying.

But she wasn't speaking; she was softly singing.

*"I shall weave you gentle dreams between dusk*
    *and morning*
*I shall nestle in your heart and whisper in your*
    *ear*
*I shall tell you sweet tales, to soothe you till*
    *dawning*
*I shall tarry close, my love, you need have no*
    *fear . . ."*

Rathina was also listening, her forehead wrinkled.

"What is that?" asked Anita.

"An old nursery rhyme," said Rathina. "A lullaby our mother used to sing to us."

*I shall weave you gentle dreams . . .* Why did that fragment of the lyric stick in her mind?

"'Tis a pretty tune," said Rathina. "I have not heard it sung for many's the long year, but Zara used to play it upon the flute." She rested her fingers under Zara's chin and lifted her head to look into her face. "And shall again, if the wish of my heart comes true." She gazed into the blank eyes, then kissed the pale forehead. "I know not how this has come to be, Zara, but your return has lifted such a burden off my soul! Such a heavy burden!"

Anita looked at Rathina. There were tears in her eyes.

*Why can't I remember? I want to remember!*

The cab slowed down. "Here we are: Nineteen Eddison Terrace," said the driver. Jade fished the fare out of her jeans and they all piled out of the cab. Rathina and Anita stood on either side of Zara. She didn't need holding up, but she seemed to have no idea where she was.

Realizing she'd left the house without any keys, Anita walked up the front steps and rang the bell.

*Hi, Mum. I'm home, and I've brought some friends with me. You'll never believe where they come from! Oh! Yes—you will. I'm the one who can't believe it. . . .*

The door opened. The first expression that passed across her mother's face was relief, then she looked beyond Anita and saw the other people gathered on her porch.

She opened the door wider. "You'd better come in," she said quickly.

Anita passed into the hallway, followed by Rathina and Zara, then Edric, and finally Jade. Mrs. Palmer closed the door. She gave Jade a resigned smile. "Hello, Jade," she said. "Welcome to my world."

# VIII

Clive Palmer stood in the living room doorway. Anita was shocked by her father's appearance. He looked pale and ill and he needed a shave. But his smile was the same as ever—that big sunshine smile that could always make everything right.

"Anita!" His voice was tired but happy. "Welcome home!"

She hugged him. There was an antiseptic odor on his clothes and skin—a lingering hospital smell. She wasn't sure what to say. She wasn't sure what he knew.

"Mum says you've been ill," she tried. "That was silly of you!"

"I know. Trust me, eh?" He held her tightly—like a father who has not seen his daughter for a long time. "I'm on the mend now, though. They threw me out of the hospital. Didn't want me lying around for no good reason when there were ill people needing a bed." He drew back a little and took her face between his hands. "Your mum tells me you've forgotten a lot of things."

She nodded. "I kind of have." His eyes slid away from hers, and she saw a new look come over his face as he focused on Edric and Rathina—uneasy and a little resentful—as though he was seeing people he had hoped never to meet again. It was an odd look, and it made her uncomfortable. Did he know something about them that she didn't?

"Greetings to you, Mistress Mary," said Rathina, bowing a little to Anita's mother. "And to you, Master Clive—I am glad indeed that your ailments are not so severe as Tania feared." She shook her head. "Fate plays a strange hand, indeed! We condemned you and banished you for a crime you did not commit—and now we come seeking your aid, and hopefully your forgiveness."

"You're welcome to both," said Mary Palmer. "Of course you are."

Clive Palmer's eyes widened. "The dream was real, then?" he said. He looked at Anita. "You came to me—a week ago—in the middle of the night. You told me the sickness in Faerie wasn't my fault. I thought I'd dreamed the whole thing. But it seemed real. Was it real?"

"I don't know, Dad," said Anita. "I don't remember."

Mr. Palmer looked sharply at Edric. "We had nothing to do with the illness in Faerie? Is that right?"

"It is, sir," said Edric, gazing steadily into Clive Palmer's eyes. "And I'm sorry for the part I played in blaming you. I hope you can forgive me."

Mr. Palmer looked away.

Rathina's voice broke the awkward silence. "I'd lay my sweet sister down, if a bed can be found for her," she said, her arm still around Zara's waist. "Mayhap sleep will restore her to us more fully. She has come to us from so very far away."

Anita's mother looked into Zara's blank face. "Your sister, you say, Rathina? I've not met her, but I've seen pictures of her—portraits—on the walls in the Royal Palace. Is this *Zara*?"

"It is," said Rathina.

"But I thought . . . I was told she died."

"Indeed she did, Mistress Mary, and only the wise and watchful spirits know how she has come back to us," said Rathina. "A bed? If you please?"

"Yes. Of course." She moved to the foot of the stairs. "Will she be able to climb the stairs?"

"I believe so."

"Then she can lie down in Anita's room."

Zara turned her head from side to side, gazing into their faces but hardly seeming to see them as Rathina and Mrs. Palmer began slowly to climb the stairs, guiding her between them.

Jade was standing in the hall with her back to the front door, her arms folded, and a look on her face of bemused acceptance.

"Okay," she said, looking from Edric to Anita's father. "I hope you've noticed how well I'm handling all this craziness. But before my brain melts, I'd really like someone to bring me up to speed on what the heck is going on here."

"Yes, we should do that," said Edric. "Talking about it might help Tania to remember."

"Come through into the kitchen," said Mr. Palmer. "I don't know about you all, but I could do with a cup of tea. A strong one." He put his arm about Anita's shoulders. "Come on, *Anita*, let's put the kettle on."

"And so at the last, on the far western coast of Hy Brassail, Master Connor's duplicity was laid bare," said Rathina. "He was revealed as the traitor in our midst; all the time he had been leading our enemy to us across those wide and strange lands." Her face contracted in anger. "Lord Balor's minions came upon us, and although we fought them, we were subdued. A blow to my head rendered me senseless."

"We woke in a cave above the beach," Edric continued. "We were tied up, but Rathina's sword was there, and we managed to cut ourselves free. We came out of the cave, expecting to have to fight for our lives, but Balor lay dead on the beach—his body torn to ribbons." He looked at Anita. "Connor was lying nearby. He had been knocked out. There was no sign of Tania."

Anita gazed into his face. *When I went to bed last night, I was Anita and he was Evan. But now he's Edric and I'm . . . ? Who am I? What am I? And what is he? Not even human—not really. Immortal? What does that mean? I wish I could remember something. I'd give anything to remember.*

"To our astonishment, the only wakeful creature on that wide beach was the Great Salamander, deadly servant of the evil brigand Balor," said Rathina, picking up the story. "I lifted my sword, expecting the beast to attack us. But it made no move. 'Do not fear me,' it said, and it had a voice that rumbled and hissed most ferociously. 'I do not fear you!' I declared. 'As you shall learn swift enough if you do not tell us what has become of my sister. Speak the truth, monster,' I said. 'Where is the princess Tania? If you have devoured her, you shall die upon this moment!' And the monster spoke again. 'Princess Tania has flown to the land of Tirnanog that lies in the western skies,' it said. 'She is unhurt. She is with the Divine Harper.' And so saying, it turned its long head westward into the sunset. 'Have patience, she will return.'"

They were gathered at the kitchen table: Rathina, Edric, Jade, Mrs. Palmer, and Anita. She was clinging to her mother's hand as Edric and Rathina spoke. Her father was moving around the table, placing cups of tea in front of everyone.

"And we waited," said Edric. "But Tania never came back. Then, just as the sun set, we heard thunder and lightning and a noise like a rough sea—but we didn't *see* anything. The ocean was calm and there was hardly a cloud in the sky. Rathina asked the Salamander if it knew what was happening."

Rathina broke in. "'Great and portentous events!' the beast declared. 'I know not what it betokens, but the sounds that you hear issue from the airy land of Tirnanog. A storm rages there.'"

"A storm . . ." murmured Anita, touching her hand to her forehead. A stream of images had glimmered for a moment in her mind. A beach of golden sand. A long white stone. A harp. An old man with apple cheeks and gray hair and beard. And there was music—discordant music that blended with lightning, clouds, and crashing waves.

"Do you remember?" asked Edric, leaning eagerly toward her across the table.

"Something . . . just pictures in my head. I don't know what they mean."

"And as the unseen storm raged in our ears, so Master Connor came suddenly awake," said Rathina. "Wild-eyed and terrified. He jumped to his feet as though fey with madness. 'Traitor!' I called him, lifting my sword and prepared to smite him to the heart for the wrong he had done to us. But my blow never fell. For he screamed and writhed and fell upon the ground as though beset by demons. It was a fearful thing to see, forsooth!"

"There was a moment when he seemed to be out of pain," said Edric. "He looked up at us and he said, 'Who are you? Where am I?'"

"And then he was gone!" said Rathina, spreading her hands. "Like rain upon a hot stone. Quite vanished away!" She frowned. "Banished, I trust, to some deadly place where he will do penance for all eternity!"

"He's here," said Anita breathlessly. "He's in London."

Rathina sprang up, knocking against the table, rattling the cups and spilling tea. "Then lead me to him, sister—and I'll split him throat to vitals for his perfidy!"

"He doesn't remember anything," said Anita, looking up at Rathina. "He told me the last thing he remembers is the two of us going to his flat. Then it's all blank till he woke up this morning."

"Lies to mask his deceits, I'll warrant!" said Rathina as Mr. Palmer took a cloth to wipe up the splashes of tea.

"Not necessarily," said Edric. "I don't think it's a coincidence that neither Tania nor Connor remembers anything about Faerie. I'd guess that whatever power destroyed Tania's memory and sent her here did exactly the same to Connor."

"The Divine Harper, you mean?" said Mrs. Palmer.

"Who else?" asked Edric. "He locked up all their memories of Faerie and then sent them back into their own world."

"A strange and uncanny creature he must be," muttered Rathina, "dwelling in the clouds and dispensing a form of justice beyond my ken. Was Tania punished for seeking his help? Is that what happened in Tirnanog?"

"I don't think so," said Edric. "The Divine Harper seeks balance in all things. You give something to get something." He looked urgently at Anita. "I'm sure if we can find a way to get Tania to remember who she is, the memory of what the Divine Harper told her will be there as well."

"Excuse me," broke in Mr. Palmer, dropping the cloth into the sink, "but I think my daughter already knows who she is."

Mrs. Palmer looked uneasy. Rathina frowned at him. "Indeed she does not, Master Clive—all her Faerie self slumbers."

"Good. I'm glad to hear it," said Anita's father, looking from Rathina to Edric. "I'd like it to stay that way. So, whatever conjuring tricks you're thinking of using on my daughter, I'd prefer that you leave her be." His voice trembled with suppressed anger. "Hasn't she done enough for you . . . *people*?" He stabbed a finger at Edric. "You! You're supposed to love her. Well, show it! She was a happy, normal girl till you turned up."

"Clive . . . ?" Mary Palmer's voice was quiet but firm. "I don't think it's as simple as that."

His face pleaded. "We've got her back. How can you want her to go through all that chaos and heartbreak again?"

"I don't," said Mrs. Palmer. "But she's needed. A baby virtually died in my arms, Clive—a little baby. And more people are dying now. If Tania can help, we can't stand in the way. How could we live with ourselves?"

"And how do we know she hasn't already done what she set out to do?" asked Mr. Palmer. "How do we know this Harper didn't grant her wishes and put an end to the illness?"

"We cannot know that for sure, Master Clive," said Rathina. "Not unless we can return to Faerie—and that we cannot do without Tania. Only she has the gift of walking between the worlds."

"Uh, excuse me!" Jade raised a tentative hand. "I know I'm the newcomer here, but Evan . . . I mean

Edric—Edric found a way to get from Faerie to here, didn't he? Why can't he do the same thing backward and go take a look in Faerie?"

"It doesn't work like that," said Edric. "I was able to get here because I was focusing on Tania, on being with her, on our feelings for each other. That's what pulled me through. And even then I needed the Salamander's help. There's no way I can punch through back into Faerie."

"And 'tis worse by far than that!" added Rathina solemnly. "For the ways between the worlds have been sealed by the Conclave of Earls. Even were Tania in her right mind, I fear she could not get through by merely sidestepping. Not from here. We would need to travel from this place and find a land where the power of the Faerie lords does not hold sway. And from there, once we had passed from this world to our own, we would need to take a ship to return to our home." She frowned. "Days and weeks could be squandered in such an endeavor!"

"You are not taking my daughter on a wild-goose chase to another country," declared Clive Palmer. "This nonsense stops here." He pointed a shaking finger from Edric to Rathina. "I want you out of my house!" he said. "You're not welcome here!"

"You would condemn all of Faerie to despair?" Rathina gasped.

"To save my daughter? Yes, I would!"

"No, Dad!" It made Anita's heart ache to see how this was affecting her father. He turned to her, his face full of fear. "I don't want that. I have to help if I can!"

He stared at her, then fumbled for the back door, walking unsteadily out into the garden.

"I should go to him," said Mrs. Palmer. She looked from Edric to Rathina. "He's still not completely well," she said. "This has been a great strain on him. He doesn't mean to belittle your problems—he's only thinking of Anita."

Anita got up from the table. "I'll go be with him," she said to her mother. "Stay here, please."

"I'll make some more tea," her mother said with a nod.

Anita walked to the open back door. Her father was down by the rosebush, his shoulders slumped.

"Jade? Does your mum know you're here?" she heard her mother say.

"Not exactly, Mrs. P.," Jade replied. "I kind of skipped out before she got home. The lily pond got wrecked. I need time to come up with a plausible explanation for what happened. Don't worry about it—it'll be fine."

The voices faded out of Anita's consciousness. She could think only about her father now. She stepped into the garden and walked toward him.

"Dad?"

She had been beside him for close to half a minute, and he hadn't looked at her once, nor said a single word. His hands were pushed deep into his pockets and his head was down, caught up in his own thoughts.

The lawn was churned by tire tracks. The back fence broken. Physical proof that Faerie was real—that Anita Palmer was also Princess Tania Aurealis.

"The roses are doing well this year," her father murmured. "This particular strain is called Deep Secret. It's a hybrid tea rose. I bought it for the fragrance." His voice cracked with emotion. "You always loved the smell of roses when you were a child."

She stooped toward the dark red roses and breathed in deeply so the powerful, sweet scent filled her head. "I still do," she said gently. She reached out to him, tugging his reluctant hand out of his pocket and twining her fingers with his. "You hate all this, don't you? All this Faerie stuff?"

"I hate what it does to you," he said. "You don't remember how it was tearing you apart. This is the first time since your birthday that you've been yourself. And now . . ." He choked and was unable to continue.

She squeezed his hand, folding her other hand around his arm and pressing close against his side. A thick lump filled her throat.

There were tears in his voice when he spoke again. "I'm afraid I'll lose you," he said. "I'm afraid you're going to go away from me and never come back."

"I'll never do that."

"You can't make that promise. You don't *know*."

"Well, that's certainly true." Anita sighed. "In fact, apart from Jade, I'm the only one here who doesn't know a single thing about Faerie." She looked into his eyes. "You and Mum have been there, Dad! You've seen stuff I've totally forgotten. It's all just words to me right now—but you know it's real." She paused, gathering her thoughts. "I'm part of their world, Dad, even though I can't remember it. They came and found me because they know I can help. I can't let them down."

He smiled bleakly. "I know, sweetheart. I know."

She clung to him. "This whole thing is unbelievably scary, Dad. I need you on my side so that I can do whatever it takes to help them." She looked into his face. "I'm not a big hero, Dad—I'm totally freaked—but a whole country full of people needs me." She could almost have laughed! Saying it out loud didn't help at all. It still sounded insane.

Her father looked at her. "So? You want my blessing? Is that what you need from me?"

She squeezed his hand even more tightly. "Please."

"Then you have it," he said.

"Thank you. Thank you *so* much!"

Muffled cries sounded from the house. Edric appeared at the back door and called to them.

"It's Zara. She's awake!"

# IX

Anita ran in from the garden.

Zara was standing in the kitchen doorway, flanked by Rathina and Edric, her flowing Faerie gown a stark contrast to their everyday clothes. Her face was drained of color, but her eyes had a new light in them.

"Come in, Zara," said Mrs. Palmer, pulling out a chair from the table. "How are you feeling?"

"I feel newborn. . . ." murmured Zara, sitting down.

"May I get you a drink?" Edric suggested, moving to the fridge.

Zara nodded. "By your courtesy, Master Chanticleer."

Anita was aware of an air of suppressed excitement in the room, as though everyone was being careful not to overwhelm the pale princess with their attention.

Anita stepped forward, and Zara seemed to notice her for the first time.

"Tania!" she said, and her voice was strong and happy. "I have seen you so often in my mind—but I never dared hope to embrace you more!" She jumped up and ran into Anita's arms.

"I don't remember you. . . ." Anita said awkwardly, folding her arms stiffly around the girl. "I'm sorry." She gave Edric an uneasy look over Zara's back.

"It matters not," said Zara. "You were in the same pickle when first you came into Faerie. And a merry time we had of it convincing you of your birthright then!"

"Indeed," Rathina added, smiling. "Most stubborn you were!"

"There is no need of persuasion this time," said Zara. "Be seated, sister mine, and we shall see what we shall see."

"I'm sorry?" Anita said.

Zara laughed. "Sit! Sit! I would run barefoot through your mind." Quite gently, but purposefully, she pressed Anita into a chair. "I will return your memories to you, Tania. I have new skills now that I am . . ." She paused, her face clouding for a moment. "But no matter. Let's to business."

Anita looked anxiously at Edric.

"You'll be fine," he said, resting the forgotten glass of milk on the table and crouching at her side. "And if this works . . ."

"I'll remember?"

He nodded.

Jade looked dubious. "Is this going to be like one of those TV shows where some guy hypnotizes people into thinking they're chickens?" she asked.

"Hush," Rathina murmured. "I know not what is coming."

The kitchen became silent. Anita was aware of all eyes on her. Her father and mother were standing together at the back door, watchful but unspeaking.

Anita felt Zara's hands come down lightly upon her head.

For a few moments nothing happened. Then Zara began very softly to sing.

> *"Spirits of love, let the lost child return*
> *Spirits of joy, make her gentle and strong*
> *Spirits of air, let her thrive and grow*
> *Spirits of blood, let her veins be warm*
>
> *"Spirits of fire, light a spark in her green eyes*
> *Let it grow in your eternal flame*
> *Spirits of life, let her remember times past*
> *Bring her back to herself and to me*
>
> *"Spirits of water, flow through her and make*
> *     her whole*
> *In the sea that has no shore, the sea of memory*
> *Let her swim in you and know you and love you*
> *Let her learn and become and be*
>
> *"Spirits of earth, let her walk again upon you*
> *Through the meadows of your land's grace*
> *Let the sunlight shine upon her beloved face*
> *Let her true self run free"*

As Zara sang, Anita felt warmth rippling through her from the princess's gentle hands. It seemed to her that Zara's voice was joined by others—soft, dulcet voices and deep, sonorous voices all singing counterpoint and descant to the aching melody until her head was filled with song.

An image poured into her mind like a flow of soft golden light. Endless green hills folding away to a blue horizon. And herself—hand-in-hand with Zara—running through the tall grass. Looking about them as they ran. Searching for something. It was an early morning and the dew was like honey on her bare feet and the singing was all around them.

"It is not enough." Zara's voice was a sharp knife through the song. "I cannot do this thing alone. Master Edric—take her hand now."

Anita's heart throbbed in her chest. A warm hand slipped into hers, and she felt enveloped in a deep love and understanding. In her vision she turned her head, seeing with a rush of joy that Edric had appeared at her side, running through the pastures with her, searching with her.

"And yet more," said Zara. "Master Clive, Mistress Mary—lay your hands upon your daughter—she is in need of your love."

Anita felt hands coming to rest on her arms. From the blue infinity of the sky, her Mortal mother and father appeared beside her—running with her. Her heart filled with happiness.

"Sister—she needs more. And you, Mortal girl,

come, join the dance, let none hold back when all are needed."

Suddenly Rathina was there at her side in her vision, and Jade, also, staring around as though stunned to find herself in such a place.

*Is this real, then? I thought it was all in my head. . . .*

They were no longer running now. They were upon a hilltop crowned with huge blue crystals that threw out a vibrant light. It was night—a night of huge and pulsing stars. They were in a ring, hand-in-hand, dancing in a circle among the shining stones. The air was like spice and the grass was alive beneath their feet.

Anita could feel the love of her family rushing through her. The love of her mother and father, the love of Jade and her Faerie sisters; and deepest of all, like a warm hand that cradled her heart, the love of her own Edric.

Faster and faster they whirled, forming a chain that threaded in and out among the great blue crystal stones.

Then there was no ground beneath her feet. She was soaring upward through the night.

She was winged, alone, suspended in darkness, surrounded by stars.

Every star was a memory, rushing at her in a hail of sharp light, pouring into her eyes, filling her mind.

She saw a vision of a solemn-eyed, brown-haired girl with a sighing voice. "He had a mausoleum of white stone built to honor our mother. . . ."

Herself, kneeling on a forest path, clutching a leather-bound book.

That same sad voice, but terrified now. "I am in a small dark room, in a hovel, lying in a bed with filthy sheets over me. . . ."

She saw Zara and herself being helped into a row-boat by a man in sky blue livery. A silver galleon lay at anchor in a wide bay.

A freckled girl with red-gold hair cut at the shoulder. "Are there cows in the Mortal World?" she was asking.

Edric's voice. "I've got house keys and some coins on me. . . ."

A riptide of gray unicorns with mauve manes and purple eyes.

A withered heath. A battle. Herself standing, a sword in her fist. The memories were coming at her too fast. There were too many—too insistent—heaping into her mind until she was lost under the weight of them.

Screaming and clawing, she felt herself drowning in memories.

The last thing she saw was a great whaleback of white rock jutting out into a crashing ocean. . . .

Tania was in a boat on a wide dark river. It was night. She knew there were other people with her, although she could not see them. She could hear uneasy horses. The stamp of a hoof. A snort in the darkness at her back. Was this a dream or another memory?

A woman stood before her. An ageless woman in a dark cloak. A woman with a sweet, round-cheeked face and clear blue eyes.

The woman spoke gently. "Do not fear. You are strongest where you are split—and I see your many selves, plucked out of time, coming together to heal you when your need is greatest." The woman released Tania's hand, and she and the boat and the river began to drift away.

"No, wait!" Her own voice was shrill in her ears. "What does that mean? I don't understand!"

She was being held down, stifled in a dark place. Panic erupted through her as she struggled and fought, unable to escape, unable to breathe.

There was a pale light above her. She clawed frantically in the darkness. She had to get to the light. She *had* to.

# X

Tania Aurealis, princess of Faerie, seventh daughter of King Oberon and Queen Titania, awoke in the gloom of her bedroom in North West London.

She sat upright, gasping for breath. Sharp, thin lines of light shone at the edges of the curtains that covered her window. She was fully dressed, save for shoes, and she was in her bed under a thin white duvet patterned with pink roses.

The Faerie part of her had come alive again—and she remembered everything.

*Everything*. From the moment when she had been sitting in her hospital bed reading the story of her own life from the book that had been blank pages only a few minutes previously. From that to the moment upon the white stone in Tirnanog when the sea had raged and the sky had grown dark and the Divine Harper's outstretched finger had touched the center of her forehead and her mind had exploded.

Scrambling out of bed, she glanced at the bedside clock: 7:03. Just after seven o'clock in the evening.

She ran to the door and flung it open. She could hear subdued voices from the kitchen.

Racing down the stairs, she arrived breathlessly at the kitchen doorway.

They were all there, gathered at the table. Her Mortal mother and father; her two Faerie sisters; her best friend, Jade—and the love of her life, Edric. Her darling Edric!

The voices stopped and every face turned to her.

"Anita . . . ?" her father asked.

"Tania?" Rathina ventured cautiously.

She laughed. "Yes!" She gasped. "Both!" She stepped into the room. "I remember everything. The Faerie part of me has come back!"

Edric stood up and she stepped into his arms, holding him, closing her eyes, and breathing him in. She could hear other voices, and feel hands on her shoulders and arms.

She pulled away from Edric and turned to embrace Rathina and Zara.

*Poor Rathina!* Doomed by love—fated never to be absolved of the terrible deeds done by her under Gabriel Drake's thrall.

And Zara, murdered on Salisoc Heath. But alive again now!

"Thank you," she said, hugging Zara even more fiercely. "Thank you so much!"

Almost in tears, she turned to her mother and father; their arms enfolded her and she held them tightly.

Her mother gazed deep into her eyes. "What would you like us to call you, sweetheart?"

Tania drew back a little, looking at her father. "Would it be bad if I said Tania?"

He smiled. "Not at all," he said. "Tania it is." He touched her cheek with his fingertips. "'What's in a name? A rose by any other name would smell as sweet.'"

She took his hand, recognizing the quote from *Romeo and Juliet*.

"Smart man, Shakespeare," added her father.

Jade pushed forward and threw her arms around her. "So, who are you now?" she asked. "Are you *you*, or are you *her*?"

"I'm both," said Tania.

"I knew it! Total schizoid!"

Tania laughed. "Not really . . ."

She turned again to Zara, taking both her hands, gazing into her eyes.

"How?" she asked. "How can you be here?"

"It is a curious tale," said Zara. "The story of one who stood at the gates of Albion but did not pass through into the Blessèd Realm." She drew one hand away from Tania and reached out toward Rathina. "How my journey began, I cannot say," she told them. "I do not remember my death."

"I do," murmured Rathina, taking Zara's hand, her

face pale and gaunt. "All too well."

Zara squeezed her fingers. "Hush now," she said. "All that passes has its purpose in the great tapestry, and you shall see that my death was not vain."

She smiled around at the others. "I stood upon the threshold of Albion and the gates swung wide to welcome me in," she continued, her voice as sweet as music. "But I could not go through. Something held me back. I turned and it seemed to me that I could see the realm of Faerie far, far below me, set like an emerald in the azure sea. A voice spoke to me. 'Great perils beset the Immortal Realm—wouldst thou stretch out thy hand to bring alms to those whom thou hast left behind?' And I said, yes, indeed I would, if I can. And the voice said, 'Thou art dead, child of Faerie, and thou mayst not return to the land of thy birth, but these gifts I will grant thee. There is one who belongs both to Faerie and to the world of Mortals—through her shalt thou work thy wonders. Within the borders of Faerie thou may come to her only in her dreams.'"

*I shall weave you gentle dreams . . .*

Of course! That was why that snatch of nursery rhyme had stuck in her mind.

Tania gazed at her sister, her throat constricted and tears pricking in her eyes. "You were the Dream Weaver!"

"Indeed, I was," said Zara. "I could not reveal my true self to you—'twould have ruined all."

"I resented that spirit taking over my body," said

Rathina, her eyes shining. "But right glad of it am I now! Had I but known . . ."

"Never was I told the true nature of the great peril that hung over Faerie," Zara continued, taking her sister's hand. "I knew only that it came from the north and that it had sickness on its breath and mayhem in its heart. But the voice that spoke to me at the gates of Albion told me of the path that needed to be trod if the dread was to be thwarted. And so I slipped into Tania's dreams and did what I could to guide her on her way. And beyond the shores of Faerie, I was able to enter Rathina's body for a while and tell more. Always too little—but every word was a stepping-stone to quest's end."

"But why were you not given greater powers?" asked Rathina. "Why could you work only through hints and guesses?"

Zara's forehead wrinkled. "Are we not to strive and contend against great evil?" she asked mildly. "Is the fight to be denied us? Nay, sister, the journey is as important as the goal—endeavor and endurance both have their parts to play in the Great Design."

"I get it," Jade said, frowning at Zara. "At least I think I do. You can't just be handed this stuff on a plate, right? You can be helped along, but you have to do most of the work yourself."

Zara smiled. "A wise Mortal, you are," she said.

Jade blinked at her. "Oh. Uh. Thanks. . . ."

Rathina gave a sudden choked cry and threw her arms around Zara's neck. Tania saw tears glinting on her dark lashes, and she could feel joyful tears filling her own eyes.

"It is blessèd indeed to embrace you once more, beloved sister," said Rathina, her voice choked with emotion. "I have shed tears enough to drown entire mountains for the loss of you!"

"Then weep no more," said Zara, kissing Rathina's forehead. "Be comforted and open your heart to full understanding. Had I not died, your quest for enlightenment might never have been accomplished."

"I'm not sure it was accomplished," Tania ventured. "At least not in the way we had hoped."

"What did the Harper tell you?" asked her father. "Did he explain how you could destroy the plague?"

Tania looked unhappily at him. "He did in a way," she said. "But he also told me that it was impossible."

"No!" gasped Rathina. "That cannot be. After all our toil and travails—it would be too cruel."

Tania told them all what had passed between her and the Divine Harper on the endless golden seashore of Tirnanog. She saw the encounter vividly in her mind as she spoke.

She could hear the Harper's resounding voice ringing out in response when she had asked him to end the plague by renewing the covenant. *There are but two ways for this to be done. Either Oberon must come to me—or I must go to him. But I cannot enter Faerie, and the King must not leave his Realm, for if he does he will lose his throne to Lear for all time."*

And her own alarmed response: *"No! That can't be*

*right! That's impossible!*" Lightning had forked across the dark sky, stabbing at the hills, tainting the air.

The Harper's voice had slashed through the storm. *"It is not impossible. Nothing is impossible."* Then his gaze had sparked as though there was lightning in his eyes. *"Your question is answered, Tania of Faerie, Anita of the Mortal World. Now you must give me that which was offered. You must render up the dearest wish of your heart."*

She now bowed her head. "And then I woke up in my bedroom here. And it was all gone. All forgotten . . ."

She looked up again, seeing horror in Rathina's face and shock and confusion in the faces of Edric and Zara.

"Our father has an older brother . . . ?" said Rathina breathlessly. "I never knew. Father and Uncle Cornelius never spoke of it."

"They didn't know, I don't think," said Tania. "Their memory of Lear was taken away by the Divine Harper when the first covenant was made."

"That Divine Harper guy sure likes wiping people's minds!" murmured Jade. "Great party trick, but annoying all the same. What's the point in telling Ani—in telling *Tania* all that stuff and then making her forget it?"

"It was because of the dearest wish of her heart," said Edric. He looked at Tania. "To find out what you needed to know you had to offer up the 'dearest wish of your heart.' Now I understand why this happened. You did it yourself, Tania—although you didn't mean to."

"The dearest wish of your heart was to be Tania of Faerie," broke in her father, staring at her with a new awareness in his face. "I never realized it meant that much to you. . . ."

"Neither did I," Tania said. She looked at Edric. "I thought I would lose something else." *You! I thought I would lose you, Edric!*

"Now we know the true nature of our foe," said Zara. "Of all ends to your quest, this was the furthest from my thoughts. That a son of the house of Aurealis should wreak such destruction upon his own people. 'Tis far beyond my reckoning! Deep perfidy, indeed!"

Mr. Palmer looked at Tania. "What do you intend to do?" he asked.

"I have to return to Faerie," she replied. "I can't do anything from here."

"Then we must quit this land and seek the long road home," said Rathina. "Tania, do you remember how to pass between the realms?"

Tania smiled. "Yes, it's all here," she said, tapping her forehead. "But I don't think we need to leave London to do it." She paused, gathering her thoughts. "I had a dream. A *kind* of dream while I was upstairs." She looked at Rathina and Edric. "Do you remember what Coriceil said to me when we crossed the river to Erin? She said I am strongest where I am split—and that she could see my other selves 'plucked out of time and coming together' to help me when I needed them."

"Your other selves?" said Mrs. Palmer. "Oh! You

mean all those poor children who died before they reached sixteen?"

Tania nodded. "I don't know how, exactly, but I think they'll be able to help me get back to Faerie."

Zara's eyes widened. "Perhaps they will!" she said. "And especially so if you call upon the Power of Seven to aid you."

"Seven is indeed a potent number," added Rathina, looking at Zara. "Is it possible that Tania can pluck six of her Mortal selves from the past to join with her?"

"I believe it is," said Zara, taking Tania's hands in hers. "You must become seven souls that are but one soul reunited. You must gather them to you, and you must use the power that flows through you to dash aside the barriers between the worlds and step into Faerie."

"I'm sorry," broke in Mr. Palmer. "I don't understand. What do you mean when you say Tania needs to *gather* her past selves? How can she do that?"

"Tania's Immortal Faerie soul came into the Mortal World five hundred years ago," said Zara. "But her first walking between the worlds weakened her body and she fell ill and died. It was only her outer shell that perished; her Immortal soul leaped free and sought another body, another girl child about to be born." Zara's face creased with sadness. "The soul of a Faerie is a bright light and burns fiercely. But by misfortune or ill happenstance or sickness and disease, the children through which the soul passed died in their childhood—until there came into the world a Mortal body and spirit equal to the task of housing the soul of a Faerie princess—one who could walk between the worlds."

Jade's voice was full of astonishment. "So, this Faerie soul has been body-hopping for five hundred years . . . until it found Tania?"

"That is so," said Zara. She looked questioningly at Tania. "You know the faces of some of your previous selves. Did it not seem strange that out of all of them, you are the only one to resemble Queen Titania? The only one to have the face of the sister who first walked into the Mortal World five centuries ago?"

"I never really thought about it before." Tania swallowed. "So, I was always the *one*?"

Zara nodded. "If not you, then no one," she said. "Yours are the spirit and the body in which all hopes and desires are housed." She smiled into Tania's eyes. "Alone, you do not have the power to break through the barriers set up by the Conclave of Earls. But with six of your past selves at your side, I think the walls will crack and tumble. The strength of your soul will be doubled and redoubled by your other selves, like a candle's light reflected in a circle of mirrors."

"But how can I reach them?" asked Tania. "They're dead. They died a long time ago."

"I think I can help you to find them," murmured Edric. His expression was pained. "I know I promised not to use the Dark Arts again, but it was the Dark Arts that brought me here, and I'm still myself." He frowned. "I can control the power; I'm sure I can—so long as I use it for good."

Tania looked uneasily at him. The Dark Arts were dangerous and she hated him using them. But perhaps it *was* possible for him to control them? For a while at least.

"Be not so sure," muttered Rathina. "Not all those devoured by evil were born with a tainted soul!"

"That is true," said Zara. "But Master Chanticleer must take the risk—there is no other way. It is only through his knowledge of the Dark Arts that the portals into the past can be broken open and Tania's previous selves brought forth." She turned to Edric. "But be wary, Master Chanticleer, and do not presume overmuch on your own fortitude. Greater men than you have fallen to ill deeds by using the Dark Arts."

Tania winced. She was talking about Gabriel Drake. He of the charmed, silvery eyes—the man who had almost been the death of her and of many others. The thought of Edric's eyes glazing over forever with evil silver made the blood freeze in her veins.

"I know the danger," said Edric quietly.

Zara gave a grievous smile. "No, you do not—and it is good that you do not, for if you were to look into the depths of that black abyss, your heart would stop in your chest."

Tania reached for Edric's hand. "I won't let anything bad happen to you," she said, hoping fervently that this was true. "I won't!"

Gripping her hand tightly, Edric lifted his head. "My lady Zara," he said, a hint of his Faerie heritage coming into his voice. "Tell me what I must do and I shall do it."

Zara held his gaze then nodded. "You must call up the spirits of Stromlos and of Eidolon—the spirits of death and loss. You must harness them to your will and use them to open a path for Tania into the past. And Tania must walk that path and draw six of her lost selves out of their own time and into ours." Zara stood up, her voice echoing, her arms spreading. "And when all are gathered, you must channel your powers through Tania and through her other selves, and thus will the ways between the worlds be opened once more."

She looked at Tania, and the light in her eyes was fierce.

"I do not say that you have the power to defeat Lear once you have entered Faerie, my sister," she said. "But I do know that if not you, then no one. This is the time, my friends! This is the place. Upon this moment we shall do such deeds as shall resound down the ages, or if we fail, then the darkness will triumph and the light be extinguished forever!"

In the shocked silence Jade's voice was only just above a whisper. "So . . ." she murmured, "no pressure, then . . ."

# XI

Tania found herself lying sleepless in her darkened bedroom with wide-awake Rathina at her side and Zara seated on the sill of the open window singing quietly to herself and gazing out into the starry London night.

Mr. and Mrs. Palmer had persuaded the reluctant Tania and Edric that they needed to rest before undertaking their task. Tania lay looking at Zara and remembering how she had first met her sister, at the door of her other bedroom in the Royal Palace of Faerie. A newly discovered memory, but of something that seemed to have taken place entire lifetimes ago.

Edric was on the couch downstairs and Jade was in the guest bedroom. Jade had been adamant not to be sent home: "You think I'm going to miss out on all this? No way! I'm staying right here."

"Will you not at least lie down, Zara?" Rathina asked now, watching their sister with anxious eyes.

"I need no rest, Rathina," Zara replied gently. "Nor ever shall."

Tania leaned up on one elbow. "Zara?" Her voice was tentative. "I'm sorry, I don't really know how to ask this, but what are you?"

Zara smiled, her face bathed in starlight. "Do you fear I am a ghost?" she asked. "That I am the unquiet dead doomed to walk the world?"

"Well, something like that. . . ."

Tania was aware of Rathina alert and tense at her side. "I pray that be not so!" Rathina whispered sharply.

"I am not a ghost," said Zara. "Mayhap were I to walk the halls and fields of Faerie, it would be as a ghost, for my time there is done—but in this world I am alive, I think." She sighed but not unhappily. "For a brief time." She tilted her face upward, as though warming her skin by starlight.

"So, you're like an angel, or something?" Tania ventured.

Zara laughed gently. "An angel! 'Tis a pretty thought! The angel Zara! It is true that I am not the only Faerie soul to have come to this world to do good deeds for a while before stepping over the Eternal Threshold."

"Others who died in Faerie have come to this place?" Rathina asked.

Zara nodded. "To shed light in dark corners and to offer comfort to the abandoned and the bereft . . ."

Rathina gasped. "I knew not!"

"Nay, nor should you," said Zara. "Already I have told you overmuch of things best unknown." She looked at them. "Sleep, now. I shall watch over you."

"Sleep?" said Tania. "You're kidding."

Zara laughed and made a wafting movement of her hand. "Sleep," she murmured. "A deep and healing sleep."

Tania felt drowsy. She saw Rathina's head hit the pillow. Her own head came down, and the duvet lifted up over her shoulder, although she had not moved it.

The last thing she heard was Zara's voice, singing a soft lament.

> *"Just as you promised, the evening comes to me*
> *    with stars in its eyes*
> *The evening comes as no surprise to me,*
> *Flies to me, soft with the shadows of midnight,*
> *And takes me to the land where all roads go*
> *To the land where all roads go."*

"Tania? Daughter? Do you hear me?"

It was Oberon's voice, crying out in the darkness. Tania stumbled through the gloom, straining her eyes.

"I can't see you! Where are you?"

"In the deep dark, my daughter—where none but you shall ever find me!" His voice broke with emotion. "We are lost, my child—betrayed and lost. Cast down, bound in amber, shrouded in silence."

"Where? What happened?" Her own voice made her head hurt.

"My brother came upon us unawares. The brother I had long forgotten—the brother banished in the lost days before the covenant."

"Lear!"

"None but he!" Oberon's voice was wrought with anguish. "He came upon us as we fought to keep the shield of Gildensleep alive. Secretly from out of the frozen north, from beyond even Ynis Borealisis. Great power he has accumulated unto himself over the millennia."

"What did he do?" shouted Tania. "What has he done?"

"He has taken the throne of Faerie, my child." Oberon groaned. "And all that were powerful in the Eternal Realm are now encased in amber for all time."

She was too late! The quest had taken too long—and now all was lost!

"I'll come to you, Father!" Tania cried as the dream faded. "I'll awaken everyone. We'll walk through right now." She thrashed under the covers, desperate to wake herself up.

"Be wary of my brother, child," came Oberon's dwindling voice. "He has grown mighty in witchcraft in the years of his banishment. He will seek to overwhelm you, and I would not have you spend eternity in a prison of unbreakable amber. It is a fearful thing. Awake but frozen of limb, locked in perpetual torment, unable to act while Lear cuts a swath of darkness through both Faerie and the Mortal World!"

Tania could feel her father's fear and pain, and the growing panic that his Realm and all its people would be lost forever. She had to reassure him.

"I can beat him," she cried. "I know I can. Trust me, Father!"

"All is lost. . . ." A whisper now, from an impossible distance.

"No! It isn't!"

"All is lost, all is . . ." The voice was gone.

"No!"

"Sister! Spirits of mercy, what ails you?"

Tania felt hands on her shoulders shaking her awake. She snapped her eyes open. Rathina was kneeling over her in the bed, her eyes dark as sloes. Tania gasped for breath, trembling all over.

Zara stood over her. "What did you dream, Tania?" she asked.

"The King!" Tania said falteringly. "Our father, the King. Trapped in amber. Crying out for help!" She pushed Rathina's hands away and scrambled out of bed. "This was a mistake. We should never have waited!" She threw on some clothes and then ran for the door. "Rathina, get dressed. I'm going to wake Edric. We have to act now—it may already be too late!" She flung her bedroom door open and ran down the stairs.

# XII

The living room was lit by a single lamp that threw feathery shadows over the walls. It was still deep night beyond the drawn curtains. London was asleep, but in here a dangerous, fervid light was growing.

The furniture had been cleared from the center of the room: chairs piled together, the low coffee table upended on the couch, the television pushed into a corner.

Clive and Mary Palmer stood together by the door, their faces still heavy from their disturbed sleep. Tania noticed they were holding hands.

Jade was kneeling to one side, her eyes huge in the flickering light. Tania had not meant for her to be involved in this, or even to know about it till she awoke in the morning—but the noise made in rousing the others had alerted her, too, and she had insisted on being there when Edric "did his thing." Looking at her now, Tania wondered whether she wished she'd stayed safe under her duvet.

Edric was summoning the Mystic forces. He had called the Globus Heim into existence, and a gradually expanding ball of coruscating blue light filled the whole of the middle of the room.

Edric was at the center of the growing globe of light standing perfectly still, his hands clasped together in front of him, head lowered, his eyes full of molten silver. Tania could see his lips moving through the incandescent light of the Dark Arts—his whole body bathed in flickering sapphire, threads of light whipping around him like shooting stars.

The power of Dark Arts filled her with dread. She was terrified that something would go wrong—that the Dark would rise up and claim Edric for its own. Could she even trust him now? Might these fearful sorceries corrupt him and ruin him and turn him into a monster who would destroy them all?

Tania glanced at Rathina. Her sister's face was pale as she looked into the Mystic light. Rathina knew all too well the devilry that could be called up through the Dark Arts: deadly powers that could crush a good soul and hurl its owner into the deepest of hells.

Only Zara seemed untroubled as she watched Edric calling upon the reluctant spirits. Did she know something the rest of them didn't? Or was she beyond fear and apprehension? It was impossible to tell.

*He mustn't be killed. He mustn't be changed in a bad way. I couldn't bear it. If something terrible happens to him . . . No! I won't think like that. He's strong, and he has my love to keep him safe. This will work. It must!*

Edric's lips became still. He raised his head, eyes narrowed, like someone coming suddenly into blazing sunlight. A slight smile. He brought his arms up in two wide circles until they were palm to palm above his head. As his hands clapped together, the Globus Heim became still and solid: a blue crystalline sphere sunken a little into the floor so that there was a wide, flat disk of carpet within.

Tania swallowed hard, desperate to appear fearless as Edric's eyes fell on her. He stepped to the curving wall of the globe and reached his hand toward her.

"The spell is safe now," he said, his voice muffled from within the ball of glittering light. His hand pierced the sparkling rind of the Globus and emerged into the room. "You can step through—but don't let go of me once we begin to move back in time."

Tania stared at his hand. Hesitating. Did she trust him? Did she dare?

Zara stepped up to Tania's side. "Have no fear. His true spirit is not overthrown by the Dark," she murmured. "But heed him. You must never lose your grip on his hand when you are in the past, for if you do, you will be lost there."

Tania nodded, too frightened to speak. She glanced briefly at her parents. Seeing the distress in their faces, she quickly looked away.

She took Edric's hand. It was cool to the touch, and his skin seemed to spark, as though with static.

"This will not be as the time before when you *inhabited* your past selves." Zara's voice spoke close behind as

Tania was about to step into the Globus Heim. "That time you *became* the girls that you once were. This time you will be separate from them. But they will know you and they will trust you. Take their hands and they will come to you." She felt Zara's touch gentle on her shoulder. "And you must try not to be overwhelmed by grief at what you will see and what you know. Be strong, Tania—endure the pain!"

Tania turned her head, puzzled by Zara's warning. But before she was able to respond, she was pulled into the sphere of dancing blue light.

As she was drawn into the Globus, she felt a coruscating fire enter her, sparking and burning through her veins. She gasped for breath, a sensation like lightning flaring in her stomach, sending out tongues of flame that ran prickling along her arms and legs. Bolts of blue light flashed across her vision, hissing and spitting.

And then she was inside, and the fire was gone from her limbs. The air was charged, tingling in her throat and nostrils. She could feel the hairs bristling all over her body as though her skin was furred with electricity. The living room and the people in it wavered in a blue haze, blurred so that shadow and light merged and she could not make out their faces. It was as though the whole world had gone out of focus, leaving only Edric and her together within the mystical glow of the Globus Heim.

"Are you okay?" asked Edric. "Do not listen to the voices."

She frowned. "What voi—?" Then she heard them. Whispering and muttering. Evil voices and cruel voices, miserable voices and whining voices. Lost voices and lonely voices. All around her. Voices to drive a person insane. The baleful voices of the Dark Arts.

"You have to ignore them," Edric said, his calm voice cutting through all the others.

She turned to him. "I will." She tried not to hear. She tried not to see the silver in his eyes. She tried to trust him and to swallow the fear. "What happens now?"

"Now your journey begins."

His fingers twined tightly with hers. He turned and made a pass through the air with his other hand. It left a wake of sparkling gray filaments, like a dew-spangled spiderweb seen through early-morning mist.

Again and again he let his hand glide through the air, like someone wiping breath from a window.

As the web of gray threads expanded, Tania saw new images through them. Darkness. Buildings huddled together in a narrow street. A horrible sound. A horrible wailing and rumbling sound that came out of a night sky stabbed by fingers of moving white light.

"Step through, Tania," Edric said. "Don't be afraid. I'll be with you."

Together, and with no more sensation than moving from one room to another, they stepped out of the Palmers' living room in Camden. The menacing voices of the Dark Arts and the shimmering blue light of the Globus Heim were gone.

They were on a road that was like a black canyon between terraced houses. Although it was deep night, there were no streetlights. No window showed even a glimmer of light. The noise was worse now—as though some gigantic animals were stropping their claws along the slate-colored sky. It set Tania's teeth on edge.

"Where are we?" she asked. "What *is* that noise?"

"Bombers," said Edric.

*"What?"*

"We're in the East End of London," Edric said. "The date is the tenth of May, 1941. This will be the worst night of the Blitz."

Tania stared up into the sky. The probing fingers of the searchlights rolled pale, misshapen circles over the clouds, making the sky ghastly. Growling and roaring bomber planes moved in formation over the city.

"What do we do?" Tania asked.

"We wait." Edric's voice was oddly impassive, as though his thoughts were elsewhere. She glanced at him but looked quickly away. His eyes were glowing like two full moons.

She saw grisly red lights blooming in the sky, followed by the howl of the bombs and the roar of explosions. She gripped Edric's hand as the sky above the rooftops turned a deep and ugly crimson.

The screaming of bombs came closer. A jet of fire burst from a rooftop at the end of the street. Black smoke boiled and for a moment all the windows of the house glowed. Then, in horrible slow motion, the whole of the front of the house swelled, cracked open, and spilled out into the street. Tania pulled away, wanting to run, but Edric's hand tightened on hers, keeping her at his side.

"Don't be afraid," he said. "We're safe."

Thick, choking smoke rolled along the street.

A door was flung open close to where Tania and Edric were standing. Tania sensed the girl's fear and knew her name before she emerged from the house.

*Marjorie Saunders. Her father's away. A soldier in the war. She's nine years old. She has a cat called Muffin. Her best friend is Elsie Turner. She lives here with her mother and her gran and granddad.*

The girl came running into the street, her face transformed into a ruddy mask of terror by the flames that clawed their way out of the pall of smoke.

"Marjorie! No!" screamed a woman's voice. "Come back!"

But the girl was lost to panic. She didn't even see Tania and Edric as she ran past them.

"Catch her hand! Quickly!" snapped Edric.

Tania lunged forward and managed to lock her fingers around the girl's wrist.

"No! Get off me!" The girl struggled, wild in her fear.

There was an explosion so huge that Tania was momentarily deafened and half blinded. She felt the ground erupt under her feet. She saw the blurred outline of a dark mass toppling slowly toward her.

Then she felt Edric pulling her arm, and suddenly she was back inside the globe of shining sapphire light. Kneeling at her feet was the girl, Marjorie.

Releasing Edric's hand, Tania crouched and hugged Marjorie's shaking shoulders. "It's okay, you're okay now," she murmured.

The girl lifted her tear-stained, grubby face. A light of recognition ignited in her eyes. "Oh! I was dead scared." Tania drew the girl to her feet. She was wearing a little knitted hat and a dark overcoat. "Mum said to stay put under the stairs, but I got frightened." She ran a sleeve under her nose. "I hate that Mr. Hitler! My dad says he's gonna punch him in the nose soon as he gets to Berlin!"

"That's a good idea." Tania swallowed hard, darting an anxious glance to Edric. "Do you know who I am?"

"Of course, silly!" Marjorie said. She put her hand to the left side of her chest. "This is you," she said. "Inside me." She reached out and pressed the same palm to Tania's heart. "And that's me!" she said, smiling. "Inside you!"

Tania nodded, gazing into Marjorie's eyes.

"Tania?" Edric's voice was no more than a whisper. "There are others."

"I have to go now—for a little while." She glanced around the blue globe. "I'd like you to stay here, please. I need to find some other girls. Girls like you. Will you be okay?"

"Right as ninepence," said Marjorie.

"Good. I'll be back as soon as I can."

Taking Edric's hand again, Tania walked a second time into the glimmering spider's web . . .

. . . and came to a place she remembered with terrible clarity.

They were on a tree-lined walkway alongside the River Thames. A gray sky emptied a steady fall of rain, pattering on the ground and pitting the dark flow of the swollen river.

A shrill voice called from under a sheltering tree.

"Gracie! Gracie! You come back here this instant or I shall give you such a smack!"

"No!" called a defiant voice. "Shan't."

Tania saw a little girl in a rain-soaked bonnet stamping through puddles, her arms swinging wide.

"You'll catch your death of cold and your mama will be so angry, Gracie."

The girl laughed.

"Come out of the rain or you'll get no supper!"

*That's her nanny—her new nanny. Oh god, I know what happens next. . . .*

"Don't care!" Gracie declared.

The nanny stamped her foot. "You are the naughtiest child that ever there was!" She drew her coat tight against the rain and marched out from under the tree. "Gracie! I shan't tell you again."

The girl ran to the river's edge and went stamping along the stones.

*One of the stones is loose. She'll fall; she'll drown.*

The girl's foot came down on the insecure stone.

Her arms windmilled, and a look of alarm came over her face.

Tania and Edric ran—Edric hissing words that made Tania's skin crawl. Time slowed around them. Streaks of rain hung in the air like flecks of gray paint. The rolling river moved like molasses. Gracie tumbled haltingly through the air.

Tania was easily able to catch her hand and tug her away from the danger.

Gracie's eyes opened wide as she saw Tania, and her expression of alarm was replaced by joy. A moment later the three of them were safe inside the blue bubble.

"I nearly fell!" Gracie exclaimed, wriggling her hand free of Tania. "Mummy would have been angry with me." She turned and looked appraisingly at Marjorie. "Hello there," she said. "I really hate my new nanny!"

"I ain't got no nanny," said Marjorie. "My mum works in the munitions factory."

Tania felt a tugging on her hand and suddenly she was passing through the spider's web for a third time.

"She—she drowned. . . ." she stammered. "Or did we just save her?"

"No, I'm sorry," Edric said gently. "She still drowns. And Marjorie is killed when the bombed building collapses on her. All we've done is to take them out of their own time for a while. We can't change what happens to them."

"Why do we have to be there just before they die?" Tania choked.

"Because that's the moment when the Faerie spirit rises to leave the body and seek another," Edric said. "The Faerie soul is at its most potent in the seconds before death."

"But it's horrible!"

Now she understood Zara's warning. Now she knew why she had to be strong.

*It's too cruel! These poor children . . .*

She smelled smoke. It clogged her nostrils and made her eyes sting and water. She was in a darkened room. A bedroom. A golden-haired girl lay asleep. Bright blue ribbons were hung from the head of her bed. Blue ribbons from her golden hair.

Flora Llewellyn. She died in the fire that started in her father's attic laboratory and swept through the entire house while the family slept.

Tania stooped over the girl. "Flora?" she whispered. "Come with me, now."

The little girl's eyes opened sleepily. "Are you the White Rabbit come to take me to Wonderland?" she asked.

"Yes." Tania could hardly speak for the swirling smoke. "Yes, I am." She took Flora's hand. She heard a man shout against a sudden roar of fire.

And then they were in the blue ball and Flora was blinking drowsily at Gracie and Marjorie as a wide smile of recognition spread across her face.

Tania let go of Flora's warm hand and turned quickly away. "Let's get this over with," she muttered between clenched teeth. "I can't stand this!"

"I know," Edric murmured.

Twice more Tania and Edric made the harrowing journey—each time venturing a little deeper into the past.

There was a fourteen-year-old girl in an Empire line dress, running along a sunken pathway in evening twilight. Instinctively Tania knew her. Georgina Eversleigh—returning late to her mama and papa's house after a secret tryst with Thomas, the gamekeeper's son. They had kissed, and Georgina's mind was full of the secret glory of it when she rounded a corner and found her path blocked by two stampeding horses harnessed to a driverless Clarence coach.

Tania plucked Georgina out of the road only a moment before the horses trampled her. She came into the blue orb as peaceful and calm as had the others. It seemed to Tania that hers was the only heart being wrung by these events.

The fifth girl was sickly Ann Burbage, daughter of a great Shakespearean actor from Elizabethan times. An ashen-faced girl with weak lungs and a tight throat. She lay in the cushioning arms of her beloved Bess, gasping for breath. Tania took her hand and drew her to her feet. The girl smiled.

"It does not hurt me anymore when I breathe!" she said gaily. "The pain is gone from my chest." And then they were in the blue sphere. Ann gazed around at the other girls in delight. "Oh!" she said, her eyes glowing. "How wonderful!"

Her own eyes full of tears, Tania turned away from

the gathered children.

"It's as if they're dreaming," Edric said, seeing the anguish in Tania's face. "Their Faerie souls are burning so brightly now that they can't be afraid or hurt."

"Until we send them back to die!"

"Yes. Until then. . . ."

Tania and Edric walked together into the glimmering past for the final time. Now they were in a small dark room that stank of filth and disease. Sacking hung over the windows and the light that filtered in was gray and grainy. The room was crowded out with small, low beds. There was straw underfoot, along with slime and rotting garbage.

Tania didn't recognize the place, although it sounded an awful alarm deep in her mind.

She heard wheezing breath. Coughing. The uneasy stirring of sleepless people in pain.

She felt drawn to a bed in the corner. A figure lay under ragged sheets.

She leaned close, trying to make out the face in the gloom, and saw tangled and unkempt red hair. Green eyes stared up at her.

She put a hand to her mouth. "Oh god, no!"

The dying face was her own face, the cheeks sunken with illness, the eyes feverish in their sockets, lips drawn back, breath gusting weakly from a fluttering chest.

Now she knew why she remembered this monstrous place. Sancha had spoken of it in the library in the Royal Palace when they had linked their minds through her soul book.

She could hear Sancha's voice in her head.

*"I know how you fared when you first entered the Mortal World. You fell victim to some deadly plague almost at once . . . you became subject to all the illnesses and misfortunes of that awful place . . ."*

Tania fell to her knees at the bedside of her dying self. Her hand slipped out of Edric's. A moment passed before she realized what she'd done.

She snapped her head around, her heart palpitating, the blood ringing in her ears, her hand reaching toward nothing.

She heard Edric's disembodied voice calling from a terrible distance. "Tania! No!"

Horrified, she snatched at the empty air where a moment before he had been standing.

But it was too late. She'd let go and the link had been broken.

Edric was gone.

# XIII

For a few moments Tania was so shocked by what had happened that she could do no more than sit there on the dank and stinking floor and fight to get breath into her lungs.

She had lost grip of Edric's hand and he had vanished, leaving her stranded in the past.

A frail shred of hope remained. *He'll find a way back to me. He must. Somehow.*

Gradually she brought her breathing under control. Forcing herself to keep calm, she stared at the spot where Edric had been standing a few moments ago.

Waiting . . .

Clinging to the desperate belief that he would reappear.

She tried to blot out the stink of decay and sickness. Her eyes grew accustomed to the darkness and she stood up. The low room was crowded with beds. People lay under ragged blankets, some ominously silent, others gasping for breath or groaning in pain.

She moved silently among the clutter of beds, seeing more than she really wanted to see. A scrawny, scabbed arm hung limp over a bed frame. A head turned on bunched-up rags, the eyes seeing nothing. There were no nurses or doctors—no one here to offer help or comfort.

Time crawled by as she glanced at face after ruined face. Still Edric did not come.

A black despair began to seep into her mind.

*He isn't coming. He can't reach me. . . .*

She leaned over a bed, reaching down tentatively to shake a thin shoulder. "Where am I?" she whispered into the ravaged face.

The eyes rolled. Foul breath gusted up.

The voice was a ghostly croak. "Let me die. . . ."

She edged away, making her way back to that first bed.

*What century is this? Tania came through—I mean, I came through from Faerie five hundred years ago, so that means I'm somewhere in the sixteen-hundreds. But where?* She glanced around the room, but she saw nothing to help her get her bearings.

*I'm guessing London. I would have come through from my bedroom in the Royal Palace, and that's Hampton Court in this world. But Edric's in Camden. How do I find it?*

Desolate now, she sat on the floor beside that first bed. If Edric was able to return, he'd surely reappear right here.

She drew her legs up and rested her forehead on her knees.

A hand closed around her arm, making her cry out.

The dying girl with Tania's face was leaning over the side of the bed, her feverish eyes wide, her fingers curled around Tania's arm just above the elbow.

"Are you an apparition sent by the spirits to ease my death?" whispered the girl.

Tania's mind reeled. It was her own voice!

She didn't know what to say to the dying girl—to this princess of Faerie whose soul she shared.

The girl frowned. "You have my very cast of countenance, maiden," she said weakly. "Who are you? How is it that you resemble me so?"

"What do you remember?" Tania asked, shocked that her voice sounded so broken. "Do you know how you got here?"

The princess sighed. "I remember playing parlor tricks with Rathina. Blithe games to beguile the hours to my sixteenth birthday . . ."

"You walked between the worlds," Tania prompted.

"Ahh. Did I? Is that what happened?" She laughed weakly, a laugh that turned to a wracking cough. Tania winced.

"You couldn't find your way back."

"Alack, for evil happenstance!" whispered the princess. "Poor Lord Gabriel, left at the Hand-Fasting cauldron by a bride who would never come. The tears he must have shed." The princess began to cough uncontrollably, and it was a few moments before the convulsion eased.

"Is there anything I can do to help you?" Tania

asked. "Anything at all?"

The girl gazed at her. "Your speech is strange to my ears, maiden. And yet, 'tis beyond belief . . . but I know you, do I not? Speak true and do not fear. What are you if not a phantom?"

Tania bit her lip. *I can't tell her the truth. I can't.*

The girl released her frail grip on Tania's arms and her long, wasted fingers moved slowly, probingly toward Tania's face. Tania was repulsed by the dirty, broken fingernails, but she tried not to flinch as the fingertips touched her skin.

At that touch the world changed. A marvelous vision ignited in her memory.

Sunshine. Towering white cliffs. A sea rolling under soft summer breezes. A shining palace upon the cliff top. The music of a flute sweetening the air. Herself, a winged child, running along an endless beach of white sand, seashells crunching under her bare feet. Shouting and laughing. A small unicorn pranced in the surf, its silvery horn threaded with periwinkle shells.

The unicorn came up on its hind legs, neighing, shining hooves striking the air.

Tania stooped, picking up a shell. She fluttered her wings, rising a little out of the sand and throwing the shell into the lacy surf so that the unicorn curvetted and ran to retrieve it for her.

A voice floated on the sea-scented air. "Tania! If Percival comes home with seaweed caught in his mane and tail, it will be your task to comb out the tangles!"

Laughing, Tania looked to where Sancha, Rathina, and Cordelia sat with the picnic things around them. Zara stood close by, playing on the flute.

It had been Cordelia calling to her.

"'Tis no chore to do that!" Tania shouted back as she walked up the beach. "It is a thing most pleasurable!"

"All the same, we should be getting back," said Sancha, closing the book she had been reading. "We must not be late for Hopie's coming-of-age ceremony."

Cordelia began to gather the things up and place them in the basket. "What shall be her gift, I wonder," she said.

"We must guess!" said Tania.

"Healing, be most sure," said Sancha.

Rathina sprang up, her wings quivering at her back. "When my sixteenth birthday comes, I hope my gift shall be a warrior's heart!" she cried, shadow fencing across the sand. "Then shall I set out upon great errantry, riding upon a mettlesome steed."

"I would that your gift were the desire to be helpful, Rathina," declared Sancha. "That would be a great wonder, indeed!"

Tania heard the thud of hooves behind her. She turned as Percival came trotting up. He shook his mane, spraying salt water into her face.

Tania jerked back from the touch of the sick princess. She gasped. "What was that? What did you do to me?"

The vision had been so vivid that her head was still spinning with it.

The princess lifted herself on one elbow, staring into Tania's face.

"Lord Gabriel was a false love!" she said, her voice shocked. "His desire was not for me—but for the power to walk between the worlds."

"What?"

They stared at each other. A sudden glimmer of understanding ignited in Tania's mind. As flesh had touched flesh, some kind of sharing had happened. Something from the princess's memory had filtered into Tania's mind—and something from hers had gone out to the princess.

The afternoon on the beach under Veraglad Palace was seared now into Tania's mind—not as an image or dream but as a specific and clear memory. She had been there. She had done those things.

*More! I want more!*

Trembling violently, Tania lifted her hand and spread her fingers.

The eyes of the princess grew huge in her ashen face, as if the same understanding had come to her.

Their hands came together and their fingers interlaced.

Surrounded by plague and death, all the lost memories of Tania's Faerie childhood came flooding like midsummer sunlight into her head.

# XIV

The princess seemed less sickly now—as though something of Tania's spirit and strength had bled into her. She still looked ill, but not deathly.

Two whole life memories burned now in Tania's mind—running parallel, braided together, and yet quite separate and discrete: sixteen years of life lived in Camden and the lost sixteen years of her Faerie childhood.

"Right glad I am that Drake met a deserved fate," growled the princess. "But it hurts my soul that Rathina was used so cruelly by him. She shall never be whole again, come what good fortune may."

Tania's heart ached as Rathina's words on the golden beach came back to her. *"I hope my gift shall be a warrior's heart!"* "No," Tania said. "She won't."

A catch came into the princess's voice. "And Zara, sweet Zara, dead and yet *not* . . ."

"I know," said Tania. "I don't get it, either. It's like

a dream come true, but it's also really weird."

The princess paused a moment, as if trying to decipher Tania's words. "But a greater peril looms over Faerie now," she said at last. "Help me up, my friend! I would stand."

Tania got to her feet. She helped the frail princess up off the bed. A few faces turned to them, the dying people roused a little by the movement.

*We're exactly the same height. Everything about us is the same—down to the gold dust in our eyes.*

"This is so strange," Tania murmured.

"It is indeed." A pale smile touched the princess's lips. "And stranger still to know my sorry fate. Alas, that a girl's foolish whims set such events in motion! Five hundred years of twilight cast over Faerie. A Queen lost, a realm blighted. Had I but known . . ."

Tania put an arm around the princess's back, ignoring the smell of the rags that covered her—rags that had once been a Faerie gown. She could still see traces of fine needlepoint and hints of lilac through the grime.

The princess smiled. "You give me strength, my friend," she said. Tania fought not to be repelled by the sour scent of death that came from her mouth. "But what purpose do we now have? How are we to return?"

"To Camden, you mean?"

"Aye. To do what must be done, we must unite with the other children. Only then can we step between the worlds and seek Lear's downfall."

Tania stared at the princess. She seemed so calm,

so focused. And yet she knew that she was dying, that nothing either of them could do would change that. Come what may, she would breathe her last breath in this foul place.

The princess gave an odd, crooked smile. "And how would you act differently, my friend, if your fate was mine and mine, yours?" It was as if she'd read Tania's thoughts. "Would you faint upon your bed and call upon death to do his worst? I think not!" Her eyes flickered with a bittersweet light. "It eases my heart to know that you are in the world five hundred years hence. And that you will do great deeds!" The smile strengthened a little. "Killed the Sorcerer King upon Salisoc Heath! There's gallantry. There's a legacy to be proud of."

"Thank you."

"And now—to the purpose!" said the princess. "We must act while the little strength you have given me remains. Let's away from this place of death." She frowned. "But not via the door—guards stand to prevent any of these poor souls from fleeing." Her eyes darkened. "They fear this plague greatly—many have died." She beckoned. "Come. There is another way out."

They walked between the beds. An emaciated arm reached out, raking fingers thin as claws. Tania drew away, trying not to look into the faces of the dying.

There was a window in the far wall, little more than a rough hole in the wall, covered with wooden shutters. Together, they forced the shutters back. Through the window Tania could see a few scattered houses and a gray stone building under a clouded night sky. Trees huddled in the distance. There were few lights and no people.

Tania climbed through the window and helped the princess to follow. She struggled to get over the sill, and Tania had to take her weight on her shoulders, easing her legs out into the night. The air was sweet and fresh outside the pest house—it was like stepping into another world. Tania could hear the sound of a river from somewhere close by.

Hand-in-hand they ran at a crouch away from the ghastly hut, passing between darkened wooden houses and pausing only when they came under the deep shadows of the trees.

The princess was gasping for breath by the time they found shelter. She sat under a tree, hunched over, her face ashen, her hair hanging. Tania stood over her, staring out at the little hamlet—trying to make sense of where they might be.

"This is the hamlet of Kentisston," murmured the princess. "Do you not remember the men throwing you upon the cart and bringing you here?"

"Vaguely," said Tania. She had so many new memories—and it was sometimes tricky to sift through them. But she did remember the horrors of the jolting trip to the pest house.

Kentisston? That name meant something to her. She'd seen it somewhere. Yes! The last time she'd been in Mortal London during the hunt for Queen Titania she'd taken a few minutes to try and find out whether Camden had existed five hundred years ago.

She'd learned that in that time Camden had been no more than a few scattered houses lying in the valley of the River Fleet, to the northwest of the teeming medieval city of London. But a little way to the north—no more than a mile along a dirt track— a hamlet had lain in the Manor of Hampstead. The hamlet of Kentisston.

Kentish Town in the modern world. No more than one stop away on the tube.

She crouched in front of the princess. "Can you walk?"

"Mayhap with your aid," said the sickly girl breathlessly.

"I think our best hope is to go to Camden. It's not too far—south of here." She frowned. South? Which way was south? Oh yes, now she remembered—they had come into Kentisston from the south. There was only that one roadway. Find that and their path would be clear ahead of them.

The princess used Tania's offered arm to climb to her feet. "You hope to make contact with the children there?" she said. "Yes, 'tis a plan not without merit. Give me your shoulder, my friend."

Tania supported the princess as they made their way along the eaves of the woodland, skirting the buildings, avoiding any contact with people.

The road south was rutted and muddy. They kept to the edges, where hoof and wheel had not churned the ground to a sticky mire.

They moved slowly, pausing often to allow the princess to catch her breath. At these times she would sit under the trees, her head down, her chest heaving, while Tania stood close by, watching the road and dreading the sound of a horse or a wagon. The princess was too obviously sick; Tania had bad feelings about how a plague victim might be treated if found at the roadside. She could be killed to prevent the illness spreading.

Tania's thoughts strayed to Edric and to the girls they had already gathered. Edric must be frantic. Would the girls understand what had happened? Would they be able to help?

The starless night stretched on and on as step by slow step the princess leaned more heavily on Tania's shoulder.

Rooftops appeared from the darkness.

*Camden?*

*Please let it be!*

Tania let the princess slip down into the grass at the roadside. Her body ached from the weight, but she pushed away all thoughts of fatigue and discomfort.

Stepping into the middle of the road, her eyes toward the rooftops, she worked to clear her mind of all thoughts but one.

*Marjorie? Gracie? Are you there? Flora? Can you hear me? Can you feel me? Georgina! Ann? I'm here! I'm right here!*

There was nothing. The night lay over her spirit

like a dead body. This agonizing journey had been a waste of time—a waste of effort.

She tried again, concentrating until her head throbbed.

"Edric?" she called. "I need you to find me!"

Silence as still as the grave.

But then . . . a twittering among the trees as of tiny voices calling from afar.

She stared around, trying to home in on the direction from which the voices were coming. But they were all around her now—a whole band of female voices all speaking over one another.

"One at a time!" she cried, her hands over her ears. "I can't understand you!"

One voice rose above the others. Georgina's voice. "Go to the light! We are there!"

A moment later Tania saw a flicker of movement in the trees.

It was a bright ball of blue light, about the size of her clenched fist, and it was moving steadily toward her.

It hovered a few yards away. Full of new hope, Tania ran to the princess and drew her to her feet.

"We have to follow the light," Tania said.

"There are sweet voices in my mind," murmured the princess.

"Yes. In mine, too." Tania half carried the princess toward the ball. It moved away, guiding them deeper into the trees.

The shining sapphire ball halted in a clearing.

The voices were an urgent chorus now. *Come, Tania! Come to us! We can see you now! Oh, come to us! Quickly!*

She stepped toward the light. A deeper blue blossomed at its center, and a hand reached out from nowhere. Around the wrist was a thin leather band strung through a black jewel.

Edric. The jewel was black amber to protect him from the curse of metal.

Clinging tightly to the princess, Tania took hold of his hand.

# XV

Tania gripped Edric's hand and held on with all her strength. She hooked her other arm around the princess's waist as they were dragged by the Dark Arts from one century to another.

There was carpet under her feet and a blue light surrounded her.

Her mother's voice rang out. "Edric! You found her! Oh, thank the lord!"

Tania gazed around. The five girls were in the Globus with her. They were holding hands and gazing at her and the princess with eyes full of gladness and calm understanding.

"We helped bring you back," said Flora. "You would never have got back without us."

"I know," said Tania. "Thank you."

"We *had* to rescue you," added Georgina. "We have important things to do together."

"We know everything," said Marjorie. She frowned.

"I feel like I should be scared and sad . . . but I'm not. Isn't that peculiar?"

"There is great wisdom and strength in the Power of Seven," said Edric. "The wisdom to see your own fates and the strength to face them with fortitude."

Beyond the limpid ball of sapphire light Tania could see swimming faces.

The curtains had been drawn back from the windows of the Palmers' living room, and the light of dawn was filtering into the room.

Jade's voice. "Way to go, Edric! You're *awesome!*"

And Rathina: "Praise the goodly spirits, she is found!"

Zara's voice was calm. "Did I not say all was not lost?"

Edric walked Tania and the princess out of the ball of light. The five other girls followed, still holding hands. Tania felt dizzy and drained. But she had succeeded! She'd survived the challenge.

"By the rood!" murmured Rathina, gazing saucer-eyed from Tania to the princess. She reached out tentatively and touched the princess's ragged clothes. "This was the very gown you wore when you . . . when you disappeared." Her expression crumpled.

The princess put her arms around Rathina's shoulders. "It was not your fault, Rathina, that I was lost to the Mortal World. Gabriel Drake had great and terrible power over you. Your mind was not your own."

Rathina lifted her tear-streaked face. "I would die a thousand deaths to roll back time to the first moment I set my eyes upon Lord Drake," she said grimly. "A crystal blade through the heart would be his payment for the evil he was to do!"

Tania's father stepped forward. "Are you all right?" he asked. He turned his eyes to the princess. "Both of you?"

"Thank you, Master Clive," said the princess. "My sickness abates for a while. The good spirits allow me the strength to do what must be done ere the end."

"Unbelievable!" breathed Jade, looking from Tania to the princess. "Two of you! As if *one* wasn't enough." She took the princess's hand. "Hi—I'm Jade."

"Aye, I know you well, most loved friend of my friend."

"Excuse me?"

"We both have the same memories now," said Tania. "A thing happened when we touched. She knows everything I know, and I know everything she knows." She looked from Edric to Zara and Rathina. "It's all come back!" she said. "I remember everything!" She looked at Zara. "Like the time we were on the *Cloud Scudder*, on our way to visit Chalcedony for the Masquerade of the Wingèd Moon. You lost your flute overboard and Father—Oberon, I mean—he asked the sea creatures to search for it for you, and a dolphin found it!"

"I remember it well," said Zara with a smile. "And I

rejoice that you know it also."

Tania turned to Rathina, full of excitement. "And you!" she said, emotions thick in her throat. "For weeks before your tenth birthday you were dropping huge hints about wanting a horse. And on your birthday the King and Queen gave you a wooden statuette of a horse, and you tried really hard to look pleased."

"And 'twas not till eventide that they relented of their teasing ways and I was blindfolded and taken to the stables," said Rathina, her eyes welling with tears. "And there I met for the first time my noble and beautiful Maddalena!"

"So?" asked her father. "How does it feel to remember everything?"

"It feels good, Dad," Tania said, taking his hand. "It feels really good."

Mrs. Palmer glanced over to where the five girls stood watching them. "Do they know what's going on?" she asked in a low voice. "They seem so normal. As though nothing extraordinary has happened."

"They are in a state of grace," said Zara. "They know where they are, Mistress Mary—and they understand *everything.*"

"Can you not feel it?" said Rathina. "Their Faerie souls burn like suns. With my eyes closed I can feel the warmth of it."

Edric was standing a little apart from them, his brow creased. A glow like trapped moonlight seeped from between his eyelids.

Tania went to him and kissed him gently. "You

found me," she whispered.

"You found *me*," he replied, his voice a little strained.

"We found each other."

He opened his eyes and the silvery light flared. "Always!" he said.

Tania bit her lip. *Don't be scared by the light! It's Edric. It's not Drake. Edric will never harm you.*

Edric turned his face away. "I cannot maintain the Globus Heim for much longer. We need to try and get into Faerie soon, or I won't have enough power left."

"Indeed, it is most imperative you act swiftly," agreed Zara.

Tania nodded. "What do I need to do?"

"The Seven must step together into the blue Globus," said Zara. "Stand you with your other selves, and with Edric at your back." She glanced at him. "You know what to do, Master Chanticleer?"

"I do," said Edric.

Tania looked at the princess. She had moved to be with the five other girls, and she was speaking softly to them.

"Is there really no time for . . ." Tania had been intending to say, *"time for them to enjoy being alive for a little longer."* But she knew it wasn't possible.

Zara had said they knew *everything.*

*They know they're going to die.*

The princess took Marjorie by one hand and Flora by the other. The other girls linked hands again.

"We are ready," said the princess.

Tania turned to her mother and father. "I'll find a way back here," she said earnestly. "I don't care what gets in the way—I will find a way back to you."

"I'm sure you will," said her mother, hugging her. "Take care of yourself, please." She smiled. "You're the only Faerie princess daughter we've got!"

"I will." Tania gave her father a fierce hug.

"That's my girl," he said. His mouth came close to her ear. "I'm more proud of you than I can ever say," he murmured. "Come back soon, okay?"

"Absolutely!" said Tania, breaking free. She looked at Jade.

"Thanks for everything," she said.

"No problem." Jade grinned. "Kick some bad-guy butt for me!"

"I will." She turned to Zara. "Are you coming with us?"

"Alas, I cannot." Zara sighed. "The realm of Faerie is closed to me." She smiled ruefully. "Indeed, I have also fulfilled my task in this place—it is time for me to step over the Eternal Threshold."

Mrs. Palmer came forward and put her arms around Zara, pressing her close. "Your own mother was never able to say good-bye to you," she said, her voice full of tears. "Let me do it for her."

They hugged, and Mary Palmer whispered something into Zara's ear that Tania didn't catch. They parted and Zara lifted her hand to touch Mrs. Palmer's cheek. "Thank you."

Wordlessly Mary Palmer walked back to stand

beside her husband. His arm came up to circle her shoulders.

Rathina stared at Zara. "No!" She caught hold of her sister's hands. "You cannot go! I will not allow it!"

"There is naught you can do to prevent it, Rathina, my love," said Zara. An odd echo had come into her sister's voice, as though it was already sounding from far away. She leaned forward and kissed Rathina on the forehead. "I do not say you will ever be entirely free of pain, Rathina, but I tell you this—someone will come. Someone to soothe your agonies, someone with a healing heart . . ." She began to fade. Rathina's hand fell through Zara's fingers. Rathina stumbled, trying to catch hold of her, but her smiling sister was gone.

A trill of laughter sounded out of nowhere, followed by a series of rising notes on a flute, playing a melody more achingly beautiful than anything Tania had ever heard. Then . . . silence.

Princess Zara Aurealis, fifth daughter of Oberon and Titania had passed from the Mortal World and had entered forever the hallowed land of Albion.

"We should go," said Edric, taking Tania's hand.

She reached for Rathina's hand, and together the three of them stepped through into the blue globe. The princess was close behind, leading the five girls.

Tania could see her mother and father and Jade as wavery images through the blue haze.

"Stand in front of me," Edric told her. "All of you— link hands now."

Tania stood staring into the blue shimmer, Rathina on one side, the princess on the other. The other girls stood with them in the globe—hand in hand in hand in hand.

"Ready?" asked Edric from close behind.

"Yes."

For a moment there was nothing. Then Tania felt a lightning sharp pain strike the back of her head. It bore through her skull and burst in her brain. A blue light filled her mind, like water rushing through her, sending her senses tumbling and rolling on its flood. But deep inside her head, the blue light was met by a blaze of purest white that burst upward like seafoam on rocks.

She felt a sparking, streaming power pulsing in her body, passing along her arms, entering Rathina and the princess, moving through them and into the other girls. Into little Flora and Gracie, Georgina and Marjorie and Ann—until they all blazed with the scintillating white energy.

Tania felt it building within her—like a slow explosion until, at last, she had to let out a shout.

The others cried out with her, and from their mouths came shafts of brilliant white light. Spears of dazzling white light darted from their eyes.

"Take the step!" Tania could only just hear Edric's voice.

She gripped Rathina and the princess hard and made the impossible side step that would take her between the worlds.

Everything was white. It was a white so incandescent that Tania felt as though she had become the light, that she had shed her body and melded with something eternal.

She heard a voice.

"Wait for me!"

There was a curious tugging to one side as she stepped through the skin of light and found herself standing in a grove of aspen trees, in a glowing Faerie dawn.

"Oh, wow!" said a shaking voice. "That was totally amazing!"

# XVI

Jade was clinging on to Georgina's hand and looking like someone who had just been dragged into another realm.

"Jade! You idiot!" yelled Tania. "Have you any idea what you've done?"

"Chide her not, sister," came Rathina's voice. "Does the rhyme not say that only those who love you and whom you love may pass between the worlds with you?" She smiled. "Be glad, then, for the love of your friend, and give her good welcome into the Realm of Faerie." She took a deep breath. "I have longed for pure Faerie air in my lungs. It is nigh on twenty days since last we were here!"

Jade was gazing around with her mouth half open. The light of a fresh dawn was washing over the rolling green hills, sweeping down to the gardens and walls of the Royal Palace. Halls and battlements, spires and towers wound away into the hazy distance under a clear blue sky, the rising sun glinting on a thousand windows.

But Tania had no eyes for the beauties of Faerie. "No! We have to take her back—it's too dangerous!"

A weak voice gasped at her back. "No time . . ." She spun around. It was Edric; he was on his knees, panting for breath.

She dropped to his side. He lifted his exhausted face to her. The effort of forcing them through the barriers between the worlds had cost him.

She reached a hand toward his cheek, but he swatted it away, his lips tightening. The silver in his eyes had changed to a sickly off-white, cold and lifeless as stone.

"Leave me!" he snarled. "Go! Get out of here!"

Fear tugged her. "Edric . . . ?"

"Get away from me!" he howled, his whole body shaking. "Go and do what you came here to do! Otherwise it's all been pointless." He reared up on his knees, throwing his hands over his ears. "No! Be silent! I won't listen!"

Tania guessed that he was hearing the voices—the evil voices that swarmed in the Dark Arts. But what were they saying to him? *Come to us. Be one with us. Surrender yourself to us.*

"I won't leave you like this!" Tania shouted.

Edric dropped onto his hands, gasping for breath. He looked up at her, his eyes shadowed by his hair. "The journey exhausted me, but I will be all right." He gulped in more breath, his fingers clawing at the ground. "Go and confront Lear while . . . while the light is strong within you. It will not last long; it burns too fiercely." He grimaced. "Please, Tania—go!"

Hands drew her to her feet, Rathina on one side and the princess on the other.

"Trust he will survive," said the princess. "We have other matters to attend." She stared into Tania's eyes. "Look at the children, my friend. See how they shine!"

She was right. The five girls had formed a circle around them—and they were blazing with a pure white light that seemed to flow through them like quicksilver and to pour like sunbeams from their eyes and fingertips.

The princess was burning with the same heavenly light. Tania lifted her hand and saw the white beams shooting from her own fingertips.

She turned to Jade, who was on the outskirts of the blazing group, looking awestruck. "Stay with Edric," Tania called to her. "Make sure he's all right."

Jade nodded.

Tania turned to Rathina. "You should stay back as well," she said. "If we fail, you have to get away from here! Hide from Lear. Keep yourself secret. Build an army to fight him."

Rathina's eyes narrowed. "You have a power far beyond my ken," she said. "I will do as you say, but if you cannot defeat Lear with the light that burns within you, then I fear his rule shall never be broken."

Tania took the princess's hand. "We won't fail," she said, feeling even more potency flowing into her as their fingers linked.

"He is in the Throne Room," said Georgina, taking Tania's other hand. "I see him in my mind."

"I think he knows we're here," added Marjorie, taking Georgina's hand. "He's sitting there waiting for us. He's not scared of us at all."

"Then let's make him scared," said Tania as the other girls also joined hands.

Linked by their hands, the seven girls began to run down the long grassy hillside toward the endless battlements and rooftops of the Royal Palace. As they ran, the light washed around them, strange as starshine, wild as the moon, potent as the noonday sun.

Sad sights met Tania as they came closer to the palace. The beautiful gardens that lay before the Royal Apartments had a stain upon them that made her heart ache. All along the yellow pathways the grass was dug-over and seeded with graves. The plague had claimed many lives here. Bereavement and despair hung in the air.

*The dead of Faerie shouldn't be under the earth. They should fly to Albion.*

The fact that the survivors had no time for the proper funeral rites was shocking. Would those taken by the plague *never* get to the Blessèd Realm? And how were the people faring now that the Gildensleep shield was no more? What terrible toll of life had Lear's sickness taken on Faerie?

*There's no time to think about things like that! Maybe this can all be put right later. If we live through the next few minutes . . .*

Together the Seven who were One came in under the tall redbrick walls of the Palace. Wide brown steps led them to a gatehouse with double doors locked against them. But as they came to the top step, the locks burst on the arched doors and they swung smoothly open.

They came into an entrance hall, the light they gave off splashing high on the sculpted walls. There were green and white tiles beneath their feet. Tall candelabrum lined the way to a staircase of carved wood.

Where were the merry courtiers who had gladdened this place? Where were the music and the laughter and the chatter of winged children? The rich gowns of the Faerie ladies and the flashing crystal swords of their gallant lords?

Tania shivered and felt that same shiver run through the other Six.

"Don't be scared," she said, and at the same moment from the mouths of all the other girls came the same words.

"Don't be scared."

*It's like we're blending—become more and more a single person.* A single being with seven minds and seven hearts and seven souls.

The Power of Seven.

They swept up the stairs and made their way through empty galleries and hallways toward the Throne Room.

As they came closer, Tania became aware that their light was fading—as though some premature night was being conjured within the Palace—a wicked, vile night filled with ghosts and terrors.

They stood at the tall closed doors of the Throne Room, their pure white light beset all around by the dark. In the gloomy corridor Tania could see half-formed shapes moving. There were hideous, leering faces with long forked tongues and hungry eyes. Hands and claws tried to reach into the light. But the glow burned them, and the hands were snatched away with howls of frustration and pain.

Monstrous, humped shapes lurched around them with fiendish yellow eyes. Laughter gurgled from gaping throats. Eyes watched.

Fearlessly the Seven moved forward together. The doors trembled but remained closed.

Tania felt an intense hostility pushing against her from within the Throne Room. She concentrated her mind and pushed back. The doors quivered and opened a crack, revealing a thread of lurid red light.

A voice rang out from behind the doors. "Tania— help!" It was her Mortal mother, her words echoing and re-echoing.

And then Clive Palmer's voice sounded. "Please, Tania. We need you—help us. The light you're giving off is hurting our eyes!"

Edric's voice called. "Let go of the others, Tania— that's the only way to stop our pain! We'll be killed otherwise. And it will be your fault!"

"No!" Seven voices rang out in chorus. "It isn't *you*!"

"It is us, Tania," called Mary Palmer's voice. "He came through to the Mortal World—he trapped us and brought us here. He says he will kill us unless you surrender yourself to him."

"He means it!" Jade's voice. "He'll kill us, Tania—he's not kidding around. Give up, Tania—otherwise we're all dead."

"If you love us, let the others go," called Tania's father. "Let go of their hands. You know they're all going to die anyway. What does it matter when?"

"They're all going to die, Tania," came Edric's voice. "You're damaged goods, Tania; you're a half-thing. You never should have been born."

The voices beat at Tania's mind like hammer blows. *They're not real! They're not real!* These were tricks and deceits sent out to keep the Seven from entering the Throne Room beyond the closed doors.

Lear must fear them!

Tania took a deep breath. "Shut! Up!" she howled, and the others howled with her. The light blazed out from them, and the doors of the Throne Room burst inward in shattered splinters.

The long room was lit by a macabre red glow, the color of blood. A host of candles flickered across the floor, like a thousand ghost lights writhing over a tormented graveyard. A slender path of darkness threaded through the candles, leading to the King's throne.

The throne itself was shrouded in gloom. A figure sat there in deep darkness. Tania felt malicious eyes on her. She sensed a mind brimming with hatred.

"Welcome, niece," said a deep, husky voice. "I have been expecting you." There was a low laugh. "Come,

would you embrace your uncle, child? Would'st thou
nestle in the arms of one who has longed for this
moment for more years than you can imagine?"

Tania felt the pressure of the darkness all around
her—all around the Seven.

"It hurts!" came Ann's gasping voice. "It hurts in
my chest!" Her voice rose to a wail. "Bess! Help me! I
can't breathe!"

And Flora's voice cried out, "Burning! Burning!
Burning! Daddy! Dadd-ee-ee!"

Tania felt their power dwindling as the dark
pounded away at them.

She heard Gracie choking and turned to see the
girl bent over, coughing up water.

With a cry Georgina began to twitch and contort—
writhing and screaming as invisible hooves beat at her.

"All is lost," groaned the princess, and suddenly her
hand was weak in Tania's grip. All the strength and
purpose were gone from her eyes, and her face was
pale and withered again, plague-wracked and close to
death.

The light was fading. The Power of Seven was
breaking apart.

She could hear Marjorie moaning softly, her breath
bubbling as though her throat were filling with blood.

They had not struck a single blow against him.
Lear was ripping them to pieces.

*No! Not like this! I won't let it end like this!*

Gripping the hands of Georgina and the princess,
Tania ran forward down the path of darkness. The

others came with them, brought along in their wake, crying and groaning.

Tania focused her mind on their light, seeing it in her mind like a spring coiling and coiling—tighter and tighter—straining to burst.

They were almost at the throne now. Lear was leaning back, watching her with dark, impassive eyes.

The sight of his face was shocking. So much of Oberon was there! But oh—how warped, how deformed and twisted! His hair and beard were grizzled, and his features were webbed with fine lines, like veins under the parchment skin.

The simple white crown of Faerie lay on his head at a careless angle, as though he mocked the very thing he had so long desired. His eyes were dark and deep-set, like storm clouds, and his lips seemed to be caught in a permanent sneer.

"It seems that you have some powers, niece," he said. "Some *little* powers."

"Yes! We do!" Tania shouted, six other voices calling out in chorus with hers. Tania let loose the coiled spring of light.

It blasted out of her, roaring and rushing as it beat against Oberon's evil brother like a tidal wave.

"No!" shouted Lear.

Tania gasped for breath as the flood of white light hammered into the throne.

They had the power. They could defeat him!

The cascade of white light began to diminish, to dim and fade away.

She felt weak and drained.

There was mocking laughter. Lear sat at his ease in the great Throne of Faerie, smiling a little. He was unharmed—unaffected by their attack.

"And did you think 'twould be so easy to thwart me, niece?" he said. "A fool, and seven times the fool, you are!" He lifted his right arm, and a red fire flowed upward from it. "Give greetings to your kinfolk, Tania Aurealis—for you are about to join them!"

Red light spewed out above the throne and Tania saw a sight that stopped her heart.

Suspended in the air over Lear's head were five amber globes—five amber prisons. And trapped inside were the King and the Queen, Eden, Hopie, and Sancha.

"And now, seventh child of my loving brother, you shall join your family in the sleepless death!" A ball of amber light ignited in Lear's fist. "A sweet good night, my child—may demons gnaw at thee until the end of the world!"

Lear flung the amber ball toward her. She was thrown backward off her feet by the impact and an avalanche of yellow flame engulfed her.

# Part Three:

# The Festival of the Pure Eclipse

# XVII

Tania's body and mind were engulfed in amber flames. Her back arched, her arms spreading wide. She was hanging suspended in the air by Lear's sorceries. There was no floor under her feet. There were no hands holding her hands.

A voice chanted through the flames.

> *"Faeries tread the Faerie Path*
> *The amber vessel will not hold*
> *The princess with the heart of gold*
> *When true love foils usurper's wrath!*
>
> *"The Power of Seven fragile be*
> *When beset by foe of bloody hue*
> *But love shall tame the deeper blue*
> *Dark Arts shall set the Princess free."*

Blue flames licked among the yellow, weak at first, coming and going, as though struggling to survive.

But gradually the blue grew stronger until there was more blue than amber—until all at once the amber fire was snuffed out and Tania dropped jarringly to the ground, her legs collapsing under her.

"Tania!" It was Edric's voice, calling from the doorway. "You have the strength! You must do it! I will hold Lear's power in check for as long as I can—but you must strike him down."

She stumbled to her feet. "How?"

"Take the crown!"

Lear's voice roared like a furnace. "Never!"

Amber contended again with the blue, the flames like interlocked fingers struggling against one another.

Amid the flames Tania sought focus. She looked around herself. The six girls were with her in the amber fire, blazing with such light that they were little more than bleached silhouettes in the flames. But each stood alone and none were holding hands any longer.

Tania struggled to move her limbs—to gain some control of herself. It was like fighting floodwater. Every twitch of a finger or foot was bought only by huge effort. But she would not give up.

She turned her head. Edric stood just inside the doors of the Throne Room, bathed in blue light, Jade to one side, Rathina to the other. And from Edric's outstretched hands, a geyser of blue fire was gushing toward her.

*Together!* She could hear Edric's voice in her head now. *Together we can defeat him!*

"Yes!"

Tania waded forward into the amber flames, buoyed up by the blue-white light.

The six girls followed, forming a semicircle behind her, their potency guiding her, driving her forward as she came to the steps of the throne.

Lear was leaning forward now, his knuckles white as he gripped the arms of the throne, his face contorted and hideous as he fought against both the white and the blue light.

He stared at her as she stood in front of him, his head thrust forward, his lips drawn back in a feral snarl.

Supported by light and love, Tania reached forward, beams of white spinning out from her fingertips.

Lear's eyes followed her, but he did not move—as though he was pinned to the throne by a force he could not overthrow.

He howled as she closed her fingers around the crown and lifted it from his head.

Words came into her mind and she spoke them aloud, the incantation pouring from her mouth on a shaft of light.

> *"Thy heart is a withered stone*
> *Thy soul groans aloud*
> *Let the four winds bear thee hence*
> *To whence thou came*
> *Broken vessel—shattered spirit*
> *Get thou back to Ynis Borealis*
> *And trouble us no more!"*

She lifted the crown high. "Ill fortune devour you, Prince Lear Aurealis! Thou art banished! Get you hence!"

Lear tried to rise from the throne, but before he could move, the world was engulfed in a discharge of power that sent Tania spinning head over heels through a universe of howling white light.

Tania stood in a place that was no place—in a white void. She was hand-in-hand with her other selves. She knew this was but a fleeting moment before the children were to return to their own worlds and to their deaths.

The princess stood opposite Tania. There was no hint or taint of illness in her radiant face, and her lilac Faerie gown was now fresh and lovely.

"We shall meet again, when desperate need calls . . ." said the princess. " . . . one final time. . . ."

"Don't be scared," added Gracie. "We'll help you."

"In darkest noon," said Ann, her eyes dreamy, her breath coming easily, "by a gray river with banks of solid stone in a world set all afire . . ."

The Six broke hands, and they were drawn back into the white void.

"Thank you," Tania called after them.

She was alone now.

She gave a deep sigh and turned, sidestepping away.

Lear was gone.

Wreaths of white smoke floated through the Throne Room, half shrouding the damage and chaos caused by the Banishing Spell. The throne itself was smashed to stone shards, pieces of it scattered across the floor among the fallen and snuffed candles. The tapestries that hung over the walls were ripped to shreds. The tall elegant windows had lost all their glass, and cracks ran up the marble frames.

The only things undisturbed by the explosion of energy were the five amber prisons. They floated still in the upper air of the room, each with its pitiful captive.

"That's what I call a firework display!"

Tania turned at the sound of Jade's voice. Jade and Rathina and Edric were still by the door. Edric's head was hanging.

Tania ran to him. "Edric?"

He lifted his head, his brown eyes unfocused, his face drained. "Is Lear gone?" he whispered.

"I think he is," said Tania.

"Good." With a weary smile Edric crumpled unconscious to the floor.

Jade dropped to one knee, two fingers pressed to the side of Edric's neck. "Just feeling for a pulse," Jade said. "There it is. Strong and clear." She looked into Tania's eyes. "He's fine. Exhausted is all. He was pretty much wiped out *before* he made us bring him here." She glanced around the wrecked room. "The boy did good, though."

Rathina helped Tania to her feet. "Have the other six gone?" she asked.

"Yes."

Rathina sighed. "This is a sad victory." She frowned.

"If victory it be. Lear is bested, I deem, but what damage has he wrought in Faerie?"

Tania turned to look at the five floating amber globes and the crumpled shapes within them. "We need *Isenmort*," she said. Only the touch of Isenmort—of metal—could open the eternal prisons.

"I have none," said Rathina. "I lost my sword on the beach under Tirnanog."

"What's Isenmort?" asked Jade.

"Metal."

"I've got some spare change in my pocket," she said hopefully, digging out a small handful of coins.

Rathina took them. "Come, sister, let's play out the last act of this drama," she said, striding down toward the smashed throne plinth.

Tania followed her.

Rathina positioned herself under the prison where Oberon was crouched. She tossed a coin into the air. It spun, glittering in the clear light that poured in through the broken windows. At the height of the toss the coin struck the underside of the floating ball.

It stuck to the amber shell, and within moments Tania saw gray tendrils spreading out over the amber. She strained her neck, watching the King as the ribbons of gray converged and spun out higher.

There was a crack like distant thunder. Fissures swept over the globe. A golden light poured out, and with it a booming, rejoicing voice.

"Free!" roared the King. "I am free!"

He stood on the golden air for a moment, stretching

his cramped limbs. He looked at Tania and Rathina and smiled. He reached down and from the debris that was strewn across the floor, his crown leaped up to his hand, whole and unharmed.

"Father!" Rathina cried. "Praise the good spirits!"

"And praise the love and courage of a King's children!" called Oberon, placing the crown on his head. He turned, stretching out a hand. Golden light bathed the remaining four amber prisons.

"Be free, my wife, my love. Be free, my children, custodians of my heart!"

The globes broke and dissolved, and Titania and Hopie and Eden and Sancha floated softly to the ground on clouds of gold.

Tania threw herself into their arms. She could do nothing more than hold her mother and her sisters and weep with joy.

As they stood there in the ruins of the Throne Room, crystal bells began to ring out from distant towers. The peal of the bells was picked up and answered from farther away, the glorious sound doubling and redoubling all along the vast expanse of the Royal Palace until it seemed to Tania that the whole Realm of Faerie was alive with a riotous chime.

Lear was banished and the Royal Family was free!

# XVIII

Oberon strode to the broken windows of the Throne Room and stared out over the land of Faerie for a few silent moments. Tania watched him, wondering what was to come next. He turned, and his voice was strong and vibrant above the ringing bells.

"Prince Lear is banished forever," he said. "And with his passing the great plague has been lifted from this Realm—I feel it to the very roots of my soul! My people are free, and even now, throughout Faerie, the sick rise in wonder from their deathbeds and greet the glad new dawn!" A look of pain darkened his face. "But many have died and can never return. And my people are Mortal now and prey to all the ills and travails of that sorry state. Much work needs to be done ere all is as it should be in Faerie."

He looked slowly around the wreckage of the Throne Room. "Let us leave this place," he said. "Never shall the Throne Room be made whole again. The throne shall remain forever sundered and strewn in shards across the floor of this chamber, so that for all time the people of Faerie may come here and learn how fragile is the peace that blesses them, and remember those who died and shall never return."

The King showed no sign of the exhaustion that had wracked him the last time Tania had seen him. Sad as he was, he seemed as strong and powerful as he had been before the Gildensleep had drained the energy from him.

Tania wiped her sleeve across her eyes, still held safe in Titania's strong embrace. "Beloved daughter!" The Queen sighed. "You bring me such joy!" She glanced to the doorway, where Jade was kneeling at Edric's side. "Who is this Mortal girl?"

"She's Jade," said Tania. "She's my friend. She kind of invited herself along."

"A close friendship it must be, for her to have traveled with you between the worlds," said the Queen. "She is most welcome."

Tania looked from Titania to the King. "Is the plague really gone?" she asked.

"It is," said Oberon. "With his banishment all the works of Prince Lear fell into ruin. But alas for my people—so many have been lost. The evil done to this Realm will never be entirely washed away."

Eden rested her long white hand on Tania's forehead. "It has been a hard road for you, sweet sister," she said. "And, alas, for your griefs are not all told—a great loss has befallen our family."

Tania stepped out of her mother's arms.

"Where is Cordelia?" Rathina demanded.

Sancha's solemn face ran with tears, and she could not speak.

"She died," said Hopie, her voice choking. "I did what I could. I used all my Arts, all my skills—but the plague was too deep in her body."

"No!" The shout tore out of Tania's throat. *"No!"*

Rathina reeled, her face blanched. "Not Cordelia, no. Blood of the spirits, not Cordelia . . ." Eden put her arms about Rathina's shoulders.

"But what about the Gildensleep?" Tania cried. "That was supposed to protect her—it was supposed to protect everyone!"

"It saved Faerie from huge loss," said Titania. "But it was not enough to bring my daughter back to us." Her eyes were sunken with bereavement. "Her mind was gone, Tania. Even had her body survived, she would not have been the person you knew."

"It is hard beyond enduring," said Eden. "But it is done and she is lost to us. A second child of Aurealis has flown to the bliss of Albion."

"When did this happen?" groaned Rathina.

"But a short time before Lear fell upon us in the Throne Room at Veraglad Palace," said Sancha. "We had scarce time for her funeral rites before doom came from the Frozen North."

"You know who Lear was?" asked Tania.

"All too well!" declared Eden. "Great pleasure he had in telling us the tale of his life while we were locked in amber. When all was told, he brought us here to the Royal Palace, the better to savor the fruits of his triumph."

"And yet I never utterly despaired," said Titania, looking sadly but fondly from Rathina to Tania. "For I knew the strength that resided in the hearts of my two youngest daughters, questing for the good of all across strange and uncanny lands."

"And did you find Tirnanog?" asked Sancha. "Did you speak with the Divine Harper?"

"She did, indeed!" said Rathina. "And the interview cost her dear!" She glanced to where Jade was kneeling with Edric's head now resting in her lap. "And if not for Edric's endeavors, all would have been lost."

"I will tend him," said Hopie, moving quickly toward the doors. As she came close to where he lay, she paused and looked at Tania over her shoulder. "He reeks of the Dark Arts," she said uneasily. "From skin to bones it infests him."

"With good cause!" said Rathina. "Without those deadly Arts nothing could have been accomplished."

Tania looked anxiously at her healer sister. "He's all right, though, isn't he?" she asked. She remembered the deathly look of his eyes.

"I will help," said Eden, striding in her sister's wake. "All that can be done shall be done." Her fingers were already moving and sending out threads of golden light toward Edric. Jade laid his head gently on the floor and stood up, backing off and eyeing the mystical tendrils uneasily as they spun over Edric's slumped body.

"What did the Divine Harper tell you?" asked Sancha.

Tania looked at the King. "First, is Lear gone?" she asked. "Gone for good, I mean?"

"His spirit is broken," the King replied. "The same blood flows in our veins, and thus I know his fate. His power is dispersed and abated. He will not be able to enter this Realm again."

Tania grinned mirthlessly. "Then there's no chance of him stealing your throne if you leave Faerie!" she said. "That means you can go to Tirnanog and sort things out with the Harper."

"Few have come to me with a more welcome message," said the King, taking Tania by the shoulders and looking deep into her eyes. "Ahh! And I see what it was that the Harper told you. I must go to him and renew the covenant." His eyes shone. "So be it!"

"And shall the people of Faerie then be Immortal again, Father?" asked Rathina.

"With the proper courtesies and sacraments, I do believe it to be so," said the King. "Great service have you done for Faerie, my daughter. You and Tania and the Mortal boy." He turned and smiled at Tania. "Truly it is said that the seventh daughter of a seventh daughter shall work wonders!"

"Let us to ship!" declared Rathina. "The *Cloud Scudder* will surely cleave the air to Tirnanog within the circuit of a single day, and all things will be made anew!"

"In good time it will," said the King gravely. "But such a journey cannot be undertaken without due ceremony." He lifted his chin. "I shall call upon the Conclave of Earls to bless my journey."

"All will not come," Sancha said. "Aldritch of Weir will not come!"

"Can the rites be fulfilled without the lord of Weir in attendance?" asked Titania.

"That we shall see," said the King. "In the meantime let us summon the lords and ladies of the court—they shall forgather in the Great Hall and I will speak with them!" He rested his arm across Tania's shoulders. "Come, stand at my right hand, with your sister Rathina upon my left. Together you have done great deeds, my daughters—but the greatest is yet to come!"

Tania leaned anxiously over Edric. "How is he?" she asked.

"He sleeps," Hopie said. "Fear not. He will recover."

"He is strong, Tania," said Eden. "With a strength that is not all his own. It is your love that protects him from danger."

Tania smiled with relief. "Then he'll be protected forever!" she said.

"Wow!" Tania turned at the sound of Jade's voice. Her friend looked thrilled and astounded. "I can't believe how amazing this place is!" she said. "Tania, it totally *rocks*! Now I get why you were gone for so long!"

Hopie instructed two men of Faerie to bear Edric to a high, airy bedchamber in the Royal Apartments. Tania and Jade followed the slow cortege.

*I won't leave him! Not until he's better.*

As they climbed the stairs and walked the upper galleries of the palace, Jade gazed around, mouthing a silent "wow" at every new thing she saw.

Edric was laid on a four-poster bed and covered with fresh white linen. Hopie had her medicine chest brought from the princesses' gallery, and soon the sweet and pungent odor of herbs filled the air. Tania was desperate to stay with Edric—to be at his side when he awoke. She and Jade stood at his bedside, watching as Hopie muttered her healing charms and laid a wreath of white flowers by his head.

"He looks peaceful," Tania said, gazing down at his pale, sleeping face. She wondered whether there was silver under his closed eyelids.

"I have given him a tincture of passionflower and valerian to induce a dreamless sleep," Hopie said. She gestured to the bunch of small white flowers lying on his pillow. "Anise will ward off dark dreams, and I will distill the orange flowers of aloe to keep evil at bay."

Tania sat on the side of the bed and took Edric's hand. "Will he be himself?" she asked.

"You fear that he will not?" said Hopie.

"He was strange—just for a few moments, when we first got here. He wasn't himself. And his eyes . . . they were dead." She swallowed hard. "There are voices inside the Dark Arts—bad voices. I heard them, too, just for a little while. But if they're in his head all the time . . ." She looked fearfully at Hopie. "What must they be doing to him?"

"The Dark Arts are savage and deadly," said Hopie. "But I do not believe he has been damaged by them. Not thus far." She rested her hand on Edric's forehead. "No. He will recover and be himself, I believe, so long as he never uses the Dark Arts again."

"Good," said Tania. "Then I'll just sit here and wait for him to wake up."

"There is nothing for you to do here, Tania," Hopie said. "He will sleep the day out now. Return at dusk, and be here when he awakens."

"I want to stay," Tania said firmly.

"'Twill be a long and unnecessary vigil when all else in Faerie is awakening," said Hopie. "Go! Show your friend that Faerie is a world of wonders as well as of torments."

Jade smiled. "I kind of already got that, thanks," she said. "But I wouldn't mind taking a look around. I wish I'd brought my mobile with me—I need some pictures of this place. No one's going to believe me when I get back otherwise."

Tania looked uneasily at her friend, but she didn't say anything—there was no purpose in alarming Jade until she knew for certain whether the barriers between Faerie and the Mortal World were still in place. They'd been able to get through this time, but who knew if it would work without Tania's other selves? She thought she knew who would be able to tell her.

She stood up. "You'll stay with him, won't you?" she said to Hopie. "And you'll let me know immediately if he starts to wake up early?"

"He will sleep till the hour before sunset," Hopie said briskly, busy with a mortar and pestle, grinding orange flowers into an aromatic paste.

Tania looked urgently at her.

"Very well," Hopie relented. "If he stirs earlier, I shall have you sent for. Now go, for pity's sake, and leave me to my work."

"This is mind-blowing!" said Jade. "You guys must really be into reading!"

Tania had brought Jade to the Royal Library—guessing correctly that she would find Sancha among her beloved books.

Jade walked to the center of the room, coming to the hub of the spiraling lines of black and white floor tiles. She gazed up to the galleries that lined the curved walls—every gallery the home to a thousand ancient tomes. Light poured in through the high domed roof, gilding the burnished wooden balustrades and stairways.

Sancha, dressed as always in a plain black gown, and with her long chestnut hair tied back from her face, was standing by a reading lectern, with a look of relief and pleasure on her slender face. "I had feared Lear might do some irreparable damage here," she said. "The destruction of knowledge is ever the first act of the despoiler and tyrant."

Tania didn't need reminding of that. She remembered how the Sorcerer King had set flames to the library a few months past. It had only been through the regenerative power of Oberon that all had been made whole again.

"I don't suppose you guys have ever considered archiving all this on a computer?" Jade asked, turning in a slow circle. "You'd save a whole lot of room—and it'd make looking stuff up way easier, you know?" She grinned. "Then you could turn this place into a multiplex cinema."

Sancha frowned at her, as though trying to make sense of what she had said. "A computer?" she commented at last. "Yes, I remember the word—you have them in the Mortal World." She smiled. "Nay, Mistress Jade, I wish for no such devices. I love my library, and I know the location of every book within these walls."

"Amazing!" breathed Jade.

"So, everything is okay here?" Tania asked, taking Sancha by the elbow and gently walking her away from Jade.

"It is," said Sancha. "Or would be if not for the clouds in your mind, my sister. What ails you? Master Edric will be well, be most sure."

"It's not that," whispered Tania, drawing her sister farther away from Jade. "I need to know something, but keep your voice down, please."

"What would you know?"

"It's about the barriers between the worlds," Tania whispered. "Jade has been talking about what she's going to do when she gets back home, but I don't even know if she *can* go back again."

"The barriers still guard the ways between the

worlds," said Sancha. "But there is no reason they cannot be removed now that Lear is banished and the plague is gone."

Tania let out a breath of relief. "Oh, that's so great!"

"It will require the combined will of the entire Conclave of Earls to speak the words of dissolution," Sancha said. "And therein lies a stumbling block, for Aldritch of Weir has quit the Conclave and denied the overlordship of the King. In other matters the Conclave can work very well without the earl of Weir—but all of those who closed the ways between the worlds must be assembled if the portals are to be reopened." She shook her head. "I do not know what inducements might bring him back to us. I fear the Earldom of Weir is estranged from the remainder of Faerie for all time."

Tania looked at her in dismay. "And Aldritch went because of me," she said. "It drives me crazy. It's like for every good thing I do here, something bad happens."

Good and bad—they haunted her! She had brought a sword of Isenmort from the Mortal World to free Edric from an amber prison, and that same sword had been used by Rathina to release the evil King of Lyonesse. She had tried to end the plague by bringing Connor to Faerie, only to be renounced by Weir as a deadly half-thing, neither Faerie nor Mortal.

"Yours is a labyrinthine destiny, to be sure," said Sancha. "But you should not despair."

"It's like I'm forever running around having to put stuff right," said Tania. She gave a forlorn smile. "When do I get to be just plain Princess Tania, Sancha?

When can I quit saving Faerie and take a vacation?"
Sancha smiled pensively and began softly to sing.

*"When the moon comes down to earth to lie*
*And fishes in the air do fly*
*When the sea doth freeze on midsummer's eve*
*And spiders unto flies shall cleave*
*When love comes easy as the dawn*
*And there grows a rose that has no thorn."*

Tania looked thoughtfully at her sister. "I get it," she
said quietly. "Never, is that it?"

"You are not made for leisure and languor, Tania,"
said Sancha. "You are the seventh daughter of a seventh daughter." She rested her cool palm against
Tania's cheek. "You think you have been tested, my
sister?" she whispered, shaking her head slowly. "You
have not been tested yet, but it shall come . . . upon
swift and shining hooves." Sancha's eyes grew strangely
earnest, her voice dropping almost to the point where
Tania could no longer hear it. "List, Tania, list—can
you not hear it? The dark steed gallops apace and will
soon be here, shaking his great mane, his eyes full of
the darkling moon."

"What's going on, guys?" Jade's penetrating voice
broke the eerie spell that Sancha's words had woven
around Tania.

She glanced at her friend. "Oh, nothing," she
stammered. She looked back at Sancha, but the weird
intensity had gone from her eyes. "We should go. I

guess you've seen enough books for the time being?"

"Way more than enough," said Jade.

"Go you into the gardens," suggested Sancha. "Eden works her arts to create a fitting monument to Cordelia. It will be beautiful, I believe."

"Yes, we'll do that," said Tania.

She left with Jade in tow. It still didn't seem like the right time to tell her friend that she may never get to go home. *Let her enjoy Faerie for the time being.* If the barriers could never be taken down, Jade would have a whole lifetime to deal with the truth. And for the moment Tania also preferred not to dwell on the fact that she would suffer the same fate.

Coming out into the gardens, Tania could hear that the bells of Faerie were still ringing. Her restored childhood memories were full of adventures and balls and festivities and explorations along the whole length of the immense palace. And now it sounded to her as though every bell tower of the Royal Palace resounded with its own sweet clarion, all the way from the western rising of the River Tamesis in the Vale of the Singing Swans to Fortrenn Quay in the east, where the running waters emptied at last into the sea.

From all the secret places and hidden corners of the palace, the beleaguered people of the Faerie court were emerging, like children waking from a nightmare to find a new dawn had arisen.

Messengers had been sent out to spread the tidings, and as Tania watched them gallop to the north and the west, she knew that the carillon of the Royal Palace would be taken up in villages and hamlets across the land.

But on every side she saw that the joy of the newly liberated Faerie folk was braided with sorrow and loss.

A woman sat on a stone bench, an open locket of white crystal cupped in her two hands, her downcast eyes on the miniature painting of a man's face.

She looked up as Tania and Jade passed. "You have saved our Realm, my lady." She sighed. "But my sweet Ardil will never return."

"I'm sorry," said Tania, briefly touching the woman's bent shoulder.

"Is all love but the overture to sorrow?" asked the woman.

"I don't know."

Aching from the sadness in the woman's voice, Tania led Jade to Princess Cordelia's menagerie.

All the creatures were gone now, and the empty huts and hutches and paddocks and ponds had a forlorn look about them. Tania could see vividly in her mind the image of her dead sister rolling on the ground with puppies gamboling over and around her.

"Where are the animals?" asked Jade.

"I don't know." Tania sighed. "I guess they went away when Cordelia died."

They came to a still, sky-reflecting pond. Eden was there, standing knee deep in the water, facing away from them, her ash white hair hanging to her waist. She was chanting softly under her breath.

"Hi there!" called Jade. "Nice weather for a paddle."

"Shh!" Tania hissed. "Don't break her concentration. Remember what Sancha said—she's making something."

"Oh. Sorry." Jade stared at Eden's back, then brought her lips close to Tania's ear. "Like what? I don't see anything."

"Watch the water," Tania said, a frisson of excitement fluttering under her ribs. Out in the middle of the pond the water was beginning to churn, as though stirred by an invisible stick.

Eden lifted her arms and the whirl of rippled water began slowly to rise from the surface of the pond, sparkling and glittering in the morning sunlight. Gradually it grew upward in the air till it was a tall column of spinning water shedding shining droplets.

Eden began to call out incomprehensible words that made the air shiver.

The pillar of gyrating water began to bend and sway and expand and split and take on new shapes.

"Ohhhh . . ." Tania gazed wide-eyed at the rippling central figure. The clear column of water swirled and rolled, reshaping itself, forming sinuous hollows and curves until a recognizable form was created. Its surface streamed still with restless white water, but its shape was now that of her sister Cordelia—her hair cut short at her shoulders, her mouth spread in a wide smile, her back bent as she stooped to pet the animals gathered at her feet.

"Far out!" murmured Jade. "How does she *do* that?"

She flicked a quick glance at Tania. "Can you do stuff like that?"

"No," Tania replied, her eyes riveted on the dogs and goats and small southern unicorns that surrounded Cordelia, on the swans and squirrels and otters and fawns and other creatures, all made of moving water but all perfect.

Eden made a final pass with her hands to fix the liquid statues in place, then turned and waded to the bank. As she stepped onto dry land, Tania noticed that her sister's ankle-length gown was dry and that her feet shed no water as she moved toward them.

"'Tis little to do to honor such a great spirit," said Eden. "But it will suffice, I hope."

"It's perfect," said Tania.

"Uh . . . could you show me how to do stuff like that?" asked Jade.

Eden smiled solemnly at her. "Would you give five hundred years to the study, Mistress Jade?" she asked.

"It takes that long?" said Jade. "Maybe not, then."

Tania looked at her oldest sister, bracing herself before speaking. "We met Zara—in the Mortal World," she said in a rush, unsure of what impact such a revelation would have.

Eden stared at her in surprise "Is it so?" she said. "In dreams?"

"No, she was real," Tania said.

"Did you speak with her?" said Eden breathlessly. "What purpose did she have there?"

Before Tania could reply, the air was filled with a

musical sound that soared louder than the unending chime of the bells. Eden lifted her head, her eyes bright. "'Tis the call to Courtmeet," she said. "Come, Tania— and come you also, Mistress Jade—to the Great Hall. Things will be spoken of there that will concern all, I deem." She linked her arm with Tania's as they walked back to the palace. "And as we walk, you can tell me more of Zara. I have not heard of any that ever returned from Albion."

"Well, the thing is," began Tania, "she never actually went into Albion. . . ."

# XIX

The doors to the Great Hall stood wide as Tania and Eden and Jade approached. Many others walked with them: the lords and ladies, knights, wardens, and serving folk of the Faerie court, summoned here by the call of the King's crystal horns.

Tania looked from face to face, her newfound memory helping her instantly to recognize many of them. There was Lord Adriano, seneschal of Trembling Bells. And Lady Hippolyta, mistress of the Royal Stables. Lady Rosaline and Lord Ross, margrave and margravine of Forestgate. Mistress Mirrlees, dressmaker to the Royal Family, trotting along with a gaggle of other ladies at her back. And there were wardens to the King in their uniforms of dove gray, and palace servants all in sky blue livery. And she saw Admiral Belial, the captain of the *Cloud Scudder*, tall and gaunt and forbidding.

"The plague was deadly indeed," Eden said as they made their way through the doors of the Great Hall.

"But many more survived than fell—and that's a thing to be grateful for."

"But what will happen to the ones that died?" asked Tania. "I saw the graves. . . ."

"And you feared they would never find Avalon?" said Eden. "Nay, have no fear. Words will be spoken, wrongs will be righted. All shall savor that blessed place."

Tania frowned. "Why is it sometimes called Albion and sometimes Avalon?"

Eden smiled. "The Blessèd Realm's full name is the Avalon of Albion," she said. "Thus either name is appropriate."

"I don't want to keep repeating myself," said Jade as they came in under the high vaulted roof of the Great Hall, "but . . . *wow!*"

Tania smiled. The Great Hall of Faerie had been one of the first places she had seen when Gabriel Drake had originally brought her from the Mortal World. And it had been the venue for the Grand Ball that had celebrated her return after five hundred years of exile. But there was more than that now—she also remembered many feasts and festivities and dances taking place here over the years.

She remembered being five years old, dancing with her uncle Cornelius, her feet upon his as they trod the measure called the Tinternell during the Masque of Winter's Turning. And she remembered when she had been just thirteen and the hall had been alive with birdsong on Cordelia's sixteenth birthday.

There were no windows in the tapestried walls of the Great Hall, and it was lit as ever by two chandeliers suspended from the ceiling, wide as wagon wheels, and by many candles that burned in sconces set upon the walls. The hall was filling with people, and at the far end, under a scarlet awning, the King and Queen of Faerie sat together on two ornate wooden chairs with high backs and velvet drapings.

"Where is Uncle Cornelius?" Tania asked Eden as they threaded their way to the far end of the hall.

"He and the Marchioness Lucina and their two sons were imprisoned by the usurper in Veraglad Palace," said Eden. "As were many others, Lord Brython and Earl Valentyne among them. Word has been sent—they will come tomorrow, 'tis to be hoped."

"Oh! I'm so sorry," said Tania, feeling guilty that she had forgotten about her sister's elderly husband. "I should have asked about Earl Valentyne—how is he, do you know?"

Eden touched her forefinger to the center of her forehead. "We have spoken," she said, obviously meaning that she and her husband had used the Mystic Arts to communicate with each other. "When Lear was banished, the plague soon fell from him, as it did from all others. He is well enough in the aftermath of his ordeal."

"And Bryn?" asked Tania, remembering Cordelia's husband—remembering how the plague had come on the day of their wedding in Leiderdale. "Will he be with them?"

Eden sighed. "I doubt that, Tania," she said. "He quit Veraglad within the hour of her death—taking a horse and riding in fury and grief into the north."

"Poor Bryn," Tania murmured. "They were only married for a couple of hours. . . ."

The movement of people into the hall came to a halt.

Tania looked around herself, seeing great lords and ladies and simple servants and attendants all mingling together.

Oberon rose to his feet and an expectant hush came over the throng.

"Much wrong has been done to this land by my brother Lear," said Oberon, his voice strong and clear. "But he is gone now, thanks to the faith and endurance of the princesses Rathina and Tania."

Faces turned, smiling. Tania hadn't even noticed Rathina standing quietly against one of the long walls. There was applause for them both. Rathina seemed embarrassed by the attention. Perhaps she thought she did not deserve praise?

The King lifted his arms and the ovation died away.

"Also deserving of your plaudits is the captain of Weir, Edric Chanticleer," he said. "May his recovery be swift and complete." There was renewed cheering, the Queen smiling at Tania and rising as she joined in the applause.

Tania winced a little at the mention of Edric's title—it was because he had been made a captain of Aldritch's guard that he had left her. She hoped that when he was better, she would be able to convince him to stay here.

*There's no way I'm letting him walk out on me twice.*

"Shortly I shall set sail upon the *Cloud Scudder* to seek the Divine Harper of Tirnanog, and to renew the covenant of Immortality!" Oberon called over the noise. "But now is the time for rejoicing, for festivities and merrymaking throughout the land." He turned to look at a slight, unassuming man who stood to one side of the two thrones. "And who better in all of Faerie to organize and oversee the revels than Master Raphael Cariotis—our chief counselor and most honored Guardian of the Precession of the Equinoxes." He reached out a hand to the man. "Come forward, Master Raphael—I know you wish to speak of wonders that are to come, greater by far than our earthbound festivities!"

Tania frowned as the man stepped onto the throne dais. She guessed he was somewhere in his late forties or early fifties. He had graying hair swept back off a large wide forehead. He had a lined, thoughtful face, a beaked nose, and a goatee and mustache. He wore plain clothing, unornamented save for an amber crystal that hung from a cord around his neck.

But what puzzled Tania was the fact that she didn't recognize him at all. Confused, she turned to Eden. "Who is he?" she whispered.

"He is as the King announced," said Eden. "Master Raphael—one of our father's most trusted advisors. He has been at the King's side for time out of measure."

She reached out a hand and touched her fingers to Tania's temple. A shock like mild lightning burrowed through Tania's brain, making her wince and pull away.

"Ow! Eden!"

"Forgive me." Eden looked deeply into Tania's eyes. "Are you sure you do not remember him now?"

Tania looked again at the man, the discomfort quite gone from her head. "Oh yes," she said as memories of Raphael Cariotis came breezing into her mind. "Yes—of course!"

How could she have forgotten him? In all affairs of the realm Raphael Cariotis had always been her father's closest confidant. A good man, and a great counselor to the House of Aurealis. And a friend to all the princesses, of course. Tania had known him all her life.

"'Tis a thing most curious that you remembered him not for a while," said Eden. "I deem there are dark places still in your mind, sister. I wonder what other people, places, and events are still lost to you."

"I remember him perfectly now," said Tania. "It was just for a moment there. But I'm sure I remember everything else."

Eden gave a small smile. "And how would you know that if the memories are hidden?"

"She's got you there!" Jade chuckled.

"Greetings to all," came Master Raphael's voice, and it was deep and soft but very penetrating. "We forgather here in auspicious times, my friends. The lords of the Starlight Dance have come into an unusual and most welcome alignment."

Tania looked at him, liking his gentle voice and his quiet authority, now quite sure that it was holes in her own memory that accounted for her not knowing him at first.

"As you all know, I have studied the skies for years beyond count," continued Master Raphael's compelling voice. "And from observing the recent movements in the heavens, I have learned that a thing is to come that has not happened these twenty-five thousand years."

Even by Faerie standards, twenty-five thousand years was a long time—whatever Master Raphael was talking about, the last time it had taken place must have been before Oberon had even gone to the Divine Harper—way, way back in the Lost Times before the covenant of Immortality.

"The constellations stand ready for the great event," Master Raphael continued. "The Phoenix falls below the horizon while the five stars of the Singing Dragon rise to the zenith of the sky. All the portents speak of the same thing: We are entering the days of the Pure Eclipse."

A murmur went around the room, mostly of bafflement, but Tania did notice that a few faces lit up with surprise and understanding.

One lord stepped forward. "I have heard of this marvel," he said. "I thought it was but fancy!"

"It is not, my lord Dozian," came Sancha's voice from the back of the hall. All eyes turned to her. "The

Pure Eclipse is mentioned in a few of the older texts and scrolls—it is a most strange and unique event."

"Indeed it is," added Raphael, giving Sancha a small polite bow. "As her royal highness states, there are books that chronicle this event, for those who seek them out." Once more he had the audience's rapt attention. "Once in twenty-five thousand years the moon of Faerie passes across the face of the noonday sun and a great shadow falls upon the land."

*An eclipse? Yes, it was in that magazine back in London, and the cabdriver was talking about it as well. So, it's going to happen here and back there at the same time. Cool!*

But Tania had no time for further thought as Raphael Cariotis continued to speak. Now his words took her breath away.

"As the shadow passes over Faerie, so all the barriers between the worlds will melt away," said Raphael. "And for that brief time, the realms of Faerie and of the Mortal World will flow together and all shall be one." His voice vibrated with the potency of his words. "Under that celestial penumbra every Mortal will be able to step into Faerie—and everything that is alive in Faerie will learn what it means to walk between the worlds."

# XX

Eden's voice broke through the murmur of astonishment that filled the hall in the wake of Raphael Cariotis's revelation.

"I had not heard of the Pure Eclipse before this moment," she said, and her voice was sober. "But if Master Raphael is correct, then we must do all that we can to lessen the chaos that such an event will create in the Mortal World."

"Eden is right," said Titania. "The people of the Mortal World are not equipped to confront the reality of Faerie—it would overthrow their minds."

Jade shot her hand up. "Uh—excuse me!" she called out. "Mortal person standing right here!" She seemed unfazed as everyone turned to look at her. "Mortal person with her mind in one piece, by the way!"

Titania smiled gravely. "Your point is well made," she said. "But you have come here with a loving friend, and of your own will. Do you think the millions that inhabit your world would react so calmly to see the walls and battlements of the Royal Palace appear suddenly among them or to have the wild unicorns of Caer Liel a-gallop along their High Streets?" She turned to address the others. "'Tis true, a single Mortal can have great wisdom and forbearance, but as a mob, they are uncontrollable—and when the sights and sounds of Faerie enter their world, they will become a frightened mob, be most assured."

"Well, okay, I guess you're right about that," Jade admitted.

"And what will happen here if we get invaded by thousands of people all carrying metal?" asked Tania. "And I'm not just talking about ordinary, everyday metal things—they have guns and knives, too. And worse weapons. Much worse." It was almost unbearable to think of the damage a slashing knife might do to Faerie flesh—not to mention the devastating effect of a bullet or a flung grenade.

"Tania speaks the truth," said Eden. "This confluence bodes ill for both realms."

"The lore masters of Faerie must come together to debate this thing," said the King. "A way must be found to lessen the effects of the Pure Eclipse in the Mortal World and in Faerie. Sancha—I charge you to call a council of the wisest of the court. Master Raphael has told me that the Pure Eclipse will strike at noon in five days' time. You have until then."

"It shall be done," said Sancha. "Master Raphael, I would speak with you—we must choose those most fitted for this endeavor."

Raphael Cariotis bowed to the King. "By your leave, sire, I would say one final thing before I depart." He turned to face the hall again. "As ominous as the Pure Eclipse may be for the denizens of both realms, I deem it also to be a great and portentous event for Faerie," he said. "The alignment of the stars is most favorable upon that time for great endeavor. By the will of the King, I would recommend that he set sail to his tryst with the Divine Harper on the evening of that selfsame day. All that I see in the skies tells me that success will mantle such an enterprise undertaken at such a time."

"So be it," said the King. "Admiral Belial! Go you now to Fortrenn Quay to prepare the *Cloud Scudder* for a great voyage."

"By your will, sire, I shall," said the Admiral, bowing and then sweeping from the hall with several other lords at his back.

"And now," continued the King, "I would have you good people depart, to congregate again at sunset in the Royal Gardens, where proper observances will be done for those who fell to the plague."

Wardens opened the double doors and the people began to filter out.

"Eden, Rathina, Tania, accompany me and the Queen to the Privy Chamber," said Oberon. "There we have a more ill-favored matter to discuss."

"That sounds nasty," said Jade. "You go—I'll take a stroll around and hook up with you later."

"Try not to get into trouble," said Tania lightly,

although the King's words had worried her.

"You know me!"

"Exactly!"

The Privy Chamber was a small wood-paneled room with wide glass doors flung open to reveal the delights of the ornamental gardens. The air wafted in sweet with the scent of alyssum and phlox and tuberose. Tania noticed that men and women were moving outside among the sad graves, covering the raw earth with sheets of white silk.

An oval, white marble table dominated the Privy Chamber, circled with chairs. As Tania and Rathina arrived, several lords and ladies were already seated with Eden and the King and Queen, and others were finding places at the table. Tania recognized them as members of her Father's inner council. Their faces were solemn.

"I have news of Weir," said the King as soon as everyone was settled. "It is not good. Since Lord Aldritch declared himself no longer subject to my rule and quit the Conclave of Earls to return to his homeland, he has raised a Mystic Wall along the borders of his earldom. I was not able to send my mind into Weir, but I felt great anger and hostility fermenting within."

"The Mystic Barrier confounds all attempts at piercing it," added Eden. "Aldritch has raised it so that we will not know what he intends."

"Has Aldritch not always repudiated the Mystic

Arts?" said one lord. "Whence comes the power he now wields—and do you fear he will turn it upon us?"

"It is true that Aldritch has never used the Mystic Arts," agreed Eden. "But there are sanctums in Caer Liel where mystical presences have long slumbered. In a deep dungeon lies hidden the Spellstone of Weir. He has awoken the powers of the Spellstone, I deem."

"But does he mean us harm or not?" asked the Queen. "Could it be that he merely sought to cut Weir off from the rest of Faerie so that the plague would not destroy his people?"

"I have spoken of this with Master Cariotis," said the King. "He fears that Aldritch is massing an army behind the barrier—that he means to lead an assault upon us."

Tania felt a shiver run through her. "Because of me?" she said. "Is he going to attack us because he wants me dead?" She remembered all too well her last encounter with the lord of Weir. It was impossible for her to forget the venom in the words he spoke to her.

*"I have no doubt but that you do us great harm! Were it not for you, Tania Aurealis, my son would still be alive! You are a sorcerer and a corrupter of men's hearts—and I will have nothing more to do with a court that seeks to defend you!"*

"Aldritch fears you greatly, sister," said Rathina. "But surely we do not need to fathom his motives in order to defend ourselves against him. If Weir desires war, then let us prepare for it! Are there not knights enough in Faerie to throw back whatever force Lord Aldritch can send out upon us?"

"Only those who have not known the full horror of war can speak so lightly of it," said the King. "And know this, Rathina, beloved child, I would pluck out my right eye—I would sever my right arm from my body—if I thought it would prevent conflict in this realm." His eyes glowed. "Weir is part of this kingdom. The people of Weir are our kinsfolk and friends, no matter how the storm clouds gather above us at this time."

Tania shivered. "Could we negotiate with Aldritch?" she asked. "Couldn't we send someone to talk to him?" She swallowed. "I could go there," she said. "Perhaps I could prove to him that I'm not a threat . . . that I'm not the bad thing he thinks I am."

"'Tis a brave offer, but foolhardy," said one of the ladies. "To put into his clutches she whom he wishes gone from this world? I think not!"

"And yet Tania has some wisdom in this," said Eden. "Belike an emissary could be found? Someone whom the lord of Weir might trust? Someone he would listen to?"

"And how would this person enter Weir when the Mystic Arts bar the way?" asked another lord.

"Oh, be most sure, any that come a-knocking upon the borders of Weir will not go unseen by Aldritch," said Eden. "The trick will be to have him allow them entry for parlay."

"We will think further on this," said the King. "One shall be found among my people. This is good counsel."

"And yet," murmured another of the ladies, "are

we to rely solely upon cool words to soothe hot hearts? Should we not also prepare for the worst that Weir might throw upon us?"

"I will speak to Master Cariotis on this subject," said the King. "But I believe that prudence dictates we call upon the knights of Faerie to muster once more upon Salisoc Heath."

Tania didn't like the sound of that—she had been involved in one battle already, and although they had been victorious over the Sorcerer King, she had hated the dreadful waste of it. The thought of war breaking out between Weir and the rest of Faerie was too heart-breaking to contemplate.

A soft knock sounded.

"Enter," called the King.

A maid opened the door, bobbing on the threshold. "By your leave, sire," she said. "Her royal highness the princess Hopie sent me with a message for Princess Tania."

Tania turned to look at her. "What message?"

"My lady, it was simply to tell you, 'he is awake,'" said the girl.

"How long have we been up here?" asked Tania.

"I have no idea," Edric replied. "Do you want to go back down?"

"Absolutely not!"

They were together alone upon the battlemented rooftop of a high tower that overlooked the gardens. A long winding stairway separated this lofty aerie and the rest of the palace.

The sun was low. The long Faerie afternoon was sinking into a golden dusk. The shadows were full of color, and the air was drowsy with birdsong and flowers. To the east and west the thousands of linked buildings and baileys and courtyards and halls of the palace stretched away beyond sight, following the meandering course of the River Tamesis. To the south turrets and spires and walls blocked the view; to the north all was rolling purple-hued hills and downs with forests beyond, leading into the heart of Faerie.

Edric was gazing north, his hand warm in Tania's.

Birds soared, climbing the sky in liquid flocks. Swifts and martens darted from rooftop to rooftop, doves gathered in sumptuous gray clusters on the battlements, their cooing as soft as a lullaby.

Tania noticed that many birds were flying around a particular tower away to their left. The square tower was of plain gray stone, its upper windows shuttered, its walls veined with strands of red ivy. The steep roof of the tower was so thick with the birds that, when one landed among them, another was dislodged from its perch. And all the time more birds circled the top of the tower, calling shrilly.

Tania had the vague feeling the tower should mean something to her, but she could not remember what. Another hole in her memory. So annoying!

"What do they find so fascinating there?" Tania wondered aloud, gazing at the tower.

"Don't you remember?" Edric asked. "Birds have

always congregated there—it's because they're never disturbed. The Dolorous Tower hasn't been used for a long time. Not for hundreds of years."

Tania frowned. "Should I know that?" she said. "I guess I should. I still have gaps."

"I'll help you to fill them in time," Edric said. "But if you don't remember, then let me warn you—don't go near the Dolorous Tower. It's falling to pieces; it isn't safe. Remember that!"

"I will," said Tania. "Edric? Look at me."

He turned his face toward her.

She smiled, squeezing his hand. "Your eyes are brown." She sighed, stroking his cheek. "I prefer them brown."

"So do I."

"And you feel . . . completely okay?"

"I feel a bit tired," Edric admitted. "But that's all. Princess Hopie mixes a powerful potion, and Princess Eden's charms have sent the bad voices packing."

Tania frowned. "Did you hear them all the time?"

"No, not all the time. They came and went."

"I hope you never have to use the Dark Arts again," Tania said vehemently. "I don't like what they do to you."

"Neither do I."

She looked into his face, wanting desperately to trust him again. Could she? Had he really survived the Dark Arts unharmed? Unchanged?

He smiled and touched her hair. She pressed against him, clinging tight.

"I hated it when we were apart," she said, his breath on her cheek, his arms strong around her back. "Let's not do that anymore."

"We shan't," said Edric, stroking her hair. "You and I—together now for all time."

She smiled into his face. "Exactly."

"Never to part."

"Never to part!"

They kissed, and for a brief time Tania lost herself in Edric's embrace.

# *XXI*

The sun lay on the western horizon, cradled in coral-colored skeins of cloud. The shadows were long in the Royal Gardens—shadows of trees and bushes and of people gathered there in silent reverence.

It seemed to Tania that most of the people from the palace had congregated on the lawns and pathways of the gardens, some grouped together, others standing alone. Children kept close to their parents, their gossamer wings folded, their faces heartbreakingly solemn or wide-eyed with incomprehension. Some men and women held babes in arms, but none of the infants cried out or made a fuss.

Tania was with Edric and Jade and Rathina and Eden. Sancha stood close by, as did the King and Queen, under the shade of a tall rowan.

A stillness came over the land as the sun dipped below the far horizon. Shadows glowed. The eastern sky was rich with the coming night.

Tania's skin tingled.

"It begins," murmured Eden.

Tania heard singing. It seemed to come from beneath the ground—a sad, slow song that made the world tremble.

The singing was of hundreds of voices: male voices and female voices, the voices of the old and the very young. As Tania listened, so the song wound through the gardens, the slow melody full of sadness.

But as the sun went down, a new harmony wove its way into the song—and it was full of hope and yearning. A countermelody grew from the original tune, a new theme that was glad and majestic.

Tania felt as if she was surrounded by song—standing deep inside the music of the thousand voices. Edric's hand slipped into hers.

Faerie stars lit the darkening sky. The white silk sheets that mantled the graves shone like moonlight. The singing rose into the sky like soaring doves.

There was an ache in Tania's heart as the lovely sound began to fade.

She looked up. From all over the realm, shooting stars were speeding into the west.

The dead of Faerie were going home to the Avalon of Albion.


"Don't you miss stuff?" Jade asked, leaning up in the large bed and looking at Tania, lying at her side. "When you're here, I mean? Normal stuff."

Beyond the open windows of Tania's bedchamber, the full moon hung low in the night sky. A gentle breeze wafted in, filling the room with the scent of evening primrose and honeysuckle.

Tania looked across at her. Jade's eyes were almost black in the flickering light of the single candle. "Some things," she said drowsily. "Mum and Dad, mostly."

Jade frowned. "What about television and movies and your computer?" She shook her head. "And your mobile phone? Doesn't it drive you crazy that you can't text the gang—or call them up—like: 'Hey, you'll never guess where I am! I'm in a bedroom in a Faerie palace, and there are these tapestry things on the walls—really nice pictures of the countryside and mountains and the sea. But here's the thing: they're alive!'" The same awe came into Jade's voice as Tania had heard a little while ago when she had first shown her friend the living tapestries that adorned the walls of her bedchamber. "Like, you're looking at a really cute landscape, and suddenly you notice the trees are moving in the wind. And then a whole flock of birds suddenly goes flying across the needlework sky. You do a double take on the whole lot—and you realize the ship is moving through the water and clouds are going across the sky, and a whole lot of other stuff besides. It's crazy!"

Tania laughed. "I'll have to show you some of my sisters' rooms," she said. "Rathina's is full of dancers. Hopie's is all wooden carvings, like a forest, but the carvings move and you can see animals padding through the grass."

Then she remembered Zara's room with its painted

seascapes where gulls flew and the waves rolled. *And is it still like that now that she's gone? Does the tide still come in and out? Are there still ships on the water?*

She pushed her thoughts away. "I just don't miss television or movies," Tania said. "And as for texting and message boards and all that, I don't even think of those things when I'm here."

"Y'see?" said Jade, as though Tania's comment had convinced her of something she'd already suspected. "You totally belong here, Tania."

"Well, yes. Half of me does. . . ."

"No way!" Jade said. "All of you does! When you told me all about this place—you know, back when I thought you were loony tunes—you made it sound like you didn't feel you really belonged here. But you so totally do. I'm here craving my iPod and my mobile phone, and you couldn't care less about stuff like that. I'm lying here thinking, 'Hey, I could go for a pizza right now. Shame we can't give the local pizza parlor a call and have one delivered.'"

"If you're hungry, we can find something to eat," Tania said.

Jade grinned. "You don't get it! I'm not hungry. The point I'm trying to get across to you is that I'm already missing stuff from my real life."

"Look," said Tania, feeling a twinge of guilt, "I'm certain we'll be able to get you back home when the Pure Eclipse hits. You have to put up with this for only five days."

"Again with not getting the point!" said Jade. "I'm not saying I'm not enjoying being here. I am; it rocks my socks! But for me it's like being on holiday—and I'm having a great time. But for you it's like this is the place you were *always* meant to be." She sat up, warming to her theme. "How long have we known each other? Ten years? Thereabouts, for sure. And there's always been this *thing* with you."

Tania stared at her. "What thing?"

"Always wanting to be someplace other than where you are," said Jade. "When you're at school, you want to be home. When you're home, you want to be out shopping in the market. When you're there, you want to be somewhere else. It's always been like you're never happy anyplace at all. My mum used to say you have itchy feet—you know, never able to stay still in one place for more than five minutes." Jade spread her arms in an encompassing gesture. "*This* is why!" she said. "All *this* is what you wanted! All your life you've missed this place and you never even knew it."

Tania blinked at her. "Oh." Jade was right—she'd always had that kind of restlessness. That was why her parents had suggested she might want to travel before going to college. That was why the life of an investigative journalist might suit her: always on the hunt for something new, always looking for hidden things.

Jade lay back again, pulling the covers up to her chin. "Me—I'm just totally ticked off I didn't bring my digital camera." She put her hands behind her head.

"Except even if I showed people pictures of this place, they'd still think I'd put them together in Photoshop. I guess there's only one way to really believe in this wacky place—and that's to visit." She gave Tania a sideways look. "It's a shame about those barriers the earls put up—we could have made a fortune!"

Tania frowned. "Excuse me?"

"I can see it now," said Jade with a wide smile. "'Faerie Tours! Been everywhere? Seen everything? I don't think so! We offer exclusive luxury tours of a whole other world! Special family rates. Money back if not one hundred percent satisfied.'"

"Jade?" said Tania, licking her fingers and reaching out to snuff the candle. "That is a truly terrible idea!"

Jade sighed in the sudden, deep darkness. "I guess so," she said. "Will you promise me one thing?"

"If I can."

"Promise when I go back, when I go home . . ." Jade's voice was suddenly quite serious. "Promise me you won't let my mind get wiped, like the thing that happened with Connor. I know I'll never be able to talk about this place—but I don't want to forget it, either. Is that a deal?"

Tania looked at her friend. How could she make such a promise? She had not been responsible for Connor's lost two weeks. And her own mind had been wiped and her Faerie self erased for a time. She had no control over what might happen.

And yet she couldn't bear to leave Jade swinging in the wind like that.

"If I can, I will," she said, turning over and drawing the covers up to her ears. "And that's a promise."

It was night. There were no stars. In her dream Tania was on the same lofty rooftop where she had stood with Edric that afternoon. Except that Edric was not there and she felt abandoned and horribly alone.

The Dolorous Tower was lit by an eerie, ghastly light, like moonlight but all *wrong*—like the kind of unhealthy light given off by rotting things, a foul and sickening glow that made her stomach turn. Birds were still swarming on its rooftop and flying circles around its upper levels, crying out in ghastly and forlorn voices. Or at least they seemed to be birds—except that there was something not quite right about them.

Then Tania saw what was wrong. She saw it because suddenly the tower was much closer—as though she had gone to it or it had come hurtling toward her. The birds were all dead. Flying but dead—their feathers rotting and matted with blood, the bones jutting from their plumage, their eyes empty, their voices spectral and horrible.

The crown of the Dolorous Tower was haunted by flocks of dead birds.

Horrible! *Horrible!* Tania tried to scream, but she had no breath.

A force hurled her through the air toward the birds. The birds surrounded her, squawking and fluttering, their loose feathers darkening the air. She threw her arms over her head as she saw the shuttered window of the tower hurtling toward her.

She smashed through and found herself in a place she knew. . . .

She had been here once before—not in her dreams but in reality. She was standing on a high gallery overlooking a huge hall made entirely of angled slabs of shining black stone.

*"The Obsidian Chamber,"* she mouthed silently. *"In Caer Liel, in Weir . . ."*

Torches lined the walls, and the angled stone threw the uneasy light back and forth so that it was almost impossible to tell what was real flame and what was reflection. The center of the room was dominated by a huge throne made of black stone. A man sat on the throne, wrapped in a cloak of black fur.

*Lord Aldritch.* Tania recognized him in a heartbeat. But a second man knelt before him, doing homage.

Lord Aldritch extended his hand, and the other man lifted his head to kiss the black rings on the wasted old fingers.

The person doing obeisance to the lord of Weir was Edric. *No, please no. Not Edric.*

His voice echoed through the great black hall. "My liege lord—I am eternally your obedient servant."

Aldritch rested his long hand on Edric's head. "Like a son you shall be to me," he said. "A fitting replacement for the child I lost—my poor Gabriel, destroyed by the half-thing Tania Aurealis!" Aldritch raised his head and his dark, dreadful eyes fixed on Tania. His voice boomed in her head. "You shall be the instrument of her doom," he cried. "A sword in the heart shall be your gift to her, Edric of Weir—and together we shall drink of her blood!"

# XXII

Tania awoke with a start.

She opened her eyes to streaming early-morning sunlight and to Jade, barefoot on the polished wooden floorboards near the window, doing her tai chi exercises.

The whole thing had been a nightmare.

Tania sat up, the terrible darkness seeping out of her mind.

"Awake at last, huh?" said Jade.

"Been up long?" Tania asked, knuckling her eyes.

"A while." Jade continued the elegant, slow-motion actions—her body lithe and fluid as she moved. "Has anyone told you that you snore?"

"No."

"Really. Not even Edric?"

"*No!*" Tania stretched, choosing to ignore the implications of that mischievous question. "I had a bad dream is all," she said. She looked quizzically at Jade. Her friend seldom spoke of her tai chi classes—too many people had made fun in the past of her slo-mo "old people" exercises. "Do all those movements have names?" she asked.

"Each and every one of them," Jade said. "This is called Wild Horse Shakes Its Mane." She made a long, slow step forward, her hands with the fingers pointing, arms flowing one over the other as she glided through the early-morning light.

"Pretty," Tania said, getting out of bed. "But don't you ever feel like cutting loose and doing something fast?"

Without any warning Jade threw herself through the air, her extended fingers slicing past Tania's throat. Startled, Tania sat back suddenly on the bed.

"That little move is known as Scooping the Moon from the Sea Bottom," Jade said with a grin. "And if I'd had a sword in my hand, your throat would be cut now from ear to ear. Don't talk to me about speed—I can do stuff so fast that you wouldn't believe it!"

"You know how to fight with a sword?"

"You bet I do—and I'm way good at it, too!"

Tania grinned, quickly recovering from Jade's surprise attack. "I thought karate was the one that did all the damage."

"Don't you believe it—just because tai chi is a soft martial art, don't assume it isn't dangerous."

"You should show some of your best moves to Rathina," said Tania. "I think she'd love them!" She stood up again and made for the large wardrobe. "Meanwhile, I'm going to get dressed and find some breakfast." She opened the wardrobe door to reveal rows of full-length gowns. "Anything in here you like the look of?"

Jade's eyes widened. "You bet!" she said. "I hope they fit."

"They fit me, so they should fit you," said Tania, standing aside as her friend began to rummage among the colored gowns. "Come on, let's get ourselves kitted out."

Jade drew out a flowing dress of green satin with gold and black embroidery at the low neck and around the ends of the sleeves and the wide, ankle-length hem. "I am going to so knock 'em dead in this!" Jade gasped.

Tania chose a simple dress of lilac and lavender. It reminded her of the dress she had worn the first time she had stepped into the Mortal World. She'd wear it in remembrance of her other self, the princess who had stepped out of Faerie on the eve of her sixteenth birthday and died in the Mortal World.

Tania was glad to leave the room; the last remnants of her nightmare lingered still among the tumbled bedclothes.

Tania and Jade breakfasted on a wide sunlit veranda. Marble steps led down to the maze, a triangular network of neatly tended hedges with a glorious fountain at its secret heart. A few other people of the court sat at nearby tables. Children were playing around the maze, some running, their wings rippling in the air—others flying in and out of the entrances and over the hedges, laughing and shouting.

Jade watched the flying children with her mouth half open in astonished delight.

"We played in the maze all the time when I was a child," Tania said, her heart filling as she gazed out over the narrow files of hedges. "Zara and Rathina and Cordelia . . . and me." She looked at Jade. *And now Cordelia and Zara are dead, and Rathina is half broken by grief.* "I used to cheat." She sighed, full of bittersweet memories. "The rules were you weren't allowed to fly once you were inside—but I'd flit up over the hedges so I got to the fountain first."

Jade looked at her. "It must be hard to lose your wings when you grow up."

"Not so hard as not remembering you ever had them," Tania said. She saw Rathina step out through the wide glass doors. She joined them at the table.

"I was remembering playing in the maze," Tania said to her sister.

"Innocent times, indeed," said Rathina, sipping from a glass of Faerie cordial. "Childhood days, all lost and gone."

Tania smiled sadly. "I'd like it if we could get together sometime soon," she said. "All of us—Eden, Hopie, Sancha. You and me. I'd like to talk about those times. Now that I remember them."

Rathina nodded. "We should do that. We should find a time and gather together in the princesses' gallery and speak of happy times before the Great Twilight, before . . ." Tania could have finished the sentence. *Before I got lost in the Mortal World, before Titania followed me . . . before the Sorcerer King was set loose . . . before Zara died, before Lear came . . .*

"But such reminiscences must wait upon other duties," said Rathina. "We have much to do, Tania. Master Raphael has allocated tasks to all of us in preparation for the festival of the Pure Eclipse." Her eyes glowed. "And I believe you have a most especial role to play."

"Do I?" asked Tania. "Such as what?"

"Master Raphael will speak to you of it, no doubt, when the time is right," said Rathina.

"And what do I get to do?" asked Jade.

"You are our guest, Mistress Jade," said Rathina. "Take your ease—gaze upon the marvels of Faerie. Amuse yourself in whatever ways you wish."

Jade looked sideways at her. "Have you ever heard of tai chi, Rathina?" she asked.

"I have not."

Jade smiled. "It's a martial arts discipline."

Rathina gave her a puzzled look.

"A kind of fighting technique," Jade said. "Tania said you might like it. I'll show you a few nifty moves when you have the time. You'll love it!"

"Thank you," said Rathina. "I shall look forward to that."

"Have you seen Edric?" Tania asked her sister. "I thought he might be here."

"I believe he is in our father's Privy Chamber, along with others of the King's council."

Tania frowned, wondering what such an early meeting might mean. "They called for him?"

"I think not," Rathina explained. "I believe that Master Chanticleer asked to meet with them."

*Odd. Why should he do that?*

But before Tania could ask more, the air was full of the high call of trumpets.

Rathina's eyes lit up. "They come," she said, getting to her feet. "Most excellent!"

"Who comes?" asked Tania.

"The cavalcade from Veraglad," Rathina said. "Come—let us greet them. It will be a delight indeed to welcome Uncle Cornelius and Aunt Lucina and Titus and Corin into our midst. And Eden and Hopie will be most pleased to be reunited with the earl Valentyne and Lord Brython, I have no doubt."


"Hey—who's the boy with the black hair and the cheekbones?" murmured Jade as the procession of riders passed through the cheering crowds that lined the bridge.

Tania saw whom she meant: a tall, black-haired young man riding with the earl marshall Cornelius and his wife. "That's Titus," she told her friend. "He's one of twins, but I can't see Corin anywhere."

"Twins?" breathed Jade. "You mean, there are two of them? Oh, be still, my fluttering heart!"

"Jade! Behave yourself," said Tania with a laugh.

A long procession of riders came across the bridge that carried the southern forest road into the Royal

Palace. Tania noticed that a few had pale scars or blemishes on their faces; people who had drawn back from the brink of death, but who would carry forever the signs of the deadly plague. As was the case with most Faerie folk, the faces of all those coming into the palace showed mixed emotions: gladness and relief that the dread was gone but also the shadow of recent grief over what had been lost.

"Titus is the son of my uncle Cornelius and his wife," Tania said. "Well, he's Lucina's son, but Cornelius's stepson—her first husband died in a fall from his horse."

Jade frowned. "I thought these people were all Immortal."

"We are . . . were, I mean," Tania explained. "But Immortal doesn't mean invulnerable. Accidents still happen."

"But not illness?"

"Right."

"No measles or head colds or heart attacks?"

Tania shook her head.

"And when they get to a certain age, they stop looking any older, is that right?"

"Yes—but I'm not really sure exactly what age that is."

Jade pointed to Titus. "But he's going to stay that handsome and hot forever, right?"

"Probably. Once the covenant has been renewed."

Jade grinned. "So, when do I get to meet him?"

Tania laughed. "Later," she said. "Meanwhile, let

me point out some other people you'll want to know." She nodded toward an ancient, wizened man riding a sturdy bay mare. "That's Earl Valentyne," she told Jade. "He's Eden's husband."

Jade's eyes widened. "Eww! I guess she goes for older men," she murmured. "But how come he looks like that? Did the Immortal thing not take with him?"

"He was already old when the covenant was agreed," said Tania. "I've told you this stuff already. Oh!" She gestured toward a large dark-haired and bearded man clad in the curious armor of Faerie: ivory white on the outside and with a mother-of-pearl inner sheen so that it looked as though it had been fashioned from seashells. "That's Lord Brython—Hopie's husband."

"Hmmm. Hunky," mused Jade. "No—I still like Titus best."

"Will you quit it with the lusting?" Tania laughed.

"It's okay for you—you've got Edric," said Jade. "You can't blame a girl for thinking of her future." She gave Tania a wicked little look. "You know how Titania got made Immortal when she married the King . . . uh . . . does that kind of thing happen a lot around here? Mortals becoming Immortal, I mean?"

"Hardly ever, so don't *think* of trying to make out with Titus so you get to live forever."

Jade grinned widely. "Oh, please—like I need an excuse to hit on someone who looks like him!" She raised an eyebrow. "You said there's going to be some kind of feast tonight, yes? A real friend would work it so I got to sit next to Titus. What do you say, Tania? Pretty please?"

"You're incorrigible, Jade!"

"But look at him, Tania—I think I'm in love!"

"You be really careful with saying stuff like that," said Tania, not quite joking any longer. "Love is forever around here." She looked over to where Rathina stood with Sancha and the Queen. "And that's not always as much fun as it might sound."

A few hours later, after the meeting and greeting of the party from Veraglad was done, Tania began to wonder where Edric could be. The meeting with Oberon and his council had been over for some time—but Edric still hadn't come to find her.

She left Jade with Rathina—her sister had agreed to take Jade on a tour of the bedchambers of the other princesses to show her the wonders and marvels that existed within their enchanted walls.

Tania finally tracked Edric down in the gardens. He was sitting on the wall of a small stone bridge that spanned a narrow brook of still green water. The bridge led to an ornate wooden gate in a hedge cut and shaped to resemble prancing horses. Beyond the gate Tania could see gently sloping parklands.

He turned his head at the crunch of her approach on the yellow pathway. He slid down off the parapet to stand waiting for her at the apex of the bridge. There was something not quite right about his smile.

"There you are!" Tania called, refusing to acknowledge the unease in his face. If she couldn't see it, maybe it would go away. "I've been looking for you all over!"

"I needed to think," he said.

She stood close to him, looking into his eyes. "That never ends well!" she murmured, joking to ward off what she feared was coming.

He sighed and drew her against him, his arms fierce around her back. The scent of him filled her.

"What is it?" she said, her voice subdued. "What's happened?"

"Nothing bad," he said. "At least . . ." He crushed her against his chest.

She edged her arms up between them and pushed away. "Just tell me and get it over with," she said.

"I need to make a decision," he said. "I was putting it off. It's a decision I can't make without you." He turned, gazing over the hedges and away into the north. "The King needs an emissary to go to Weir," he said. "Someone who Lord Aldritch might listen to."

There was a heavy silence. Clouds like white mountains floated across the sky. A robin piped from the hedge. The motionless stream smelled sickly sweet.

*This is my fault! I'm the one who suggested sending someone to talk to Aldritch! I should have kept my mouth shut—I might have known the idea would come back and bite me!*

"And you think he might listen to you," Tania said. "Is that it?"

"Yes."

She narrowed her eyes as she looked into his troubled face. "But if I say no, then you won't go—do

I understand that right?"

"You understand that exactly right," Edric said. "I pushed you away once, Tania—I won't do it again. I can't do it again."

"I see."

She walked away from him. She leaned heavily on the cool stone of the parapet and gazed down into weed green water. Silvery shapes glided just under the surface. She wasn't struggling with the decision; she already knew what had to happen. She was simply hanging on to the few moments that remained to her before the decision became real.

She turned, keeping her face as expressionless as possible. "Sorry—you can't go."

A small knowing smile touched his lips. "Fair enough. I'll go tell the King he needs to find someone else." He made to walk past her. She caught his arm.

"Why you?" she asked, her voice resigned. "Why always you?"

"Because Aldritch knows me," Edric said. "Because I'm the only one here who was born and brought up in Weir."

"It's not fair," said Tania. "What about us?"

"I'd only be gone a few days," Edric reassured her. "I could conjure a Horse of Air to take me there—I don't have the powers of the King or Princess Eden, but I could be at the borders of Weir in half a day. And back just as quickly once the job is done."

"More Dark Arts?"

"Dark Arts working for good," said Edric.

"Do the nasty voices know that?"

He didn't respond to that question.

"I want to come with you," Tania said suddenly. "You can go, but only if I go along, too."

"You can't," said Edric. "You have things to do here—important things in connection with the Pure Eclipse."

"Such as?"

"I don't know. Master Raphael is in conference with the King and Valentyne and others about it. But I know you will have a vital role to play—you can't leave the Palace." He touched her cheek. "Besides, I wouldn't take you within twenty leagues of Weir—not the way Lord Aldritch feels about you."

Tania knew he was right, although her duties were beginning to weigh her down. "Will you promise me that one day—one day soon—all these important things will be over and done and we can start to enjoy ourselves?" She looked hard into his eyes. "Will you promise that?"

He sighed. "I can't do that," he said.

"No, of course you can't." She ran her fingertips over his face. "I had a bad dream," she said. "You were in it. You handed yourself over to Aldritch on a plate. He wanted to use you to crush me."

"Well, that's never going to happen. And that *is* a promise!"

"When do you need to go?" she asked.

"Today. This morning."

She bit her lip. "So? What do you need to do? Slip

your credit card into your top pocket, grab a tooth-brush, and . . . away?"

"I need to take Oberon's ring," Edric said. "To prove I have his authority."

"When will you be back?"

"I don't know. As soon as possible. By the Pure Eclipse at the very latest."

"That's four days away."

"Four days isn't so long."

"Yes." She looked deep into his eyes. "Yes, it is." She took a long, shuddering breath. "Okay—I need you to do something for me."

"Anything."

"Turn around and go," she said. "Just go right now. Don't look back—don't say anything else. I love you and I know you have to do this, but if you don't go right now, I'm not going to have the strength to let you walk away."

He held her eyes for a moment, then turned and strode quickly off the bridge. She swung around, eyes tight shut, unable to watch him. His footsteps quickened. He was running—running away from her.

The sound struck her like knives in her chest.

# XXIII

Tania and Jade were walking the battlements under a clear blue sky. From their vantage point they could see out past the gardens and parklands to the rolling purple downs and the green eaves of Esgarth Forest stretching away into the hazy north.

"I wish I could take you on the grand tour of Faerie," Tania said to her friend. "You wouldn't believe what's out there. Fields of poppies that change color with the breeze. A castle that looks like it's made of seashells. Oh, and Crystalhenge—that's a ring of blue crystals twenty feet high and so beautiful you wouldn't believe it."

"Maybe next time," Jade said. "When things have settled down a little." She glanced at Tania. "Once Edric has sweet-talked Lord Ostrich of Weirdo out of being such a dope!"

Tania had to laugh. "Lord *Aldritch* of *Weir*."

"Whatever," Jade said. She gazed out over the battlements. "Looks like there are plenty of people responding to the party invites."

The roads to the north and west were busy with traffic: some came with laden wagons and carts; others rode upon horses, still more on foot.

Tents and pavilions were being erected in the parks and on the downs, their banners floating in the wind. Knights had set up camp on Salisoc Heath—only a few so far, the first of the army that Oberon was mustering to defend Faerie from any potential assault from Weir.

*Is Edric there yet? I wonder. He said it would take only half a day to get to Weir. No, he won't have arrived yet, not till later this afternoon. I wish he didn't have to be so . . . noble. I wish he'd just said, "Me—go to Weir? You have to be kidding! Find some other sucker this time." But of course he had to go. I just hope Aldritch listens to him. I hope he can make everything all right again. I hope Aldritch stops hating me.*

"Did Rathina show you the bedchambers?" Tania asked.

"She did," said Jade. "All totally amazing. In fact, I'm going to have to come up with some new words to describe this place—'amazing' isn't cutting it anymore. I'm thinking: Faerie-tastic!"

Tania smiled; Jade could always drag her out of her dark moods. "Do you have a favorite room?" she asked.

"I think maybe Cordelia's," said Jade. "I love the way the animals just come walking out of the wallpaper. And the birds—flying out of the walls and back in again. There was even a stag, a full-grown stag with the antlers and all. We were standing there, Rathina and me—and he just kind of turned up and strolled past. He was, like, huge!"

*Ah! So the rooms are still full of magic even after their owners have gone. That's nice.*

"That's because Cordelia's room is somehow in the forest and in the Palace at the same time," Tania said. "And what about Zara's room? Isn't that amazing the way the sea is always moving?"

Jade frowned. "Rathina didn't take me there—she said there was nothing in Zara's room now that she's dead."

"Oh. But Cordelia's room is still magical? That's odd."

"Maybe it's like a battery," Jade suggested. "You know, gradually running out of juice. The magic doesn't just go away—maybe it fades over time."

Tania nodded. "Yes, that must be it."

They saw a warden approaching them along the battlements.

He bowed to Tania. "My lady," he said. "The King requests your presence in the Privy Chamber at your very earliest convenience."

Tania turned to Jade. "I'd better go," she said. "I think I know what this is."

"No problem. I'll go find Rathina or someone else to chat to."

Tania followed the warden along the battlements—assuming that she would now learn what her part in the festival of the Pure Eclipse was to be.

\* \* \*

Oberon and Titania were waiting for Tania in the Privy Chamber, along with Sancha and Eden, Earl Valentyne and Raphael Cariotis, all of them seated at the marble table with many scrolls and documents and books open in front of them.

"I know how hard it is for you, my daughter, that Master Chanticleer was needed for the mission in the north," said Oberon. "But we each have our part to play in the coming events."

"And yours is no less important than his, Tania," added the Queen. "In fact, from what we have learned this day, your role may be in many ways the most vital—for the people of the Mortal World and of Faerie."

"Why?" Tania asked. "What am I supposed to do?"

"Hold back the flood tides of the two realms," said Eden. "Keep the two worlds apart when the eclipse comes. Come, sit and we shall tell you all that we have learned—and how you are to be the bulwark between Faerie and the World of Mortals."

Startled by her sister's words, Tania sat down.

Master Raphael began to explain. "We have had to piece together the events of the Pure Eclipse from hints and guesses and scraps. Earl Valentyne sent his mind into the Helan Archaia—to the vast Hall of Archives in Caer Regnar Naal—and has gleaned therefrom certain information that may help us to prevent the two realms from bleeding one into another."

"No power in this world can halt the progress of the Great Eclipse," said Valentyne, his voice like old branches creaking in the wind. "But in ancient documents I found a certain text that spoke of the half-child who in times to come will have the power to walk between the worlds—a half-Faerie and half-human who alone of all living beings will be able to straddle the realms."

"Me, you mean?" said Tania breathlessly.

"You indeed, sister," said Sancha. "It can surely be no other."

"What do I have to do?"

"You must stand between the two worlds while the moon covers the sun and hold them apart by the power that resides in you," said the King.

"It's your especial gift that will allow you to do this," said the Queen. "That is why you are the only one who can perform the ritual when the time comes."

Tania's mouth was suddenly dry. "But how?"

"Upon the northern downs there is a cave," said Master Raphael. "The cave leads to an underground chamber where flows the dark subterranean River Elfleet. Upon the morning of the Pure Eclipse you must follow the river to the Cavern of Heartsdelving."

Tania knew of the cave and the black river— she had even been in the cavern once, long ago. Heartsdelving was one of the greatest centers of power in all the realm. Even more potent than Crystalhenge. In Heartsdelving there was a lake, and in that lake there was an island, and upon that island there was a stalagmite—a great pillar of stone called the Quellstone Spire. Enormous power flowed through that finger of stone.

Eden spoke. "At the moment of the Pure Eclipse, Tania, you must touch the Quellstone, for then your gift will be magnified a thousandfold."

Raphael continued. "It will give you the strength to use your mind to hold back the flood of Faerie into the Mortal Realm and of the Mortal Realm into Faerie."

*I'm supposed to do this with my mind?*

"It will take great power of will, my daughter," said the King. "But the threat will not last long. The peril exists only while the moon covers the sun—and the truth is that none but you can do this thing."

"And if I fail?" Tania asked. She tried to recall what she had read over the man's shoulder in the park while she had been waiting for Connor. . . . *The longest solar eclipse of this century, lasting 6 minutes and 45 seconds . . .* She had to use the power of her mind to hold two worlds apart for nearly seven minutes.

"If you love the Mortal World and the realm of Faerie, pray to the good spirits that you do not fail," said Sancha. "Because if the two worlds merge, even for so brief a time, much that you know of both realms could be changed forever."

Tania looked at the King in alarm. "Can't *you* stop that happening?" she asked. "You're so much more powerful than I am."

The King smiled sadly. "And yet, of us all, only you belong to both worlds, Tania. The power I wield holds sway only within the realm of Faerie. This task is yours—it is yours alone."

Tania was aware that all eyes were on her now. She hesitated, torn by self-doubt, overwhelmed by the task they had set for her.

"Will you at least try?" murmured the Queen.

Tania straightened her back, her fingers gripping the arms of her chair.

"I will," she said. "If someone will guide me there and show me what to do."

"Have no fear," said Master Raphael. "I will be at your side throughout the ritual." He smiled and his eyes gleamed. "Indeed, I will not leave you, my lady, not until the Pure Eclipse is past and done and the fate of the two worlds is sealed for all time."

That night the Great Hall became the venue for a magnificent feast. Tables had been set up along the walls, laden with food and drink of all kinds. Musicians played in the gallery, their melodies a constant backdrop to conversation and laughter. The aroma of roasted meats vied with the yeasty scent of new-baked bread and with the smells of cooked herbs and spicy sauces.

All the greatest of Faerie were there: lords and ladies in their finest clothes, knights clad in the livery of many earldoms, their clothes blazoned with the heraldic charges of their homeland. The red dragon for Mynwy Clun, the white star of Anvis. The oak of Gaidheal and the sea horse of Talebolion. And from some distant corner of the realm there was a group of dour knights who wore dark red cloaks that showed no heraldry at all.

"They hail from Gralach Hern," Rathina confided to Tania, watching the curious, self-contained group as they sat eating together at the far end of one table. "'Tis a principality on the north coast of Prydein."

"They came all the way from there?" Tania said in surprise. She had traveled to the far ends of Prydein—and it had taken her many days. "How did they get here so quickly?"

"Master Raphael sent word to them some time ago," Rathina said. "Or so 'tis said."

Tania gave her a puzzled look. "When could he have done that?" she asked. "All of Faerie was under the Gildensleep shield until Lear came—and after that . . . When would Raphael have had time to send . . . ?"

"Fie, Tania! You'd gnaw entire mountains to nubs with your endless questions!" Rathina laughed. "They are here and they will give us good aid if war comes. What more do you need to know?"

"Nothing more, I suppose. . . ." Tania looked at the men again. Something about them still bothered her.

Minstrels began to play a lively dance.

"This is my chance," murmured Jade, sitting at Tania's side and watching Titus like a hawk. Tania hadn't managed to get her friend a seat next to Titus, but they were at the same table, just a few places apart. A brief conversation Tania had with Titus had revealed that Corin had been sent to the family home of Caer Ravensare to ensure that all was well there and to call the men of that lovely flower-decked palace to arms.

Jade raised a questioning eyebrow. "Are there any rules here about girls asking guys to dance?"

"None that I know of," said Tania.

"Okay." Jade stood up as people began to fill the dance floor between the tables. "Wish me luck. Here goes nothing!"

Tania watched as Jade went to where Titus was sitting. She leaned over him, whispering close. He smiled and stood up, leading her onto the dance floor.

"I wish Edric was here," Tania said under her breath as Jade and Titus joined in the dance.

"He has sterner deeds to attempt," said Rathina. "Have no fear—you'll see your beloved captain again before too long."

Tania tried a weak smile. "But all the time he's gone, it feels like he's taken part of me away with him." She sighed. "Even in a room full of people, I still feel alone, somehow. . . . "

Rathina gave her a long, thoughtful look. "Alone?" she murmured. "Yes, I can see how you might feel that." Her eyes darkened. "But imagine, sweet sister, how you would feel if the stallion of the darkling moon galloped over your heart with his brazen hooves. . . . Imagine that!" A slow smile spread across Rathina's face. "Or maybe it is that you shall not need to imagine it, Tania—can you not hear it? The horse of the night, galloping ever closer." Her eyes burned. "Ever closer . . ."

Tania stared at her in growing alarm. "Rathina?"

Then her sister laughed and tossed her hair. "You

were always the most easy child to put the goblin fright into, Tania!" she said. She stood up. "Come, let us find worthy lords to dance with—*the night is fine and the stars do shine and there's a scent on the air as old as time.*"

The Feast lasted late into the night. Tania even managed to stop fretting over Edric for part of the time as she danced with various lords of Faerie. But in the deep of night she and Jade finally wound their way wearily to her bedchamber and flung themselves into bed.

"So? How did it go with Titus?" Tania asked sleepily. "Are the two of you engaged?"

"It was nice," Jade said, unusually subdued. "I could fall for him big time, but . . ."

Tania turned her head on the pillow to look at her friend. Jade's face was blurred with moonlight. Her eyes were open, staring at the ceiling.

"But . . . ?"

"He's totally into someone else, is my opinion," Jade said. "I pulled out all the stops, you know? And he was really sweet and considerate and all that—but I got the distinct impression he wished he was with someone else. And when we danced, he was always half looking over my shoulder."

"At who?" Tania asked, intrigued by this.

"Do I look like I have eyes in the back of my head?" said Jade. "And there was something else. . . ."

"What?"

"Every now and then he'd stop and he'd say. 'Can

you hear that?' and I'd say, 'What?' and he'd say, 'Do you not hear it—the distant sound of hooves?' and I'd be like, 'Hooves? What hooves?'" Jade made a clicking sound with her tongue. "Hooves!" she said. "Y'know, Tania, I think there's something kind of wacky about some of these people."

Tania felt as if a black abyss was yawning at her back. "Did he say anything else about the hooves?" she asked.

"Just that they were getting louder all the time," said Jade. "Listen, girl—I'm wiped out. Let's get some sleep."

Jade turned over so that she was facing away from Tania. Within seconds her breathing had deepened with sleep.

*Hooves? Titus could hear hooves?*

What was going on? First Sancha and then Rathina had talked of a dark horse . . . and now Titus was hearing approaching hooves.

What was coming?

# XXIV

A dark dream.

Tania alone on the downs on a cold and windswept night. Stumbling under a moonless sky. Calling.

"Edric! Edric!"

A sound borne to her on the chill north wind. Hooves. Galloping hooves.

Something monstrous, coming for her down the long miles from the frozen north. Something with red flames in its eyes.

Red flames. Stamping hooves. A scarlet mane flying.

And then she was standing at the foot of the Dolorous Tower, ankle-deep in dead birds—more rotting feathered carcasses raining down on her. And a voice, chanting a broken rhythm.

> *"Fishes dancing in the midnight*
> *Ravens circling in the sky*
> *Light the night with Mortal beacons*
> *Screaming in the rosy light*

*Stars are shaking in the heavens*
*Mountains tremble in the earth*
*Lovers leaping from the cliff tops*
*Hungry rocks awake below . . ."*

Tania shouted into the night. "Cordelia? Is that you?"

Then everything was different and Tania was in the Obsidian Chamber in Caer Liel. The whole room was crowded with armed men. Lord Aldritch was standing on the throne plinth. Edric knelt in front of him, and the lord was addressing the crowd.

"By the ancient laws of Weir, it is fulfilled!"

Tania struggled and fought to get through the shoulder-to-shoulder throng—to get to Edric before something terrible happened.

There was a roar of approval from the congregation at their lord's words.

Moaning with frustration, Tania strove to make headway through the gathered knights of Weir. But they crowded around her, making any progress almost impossible, their cheers deafening her to the galloping hooves that thundered in her mind.

At last she broke clear of the men. Edric was standing at Lord Aldritch's side, and the lord's arm was about his shoulders and his voice was loud enough to be heard above the din.

"And now, with the ritual of Adoption complete, give thanks, my knights—give thanks that there is now a new heir to the throne of Weir!" shouted Aldritch. "A son lost—but a son gained!"

Edric smiled fiercely, his eyes blazing silver.

"Edric! No!" Tania's voice sounded weak in her own ears.

Edric raised his arms and the crowd quieted. "Great deeds we have ahead of us!" he shouted. "To arms, men of Weir! At dawn tomorrow we ride to war."

"No!" Tania screamed.

"And the first to die shall be the half-thing, Tania Aurealis!" Edric drew a black sword and lifted it on high. "And she shall never know the truth—she shall never know how she has been deceived."

From the blade of the black sword ravens flew into Tania's face, pecking and clawing at her.

As soon as it was light the next morning, Tania made her way to the Queen's apartments, hoping desperately that Titania might be able to shed some light on the nightmares that were blighting her sleep.

She remembered the first time that "Anita" had visited these apartments—the white rooms empty and cheerless and the Queen lost for centuries. But far more intense than that bleak memory were happy recollections of her childhood—speeding on silken wings up the curving white marble staircase to the domed lobby with the tall white doors, bursting in full of tales of her exploits, flying into her Faerie mother's welcoming arms, breathing in the scent of lilies.

These elegant, sunlit rooms held for her more sense of comfort and cheer than any other place in

Faerie. The Queen would unravel the dark tangle of her nightmares—Titania would soothe away her fears.

Tania found the Queen in the main room of her apartments: a room decked out in white and ivory, with a swan's down carpet and snowy couches and furniture of creamy woodwork. Tall bay windows stood open to allow the breeze to blow through white lace curtains.

Titania was at her desk in the bay window, speaking with a lady of the court—talking over arrangements for the masques and plays and entertainments that would form part of the coming festival.

Seeing the agitation on Tania's face, the Queen dismissed the lady.

"Come, sit with me," Titania said. "Speak to me of your troubles."

Tania sat at the Queen's side on a fleecy couch by the bay window. Titania drew Tania close.

"What is wrong, Tania?" the Queen asked. "Are you uneasy about the role you must play in the Pure Eclipse?"

Tania looked into the Queen's face—that face that was so very much like her own. "I'm having bad dreams."

"Tell me."

In the reassuring curve of her mother's arm Tania spoke of the dreams that had haunted her last two nights. Even talking about it aloud made her fears diminish.

"It must be very distressing for you, Tania," said

the Queen. "But these are no more than nightmares, child—they are not real."

"Are you sure?" Tania asked, looking into Titania's face.

"I am certain of it. You grieve for the loss of your sister—as you should—that is why you dream of her voice and of the birds." She smiled gently. "And as for Edric becoming Lord Aldritch's son and waging war on us— Why, fie! Tania! What a foolish fancy that is."

"And the horse?" she asked. "The galloping?"

"You yourself said that Rathina had teased you with talk of a dark horse coming," said Titania. "You were ever a most suggestible child, Tania. Your dreams were always full of strange imaginings." She pulled away a little and took Tania's shoulders between her long white hands. "'Tis time to put aside these fears, Tania—you are grown too old for such antics!"

Tania looked into her mother's green eyes.

"Not all dreams are prophetic, Tania," insisted the Queen. "Even in Faerie it is possible for a dream to be no more than a dream."

Tania smiled. "You're right," she said. "I was being an idiot." She leaned forward and kissed her mother's cheek. "I'll leave you to your work now," she said, getting up. "Sorry I was such a nuisance."

"No need to apologize, Tania," said the Queen. "I am always here for you—for any of you."

Reassured, Tania headed for the doors.

"Tania?" There was a sudden urgency in the Queen's voice.

"Yes?"

"Do not listen to the hooves, child," she said. "And do not go near the Dolorous Tower—it is a dangerous place. The Dolorous Tower has not been used for a long time. Not for hundreds of years."

She looked at her mother, puzzled a little by the oddness of this sudden warning. "Okay, I won't."

Tania closed the white doors behind her and began to descend the long winding stairway.

"Does the word 'paranoid' mean anything to you?" asked Jade.

The two friends were heading out through the gardens, intending to take a look at the preparations for the coming celebration. Trying to sound reasonably casual, Tania had mentioned to Jade her mother's parting words.

"You mean, you don't think there's anything weird going on?" Tania said.

Jade laughed aloud. "Oh, there's plenty of weird stuff going on," she said. "Everything about this place is weird, if you ask me. But if you mean do I think the Queen is going freaky on you, then no, of course not."

"But you said Titus mentioned the galloping hooves," Tania insisted. "That's four different people all taking *hooves*—and I'm hearing hooves in my dreams."

"That's called autosuggestion," Jade said. "People mention hooves—you hear hooves in your sleep. And anyway, what's so bad about hooves? Maybe hearing hooves is all part of this Pure Eclipse thing that's going to happen; have you thought of that?"

"Why hooves?"

"Why not? Does this place run on logic suddenly?"

"No, not really. . . ."

"Oh, look! Is that, like, for jousting?" Jade exclaimed, pointing to a flat grassy area beyond the gardens. "I've always fancied jousting!" Yellow and blue tents had been set up ahead of them, and a wooden barrier ran along the center of an oblong track marked out by low wicker fences. Close by, new-built paddocks housed a number of horses in fine gear, tended by grooms while richly caparisoned knights watched on. Multicolored shields were propped alongside the tents. Wooden lances, ten or twelve feet long, were gathered in frames, their sharp tips pointing to the sky.

"What are you talking about, Jade?" said Tania. "You've never ridden a horse in your life."

"I could learn."

"Or not!" Tania said. "I'm not taking you home with two broken legs and half a dozen great big holes punched through you. Oh, hi, Mrs. Anderson—yes, sorry about this—Jade wanted to try her hand at jousting!" She hooked her arm into Jade's. "Let's go look at something a little less dangerous."

Between the gardens and the rising downs the whole landscape was a noisy chaos of stalls and sideshows still being put together, and of larger covered stages being erected and rings and arenas being staked out for sporting events.

Wagons rolled by, stopping to disgorge bails of colored silk or timbers or barrels and caskets of goods and gear. Some folk were hanging rainbow bunting while others dug holes and sank flagpoles where the banners of the eleven earldoms would flutter. Except, of course, that the white unicorn of Weir was not in evidence.

*But if Edric's mission goes well, who knows? Even Lord Aldritch might join in the revels.*

Tania and Jade watched tumblers and jugglers rehearsing until the smell of something sweet being baked drew them on. A long tent housed a kitchen where pies were being made. They left the cheerful cook, each with a large slice of cherry pie in their hands.

Tania spotted Eden at one of the tents. She left Jade playing tag with some children and went to speak with her eldest sister. She was at the open mouth of a dark blue tent that seemed to be filled with small wooden crates.

"Well met, sweetheart," said Eden. "The Queen tells me you have been suffering unsettling dreams. 'Tis too bad of you, sister, to darken such a glorious time with such a thing!"

"It's nothing," Tania said. "To be honest, I'm more worried about what I have to do in the Cavern of Heartsdelving." She wrinkled her forehead. "Are you sure I'm up to it, Eden? I don't even really understand what I have to do. How do I keep the two worlds apart with my mind? How do I *think* them apart? I don't have the faintest idea how it's going to work."

"Have no fears, my sister," said Eden. "Master Raphael will be with you when the time comes—he will tell you what must be done."

"All the same, I'd like the chance to rehearse a little—just in case. Do you know what I mean?"

"You fret over nothing," Eden said. She reached out and touched the pads of her fingertips against Tania's temple. "Your mind is all turmoil and chaos!" she said.

"Tell me about it!" Tania muttered.

"At least let me do this little thing for you." Eden touched the tip of her forefinger to the center of Tania's forehead. Tania felt a small shock pass from Eden's finger into her mind.

"What was that?" she asked.

"A Traumlos glamour—a dream-dwindling charm, no more than that," said Eden with a smile. "You shall suffer no ill dreams this night, sweet sister."

"Oh. Thanks."

"And now, I have work to do." She gestured into the tent. "I am to place glamours on these firiencraft—so that the sky on the eve of the Pure Eclipse will be filled with wonders!"

"Firiencraft?" said Tania, puzzled for a moment by the word. "Oh!" She remembered. "You mean fireworks!"

Yes! She recalled now the great carnivals and festivities of her childhood, when the night would be full of music and laughter and Eden's mystically charged fireworks would make a glorious pageant of the sky!

She left her sister and went to look for Jade.

Her friend was sprawled in the grass with little Faerie children tumbling all over her. Jade was laughing so much she could hardly breathe.

"Have you ever tried playing tag with kids who can fly?" She gasped as the children grabbed at her from all sides and lifted her into the air, hauling her up out of the grass and yanking at her till her legs were swinging several inches above the ground.

One small child flew at Tania. "You're it!" she cried, skittering away, her wings whirring.

"Oh no, you don't!" called Tania, haring after her and snatching at the child as she soared up out of reach in a peal of laughter.

Until the children were called away by their parents for the evening meal, Tania forgot all her troubles in the riot and lunacy of wing-tag with the children.

When she went to bed that night, she slept a serene and dreamless sleep.

# XXV

Tania felt the need to be alone with her thoughts the next morning. She left Jade to her tai chi exercises and made her way out to where the festivities were still being prepared.

She walked through the gardens and picked her way across the parklands, seeing all the activity but feeling detached from it—even when people smiled and bowed and spoke to her. It was uncanny how alone she felt, as if she was moving through the merry crowds in a bubble of private sadness.

She felt herself drawn toward the long sloping heaths where the knights of Faerie had made camp. Very bright and heroic their tents looked, and the knights among them, on horseback or sparring on foot, in their luminous, shelly armor or in bright-colored tabards.

But the knights of Gralach Hern disturbed her still. Their tents were of a somber dark red, and they had no pennants or standards. And there were now many more of them than before—tall and dark and as silent as stones, and each bore a sword of dark red crystal and carried a red shield, and the horses that they rode were midnight black.

How had they got here so quickly—all the way from the far north? And why did no one else seem bothered about them?

Tania turned on her heel and strode rapidly back to the Royal Apartments. She needed to speak with the King.

Tania found Oberon in his Privy Chamber, alone among sheaves of documents.

*Good! I half expected Raphael Cariotis to be with him.*

The King looked up from the piled documents as Tania came into the room. She noticed that the blue signet ring was missing from the forefinger of his right hand. Edric had indeed taken it to Weir as a token that he spoke for the King.

*Edric, come back quickly. Come back safely.*

"Tania, dearest child, welcome," said the King, smiling warmly.

"Am I disturbing you?" she asked.

"Most excellently you are!" Oberon said with a laugh. "Master Raphael has set me much endeavor in the lead-up to the Pure Eclipse. I must read many documents and give signature to them, so he tells me, although I'd rather be elsewhere and engaged in sweeter delights."

"Poor you."

"'Tis naught," said the King. "And I have had word from Admiral Belial that the *Cloud Scudder* is set and ready for the voyage to Tirnanog upon the eve of that glad day."

"That's good," said Tania, moving to stand at her father's side. "Is everything all right, do you think?"

The King looked up at her. "Do you fear for Master Chanticleer's safety, child?" he asked.

"Yes, a little. I haven't forgotten how much Lord Aldritch hates me, and I've been having really weird dreams. . . ."

He smiled. "Even in Faerie it is possible for a dream to be no more than a dream," he said, his arm curling gently around her waist. "Fear no night noises, Tania; it is only the good spirits, their whispering voices. All is well in the realm of Faerie, and if Weir prove false, why, have we not knights enough to keep Lord Aldritch safe penned behind his own borders?"

*Even in Faerie it is possible for a dream to be no more than a dream.* Titania's exact words.

Her *exact* words!

"I'm worried about the men from Gralach Hern—there's something not quite right about them, I think."

"The folk of Prydein have ever been a curious breed," said her father. "You know this, Tania—but they are loyal and brave, have no fear of that. If the time comes when drawn swords must take the place of spoken words, they will prove their worth to Faerie and to the House of Aurealis."

"But there are so many of them, and I don't

understand how they are getting here so quickly. . . ."

"That is a question easily answered," the King replied. "Master Raphael sent word to them some time ago."

Rathina had said that!

Tania gently extricated herself from her father's embrace. It was strange that no one seemed concerned about those sinister knights.

"Yes," she said uncertainly, "I guess that must be what happened." She gazed closely into the King's face. He looked as he had always looked, with his golden hair and his close-cut beard and mustache and his deep, piercing blue eyes. "Do you feel all right?"

"I am a little weary of ancient texts!" he said with a quick smile. "And I'd have this matter with Weir settled."

"No, I mean . . ." She frowned, touching her hand to his cheek. "You don't feel like there's something wrong . . . inside you, I mean?"

"Nay, child, all is well."

She swallowed nervously. "Do you hear galloping horses?"

He frowned, and for a moment there was a flicker of something in his eyes. Something that came and went in an instant. The tiny, remote furling of red flame.

"Do not listen to the hooves," he said.

"Hail and well met, sire, and also my lady Tania." Raphael Cariotis's voice came into Tania's head like a whiplash.

The Guardian of the Precession of the Equinoxes was standing in the open doorway, a bundle of documents in his arms.

"Forgive me for intruding upon you, sire—my lady," said Raphael. "I have letters and missives of greetings from many of your people, sire, and I know that you would wish to peruse them." He smiled as he came into the room. "And I have certain other matters to discuss."

"That's fine," said Tania. "I was just leaving anyhow."

Master Raphael bowed as she passed him. "The noontide of the Pure Eclipse comes apace, my lady," he said. "Mayhap you will be better prepared for the trials that are to come if you seek from Princess Eden another Traumlos glamour to give you a further night free of evil dreams?"

How did he know about that?

"Yes," she said, feigning a smile. "I think I'll do that."

"Jade, please listen to me. I'm not crazy—there is definitely something going on here."

They were in Tania's bedchamber at the end of the day. Tania had not felt safe talking to her friend about her fears until she was certain they could not be overheard. Until they were entirely alone.

Jade sat cross-legged on the bed, her head tilted, face puzzled.

"Well, you'd know that better than me," she said. "So, go on. Tell me what you think is going on?"

Tania was by the open window, the warm evening breeze in her hair, the air laden with sweet scents, the moon hanging low like a white shield on the starry sky.

"I don't *know*!" Tania exclaimed. "That's the whole point! I don't know what's going on. But people are acting really strange."

"Which people in particular?"

Tania threw her arms up in exasperation. "Everyone! The King. The Queen. Eden. Sancha. Rathina—Titus! Raphael Cariotis." She shook her head. "It's like everyone I talk to is . . ."

"Yes?" Jade prompted.

"Is saying weird things . . ." Tania ended, aware of how lame this must sound to her practical friend. "Weird, coincidental things. And it's like everyone is way too happy, you know? It doesn't feel right. The plague wasn't that long ago, and Cordelia is dead, but people are running around jousting and organizing fireworks and playing tag. It's freaky—like everyone's in a dream. . . ." She stared at Jade. "Maybe that's it. Maybe this is all a dream?"

Jade shuffled to the edge of the bed. "Come here," she said.

"Why?"

"Just do it!"

Tania approached her. Jade's arm stabbed out, two fingers stiff and hard into Tania's midriff. Tania folded over, stepping back again with a gasp.

"Ow! That hurt!"

"Still think you're dreaming?" Jade asked.

"No!" Tania said, rubbing her stomach. "Definitely not, *thanks!*"

"You're welcome," said Jade. "That's one explanation ruled out. So, what else could be causing you to think people are acting weird?"

Tania wracked her brains but came up empty.

Galloping hooves. Phrases, suggestions, and warnings being repeated by different people. Bad dreams. The feeling of being slightly out of synch with everyone around her. What did it all add up to?

"What if it's not them? What if it's you?" Jade suggested. "It could be something like post-traumatic stress disorder. You've been through some really hard times recently—do you think it could have scrambled your brains a little?"

"I hope not!"

"Maybe meeting your other selves was more disturbing than you thought? And that fight with Lear—that was way unnerving." She looked at Tania. "Face it, any one of those things could have freaked you out . . . and all of them? I'm surprised you're still coherent. Me? I'd be curled up in a fetal position under the bed!"

"So, you think it's me, not them?"

"Are you certain it isn't you?"

Tania stared at her. "I have no idea how to answer that."

Jade pursed her lips. "Did you get Eden to give you another one of those no-dream whammies?"

"No."

Jade's eyebrows rose in surprise.

"Yes, I know," Tania said with sudden impatience. "Crazy girl with her crazy nightmares—give her a charm to put the lights out! But the thing is, I felt worse somehow this morning—worse for not having the dreams." She looked fiercely at Jade. "Maybe I am losing it—you're right. It's not like I don't have a good reason to be going out of my mind. But even if that's the case, I still think those dreams are trying to tell me something."

"Fair enough," said Jade. "Then I suggest we get to bed and you take a trip to dreamland again."

That was easier said than done. Jade was curled up snoring softly long before Tania even found the courage to close her eyes against the darkness.

And even then it felt as though a searchlight were strobing in her brain, banishing sleep, lighting up the inside of her head like a flashlight being shone in her eyes.

She'd never get to sleep.

Galloping hooves beyond a dark hillside. Boiling clouds blotting out the stars. A wind rushing through the trees, sounding like a thousand swords being unsheathed.

A solitary voice calling out of nowhere. "To war! To war!"

And then a dark tide of horsemen coming over the ridge, and at their head a tall figure holding a sword aloft.

Edric—clad all in black—leading the warriors of

Weir into battle in the south.

He did not see her standing in the path of his galloping horse.

"Edric! No! It's me! Stop! Please stop!"

She spread her arms, holding her ground as the charging warhorses ran her down. The first buffet knocked her sideways. She staggered, striking hard against the flank of another horse. And then another crashed into her, so that she stumbled and fell to her knees. The horses moved all around her like colossal monsters—hooves pounding so that the ground shook.

"Edric, no . . ."

A hoof came down like a hammer. Filling the world. Blotting out all life.

She was in a dark courtyard. A tall square tower reared up into the night, covered all over with red ivy. Birds circled the tower's head, screaming and shrieking. Feathers rained down like black snow, their musty scent filling Tania's head. They swirled around her, sticking to her skin, snagging in her hair as she flailed her arms to be rid of them. She was standing in a mire of dead and rotting birds. Slimy underfoot. Bones through feathers. Beaks and claws and dead, seeping eyes.

She heard a muffled voice chanting. There was the sharp chink of something hitting glass. She walked slowly around the corner and found a large round window of dirty, colored glass. She reached up—the lower curve of the sill was at the height of her chest. The voice was still there, behind the glass.

*"The wolves howl on the moonlit crag*
*The stags bellow in the deep woods*
*Come back to us, come back!*
*The whales sing, the dogs do bark*
*The owls know, the wise salmon knows*
*She is not gone, she is not gone!"*

Tania reached up and wiped her hand across the window. A face stared out at her through a pane of bloodred glass.

An insane, grinning face with flaming eyes and teeth bared to bite and rip.

And then the tower was gone and she was staring into the poison green eyes of a woman with hair like flame and lips like blood and skin as white as bone.

Long red fingernails slashed at Tania's cheek, drawing blood.

The woman's voice hissed like a snake. "You will never know true happiness, child of the riven soul. Any happiness you do find will be nothing but an illusion!"

# XXVI

"Wake up! Jade! Will you please wake up!"

Tania was wide-eyed in the gray dawn. Kneeling in a welter of bedclothes with her dreams shrouding her like winding sheets. Shaking the sleeping form of her friend.

Jade burst suddenly into life, floundering under the covers.

"What the . . . !"

"It's me. I need you to come with me. Right now."

"Tania!" Her voice was thick with sleep. "What time is it?"

"Almost dawn." She stripped the bedclothes back. "I want us to go somewhere—before anyone else is up and about."

Jade's voice was suddenly sharp. "You found something out in a dream?"

"I think so."

Jade bounced off the bed and dressed quickly. "Come on, then. What are we waiting for?"

Tania flung herself into her dress, and the two of them padded along the corridors and down the stairs. There was just enough light for them to see where they were going, and when they came out into an open courtyard, the sky was a grainy blue-gray.

The courtyard was long, cobbled, with a stone fountain in the center. No water was flowing and the fountain had an abandoned look. At the far end of the courtyard stood a square stone tower, ivy-grown, desolate . . . abandoned by all save the birds that roosted on its steep roof.

"This is the Dolorous Tower," Tania told her friend.

"The one you've been dreaming about?" said Jade. She whistled between her teeth. "The one with the dead birds?"

"Yes, that one. The place everyone has been telling me to steer clear of ever since we came here." Windows pocked the ivy-infested walls—but all were shuttered, and the sills were dark with birds.

There were no birds in the air. There was neither song nor calling. A thousand small dark eyes were on her. Watching and waiting.

Tania walked the length of the courtyard. She came to the foot of the tower. There were three gray stone steps leading to an overgrown door. A black door.

"Yes," she murmured. "Yes!" Jade trailed after her as she walked to the corner of the tower.

"What?" Jade whispered. "What are we looking for?"

"That!" Tania said, pointing to the wide circular

window, over which the ivy hung like long broken fingers. "The Oriole Glass." She looked at Jade. "They're calling this the Dolorous Tower—and that is its name; I remember now. But it hasn't been abandoned for hundreds of years. The dreams helped me to remember the truth. All through the Great Twilight this was Eden's home." Her voice trembled. "She lived here alone—going a little crazy, I think. Until I came back to Faerie and she started to get better."

"Okay," Jade said, peering at her in confusion. "And this means what now?"

"It means everyone wants me to stay away from here, and I know for sure—for *certain*—that this tower is where Eden brews her mystical spells." She turned to Jade. "Don't you see? My dreams have been trying to warn me about this place. I told you everyone was acting weird—and there's something in this tower that will explain why!"

"Something your sister Eden has done?" said Jade.

Tania stared at her. "There aren't many people in Faerie who can do stuff this powerful," she said. "My father, for sure—and maybe my mother as well. Valentyne and one or two others. And *Eden!*"

"You think she's put a spell on *everyone*?" said Jade breathlessly. Her eyes widened in the growing light of day. "A spell to do *what*?"

"I don't know," Tania said.

"Maybe it's a good spell, to make people feel better . . . you know?"

"Then why the deception?" Tania hissed, snatching hold of Jade's arm and gripping tight. "Why did she need to poke those holes in my memory? Why wasn't I supposed to know the truth about this place? Everyone's been programmed to tell me to stay away. *Why?*" The thought that Eden might be behind all this gnawed at her heart. Eden had only ever used her powers for good in the past—if her sister had turned away from that, what could possibly have happened to change her?

A silvery light came over the sky, and from some distant place a cock crowed to welcome the new day. Sharp footsteps clacked on cobbles.

"Someone's coming!" Tania said, her nails digging into Jade's flesh. "We're not safe here." She pulled her friend along the wall and around to the back of the tower.

"Is it Eden?" Jade gasped. "Has she tracked us down with that magic mojo of hers?"

"I don't know. I don't think so." Tania's voice was hoarse and urgent. "But we need to get away." The two of them ran from the courtyard, down a narrow alley where night still lingered, and across to a doorway.

Not until they had the closed and bolted door and two levels of stairs between them and the courtyard did Tania let them stop running.

"We can't trust anyone," Tania said. "We can't go to anyone about this. We can't confide in anyone. We have to assume everyone's been contaminated with this thing—whatever it is."

"Yes, I get it!" said Jade, prying Tania's fingers off her arm. "So? Do you have a plan?"

"I think so," said Tania. "Today we act totally normal—do all the things we'd usually do. We join in with the preparations and all that. And tonight, when everyone is in bed, the two of us go back to that tower, and we get inside. We find out exactly what's in there."

"I get it," said Jade. "I've seen stuff like this in movies. The spell will be in a special magic jar or in a glow-y ball kind of thing—and all we have to do is find it and smash it and everything will be back to normal!"

Tania stared uneasily at her. "Something like that . . ." she said slowly. "If we're lucky." Tania remembered only too well the malevolent things that inhabited the walls of Eden's sanctum—evil things that leered and spat and reached out with poisoned claws.

They were dangerous enough watchdogs when there was nothing special to guard—how much more of a peril would they be if a great spell was housed in the tower? Too great a peril for Tania to allow Jade to be harmed, that much was certain. No. When the time came, she'd find a way to give Jade the slip. She could not ask her friend to walk into that much danger.

But before then they had a day of pretense to get through.

A day when nothing they did must arouse suspicion.

The final day before the start of the festival of the Pure Eclipse.

\* \* \*

For Tania the hardest part of that day of deception was the need to avoid Eden. She hated herself for suspecting her sister, and had too much respect for her powers to think she could look her in the eyes and not have her thoughts and suspicions peeled open and revealed to Eden's piercing gaze.

She was so on edge that she felt as if a spotlight was shining down on her. In fact, it was only Jade's presence constantly at her side that gave her the fortitude to get through the day.

But she did what she had to do. She moved among the people—greeting newly arrived nobility—even at one point, speaking briefly with Master Raphael, responding to his polite inquiry regarding her sleep the previous night.

"No bad dreams at all, thank you," she had told him. And as far as it went, that was true—the dreams were terrible, but they were not *bad*. They had given her the key to discovering what was going on here . . . or so she hoped.

She tried not to dwell on what dark intentions could be driving Eden, if she truly was the person manipulating everyone around her. It was too agonizing to think that she had betrayed her whole family for some sinister, impenetrable purpose.

*Or perhaps it's for a good reason—perhaps she's doing this for the benefit of Faerie. Perhaps it has to be done in secret or . . . or it won't work?*

Clutching at straws!

At one point sadness intruded into the festivities for Tania. She saw a woman standing alone watching some children playing. The woman's head was half-covered by a shawl of white silk. It was Mallory, the mother whose infant boy had been the first victim of the plague.

"Give me a moment," Tania asked Jade. She went and stood at Mallory's side. The Faerie woman turned to her and a wan smile touched her lips.

"Will time heal my hurt, my lady?" she asked, searching Tania's face.

"I don't know."

"I think not," said Mallory. "But new gladness may ease the pain." She pointed to a man in among the children. He was tossing them one by one into the air. Their wings whirred as they flew around his head, laughing and calling.

"That is my husband," she said. "He is a good and loving man." She touched her hand to her stomach. "My Gyvan is in Avalon, but new life stirs within me."

"Oh, I'm so pleased," said Tania.

"As am I," Mallory murmured. She glanced side-long at Tania. "You have great work ahead of you upon the morrow, my lady, when the Pure Eclipse comes."

Tania nodded.

Mallory's fingers touched cool for a moment against Tania's hand. "The horses are galloping," she said. "They will be here soon."

Before Tania could respond, the woman stepped

away from her and joined her husband among the children.

Tania watched her, the blood throbbing in her ears, then she turned away and went to look for Jade.

During the day, a flotilla of barges and small boats had been assembled along the bank of the Tamesis. As the sun began to dip toward the horizon, musicians filled several of the boats and pushed off onto the moving belly of the wide river.

In the growing twilight people gathered in the hundreds at the wharfs and jetties and quays of the palace, the excited throng gradually taking to the boats as the minstrels began to play.

Lanterns were set adrift on the river, lit by some mystical inner glow, circling and gliding on the darkening water, shedding light on the surface—pink and indigo, turquoise and beryl green, viridian and carmine, cerise and saffron—and where they collided or swung together in eddies, creating new unnamed colors that constantly blended and changed.

Tania and Jade climbed aboard a small narrow rowboat that was moored some distance from the main congregation of royal vessels. An oarsman in pale blue livery rowed them out into midstream. Tania could see the King's great dark barge with its golden awnings and carved wooden cabin. The King and Queen were there, attended by servants as they sat at ease on deep wooden chairs. With them were the earl marshall Cornelius and his wife and two sons. Corin had recently arrived from Caer Ravensare with a contingent of knights to swell the armies on Salisoc Heath. Tania saw that Master Cariotis was also on the Royal Barge, along with Hopie and Lord Brython and Earl Valentyne.

The other princesses were on boats that gathered around the Royal Barge. Only Eden was missing.

*Where is she?*

All along the battlements and towers of the Royal Palace, light burned brightly in the growing twilight. And more torches burned along the banks of the river.

The sound of excited conversation and laughter mingled with the music as the water pageant made its gradual way upriver. Everyone was in their finest clothes, and each boat and barge contained a basket brim full of delicious foodstuffs and bottles of sweet Faerie cordial.

Moving with a languid grace on the river, the boats and barges were steered toward the single bridge that spanned the Tamesis. It was an arc of elegant white stone with a tall tower at either end. Torches were positioned along its curved span so their flickering lights were mirrored in the dark water.

The day had drained away in the far west, and now the night was full of stars. The moon hung in the north, pierced through by the black arrow of a steeple rising from the dark mass of the palace.

Now Tania saw Eden. She was standing at the apex of the bridge, dressed all in white so that with her pale face and her ashen hair, she looked like a marble statue as the vessels began to slide away into the shadows of the arch. But even under the bridge there was light—the glow from the floating lanterns illuminated the white stone of the underside to create a rippling rainbow of lambent colors.

Tania felt herself shrinking down in the belly of the boat as they approached the bridge. Jade's hand closed reassuringly around her wrist. Neither spoke.

There was cheering now and applause as Eden lifted her alabaster arms into the sky. Like a white flame, she looked to Tania as their boat came closer and closer to the bridge. Against the dark of the sky Eden seemed to have grown huge and powerful as she stood on the bridge with her fingers pointing to the stars.

*She'll see us. She'll know. She'll put a spell on us, and that'll be the end of everything.*

But Eden's face was turned upward, and although her lips were moving with some mystic incantation, the threads of rainbow light that unraveled from her fingertips went spinning up into the sky.

The music reached a crescendo, and the whole skyline of the Royal Palace was ablaze with fizzing and crackling fireworks. Curtains of red and gold and silver sparks rained down the walls; rosy mists rose with red fire at their hearts. Rockets shot skyward, roaring and whistling, curving so high that they mingled with the stars before exploding into crescents and arcs of blazing multicolored lights.

The people on the river cheered even louder, all faces turned to the skies, the whole world bathed in coruscating light as the sky erupted into balls and spiraling columns of sparkling fire. Among the boats more fireworks were lit, sending gushing plumes of red and blue and yellow and gold sparks up into the night; sparks that fell back onto the river did not go out—staying bright and burning as they whorled away under the water. In the depths of the river the sparkling lights danced, forming patterns and marvelous designs, so that folk did not know whether to watch the skies or to lean over the bows of their boats and gaze down in wonder at the submerged display.

Voices drifted over the water.

"'Tis most wonderful!"

"Princess Eden has outdone herself this night!"

The fountains of light that were still pouring upward from Eden's fingers began to form immense shapes in the sky. Tania stared, awestruck at the forces her mystic sister could command. The lights swarmed and separated and took on the shapes of people in a gigantic, luminous ring. While Tania watched, feeling impossibly tiny in that little boat on that little river, the immense sky-folk joined hands and began to dance, their colossal feet skipping across the rooftops and towers of the palace and over the uppermost branches of the trees of the southern forest.

As the sky-dancers whirled, music rang out and the firiencraft burned and blazed. Then the great starlight shapes began to break up again, to dissolve into points of dazzling light. The sparks went shooting up into the profound dark of the upper skies, lustrous and color-shifting, trailing behind them a wake of burning light so that the sky was streaked with ragged bands of ruby and turquoise and aquamarine, emerald and amber.

As the boats and barges floated under the bridge and away along the river, so the celestial lights followed them, and the music was all around them, and there was laughter and the speech of delighted and amazed voices.

"Hail to the lady Eden! Blessings be upon her!"

"All joy to the princess, and to all the Family Royal!"

"All joy this wondrous night!"

"All joy!"

Even Tania lost herself in the wonder and the grandeur of the celebrations that marked the eve of the Pure Eclipse.


"Do you have a backup plan for if we're caught?" Jade's voice was a sharp whisper in the darkness of the night.

"No, not really," Tania replied, slipping along a wall and peering through an arch to where moonlight fell soft on a long floor of cobblestones. "I'm hoping everyone else will be asleep."

The festivities had gone on into the small hours. Tania guessed that it was well past midnight when the boats finally came back downstream and moored to let their bedazzled passengers off. Tania and Jade managed to avoid contact with any of the Royal Family as they headed for Tania's bedroom. But even so, they let a good while pass before they ventured out again. After such a night people would find it hard to sleep straightaway—not with their ears still ringing with the music and their eyes still filled with the light of the firiencraft.

Tania didn't dare risk lighting a candle, so they had to move slowly and cautiously as they approached the long courtyard with the tall square towers at its far end.

Tania's nerves jangled as she stepped out into the moonlight and saw the Dolorous Tower ahead of her, brooding in its graveclothes of ivy, the birds huddled on its roof and windowsills. She shuddered, her blood chilled at the sight. Part of her was absolutely convinced that Eden would appear out of nowhere at the last moment.

Her plans for leaving Jade behind had failed miserably. Waiting for Jade to fall asleep so she could slip away had been a total waste of time. Her friend had virtually laughed in her face when Tania had tried to suggest that she should go it alone.

"This isn't a game, Jade. It's dangerous!"

"I know that. But I didn't just come to Faerie to stand around gawking and going 'wow'! I wanted to make sure you would be all right. And that's just what I intend to do, so shut up about it. I'm coming with you. Get used to it!"

Despite Tania's misgivings it was comforting to have her friend at her side—she just hoped and prayed she wasn't leading Jade into a deadly trap.

They moved along the courtyard and came to the three gray stone steps.

Tania was one pace ahead of her friend as she climbed the steps to the dark door. There was no handle. She reached forward, pressing the palms of both hands against the black wood.

Surely it would not be so easy . . . ?

She pushed hard but the door did not move.

"Whatcha doing?" whispered Jade.

"Seeing if I can get the door open," Tania hissed back.

"Is it locked?"

"I don't know."

Jade came onto the top step. "I'd get out of the way if I were you," she said. "I'm going to try something."

"What?"

"It's called a yoko geri," said Jade. "Watch and learn!"

Tania moved aside as Jade stood on the wide top step, staring hard at the door, breathing long and slow.

She brought her knee up sharply, twisting sideways from the door, rotating from the hips, her raised leg thrusting suddenly outward. The heel of her foot slammed in hard against the side of the door. With a tearing sound the door lurched inward. Jade brought her leg down, her arms lifted a little for balance. She turned and looked at Tania, a slow grin spreading across her face. "And that's why tai chi is so great!" She gestured toward the gaping door. "After you."

Tania stared out across the courtyard, her heart

pounding. Jade's side kick had not been silent. Anyone close by would have heard it. But no shadows moved through the moonlight. No one was coming for them.

"It'll be dark inside," Tania said. "Be careful."

To be honest, it wasn't the darkness inside the tower that Tania feared—it was those menacing creatures in the walls of the room beyond the entrance lobby. She had encountered them once before, and although she had gotten through, it was not an ordeal she relished repeating.

All the same, she steeled herself and stepped into the gloom. She remembered the layout of the tower. To the right an archway led to spiral stairs. To the left a simple door of gray wood was all that stood between them and the room with the monsters in the walls.

She fumbled for the latch that held the inner door closed. She lifted it and pushed the door open.

At the far end of the long, narrow room a circle of moonlight shed a little grimy light over the bare wood floor.

"See anything?" Jade hissed over her shoulder.

"No," Tania whispered. She took a step into the room. There was no sense of menace in there—just the long, sad quiet of a room seldom visited.

"Now what?" Jade whispered.

"Upstairs. It'll be dark."

"Okay. I'll stick close."

"You'd be better off staying down here—just in case."

"Tania? Shut up!"

*Well, you can't say I haven't warned you.*

Her hands groping ahead, Tania went through the arch and began to climb the stairs. This was a part of Eden's tower that she had never been in before. She had no idea what might be lurking in the upper parts—demons, deadly traps, mystical barriers—*nightmares!*

She could hear the blood coursing through her temples as she moved upward into the blind dark. The thumping of her heart seemed to fill the air.

She came to a landing. A faint seepage of light showed. Square. Like an occluded window. She ran her fingers over a wooden shutter. She found a catch and pulled the shutter in. Moonlight came in, seeming strangely bright to Tania's eyes.

It glimmered on the rising curve of the stairway. Darkness lurked around the bend of the spiraling staircase. Darkness and death and worse than death.

She continued to climb, and Jade was never more than a single step behind her.

"If Eden is here and she comes for us, get out of my way," Jade whispered. "I know a few moves that should slow her down."

"If it is Eden, she won't attack us like that," murmured Tania. "And if she finds us—trust me, there's nothing you could do that would stop her."

"We'll see about that."

Tania turned and glared at her friend. "Jade!"

"Chill out, Tania. I'm just trying to be positive."

"Be realistic. If Eden's up here, run! Don't look back—just run!"

They came to a second landing. Jade pried the shutter open so that a little more of the unending stairway was revealed in the moonlight.

Tania almost wished Eden would appear—just to get it over with. Much more of this and the fears that were teeming in her head would get too much to bear.

A third landing and a third shuttered window.

But this time when Tania pulled the shutter open, the moonlight allowed in fell on a small door. And there was something else: the sill outside the window was filled with birds, and they were all turned toward the glass, almost as if they had been perching there waiting for the shutter to be removed. Bright, beady eyes stared in at the two girls. The silence and the stillness of the birds were uncanny. Unnerving.

Tania turned away. There was a crystal bolt on the door. As she drew the bolt back with a sharp, scraping sound, she thought she heard a furtive movement from beyond the door.

Jade's mouth came up close to her ear. "There's someone in there!"

Tania nodded.

Pausing to gather her courage, she leaned into the door and pushed it open.

It was a small room, a grimy, shadowy room that smelled musty and stale and unpleasant. There was a bed and a table and a chair. A single, thin yellow candle stood in a mound of wax at one end of the table. There was a plate and a cup. A hunk of bread.

Tania heard a sound from the far side of the room.

A shadow quivered.

Something monstrous waiting to pounce? The guardian of the Great Spell?

There were more sounds—small dry sounds. The rustle of clothing, the scrape of bare feet on floorboards, an indrawn breath. The shadows in the corner of the room shifted again.

Tania stepped into the room. She paced slowly to the table. Her heart in her mouth, she wrenched the candle up. A splash of hot wax burned on her wrist.

She turned and held the candle out toward the thing in the corner of the room.

There was a soft laugh. There was a glimmer of ragged clothing—the dull sheen of bare skin.

Dark eyes glowed with candlelight.

A mouth stretched in a feral grin.

"What's this, now?" croaked a low, female voice. "More flibbertigibbets come to mock me in my despair?" There was another laugh—a gust of sound without a trace of humor in it. "Why do you bother me now?" the hoarse voice inquired. "You can't harm me. I'm quite mad, you know. Entirely mad. Mad as moonlight."

Tania took another step forward, and the grimy, wild-eyed, hair-draggled face was finally revealed.

"Cordelia!" she gasped, almost dropping the candle in her astonishment and disbelief. "Oh my god— *Cordelia!*"

# Part Four:

## The Darkling Tide

# XXVII

"Good morrow, sweet sister," Cordelia growled. "Have you come to play blindman's bluff with me? Come, we are a merry gathering, Tania." She swept her hand in a low gesture along the floor in front of her dirty bare feet. "See how my friends are gathered? Mice aplenty to sing and dance. And shall I have the spiders weave you a ball gown of finest silk and set the flies to playing sweet melodies for you upon the horse-hair fiddle?" Cordelia's wide eyes closed and opened slowly. "Or would you pluck me by the tail and tweak my furry ears and whiskers and mock me, sister?"

"Cordelia . . . ?" Tania took another step forward, unable to take in what she was seeing and hearing.

Jade's voice whispered at her back. "I thought she was meant to be . . ."

". . . dead," murmured Tania. "Yes. She is." No wonder the birds had been flocking about this tower—they had sensed Cordelia's presence. They had gathered here to be close to her.

Tania crouched, bringing the candle closer to Cordelia's face. Her sister shrank back, huddled in on herself in the corner like a wounded and terrified animal. Heartbreakingly, Tania saw that she was still dressed in the ragged remnants of her wedding gown, sky blue and gold showing among the rents and tears, some few jewels still glimmering on the bodice. But the long sleeves were gone and the hem was ripped, so that Cordelia's bare, grimy arms and legs showed.

Her face was framed with a matted tangle of tawny hair, her freckled cheeks smeared with dirt, her eyes burning like blue ice, her lips pulled back in some limbo between snarling and grinning.

"Mad as the moon when mayhem calls." Cordelia's voice was a bleak singsong. "Empty castles and empty halls." She pointed a trembling finger to the candle flame. "Is that your soul, sister mine? My, how it does shine. Come." She stared distractedly at the floor. "My mice would sing for you—we have been practicing—'tis a song fit for a king. The song of a princess set adrift on the never-ending sea."

"She's lost her mind," said Jade breathlessly. "Tania? Is this how you treat people with mental illness in this world?"

"No!" Tania gave Jade a quick look. "Not at all!"

*Why has Cordelia been locked away like this? What's going on?*

Cordelia half rose, her head drawn down on her shoulders, her back squeezed into the corner of the room. She pointed at nothing. "Look!" she cried. "See how the ducks swim on Robin Goodfellow's pond! But they must watch out for the crocodiles among the soapy suds." She held her trembling hand out to Tania, palm upward. "Do you see this stag? Did you ever see such a small stag, Tania? Why, 'twould fit in a poke and leave room enough for all our hopes and desires besides." She cocked her head. "Listen! Do you hear him? He sings songs of the deep forest." She nodded vehemently. "He has been the greatest friend to me. A great comfort, although he has no head . . ."

Tania stood up, backing away from the wretched sight of her sister. "They told me you were dead, Cordelia," she murmured. "Why are you here? Why have you been put in this terrible place?"

Cordelia's eyes flitted from Tania to Jade. "Come, uncle, you can do better than this puppet show." She poked a finger at them. "I see you! I see through your masks, uncle—do you think you are sweet, dead Zara that you can play upon me as upon a flute?"

"We have to get her out of here," said Jade. "How could anyone leave her like this?"

But something Cordelia had said had lodged in Tania's mind. "Did Uncle Cornelius bring you here?" she asked.

Cordelia grinned, padding forward and wagging her finger in Tania's face. "Fie, uncle—would you blame others for your deeds? 'Tis not honorable, indeed. We shall have to convene the parliament of owls if you persist! And to draw a veil over those sharp eyes is a thing not possible."

Tania felt a sudden rush of pity and dismay for her sister. She stepped forward, throwing her arms around Cordelia's shrunken shoulders, careful to keep the candle away from her hair and clothes as she held her close.

"I'll make it better," Tania said, tears pricking. "I promise—I'll do everything I can to make it better."

Cordelia's body was cold—so terribly cold. But as Tania's warmth seeped into her sister's icy flesh, she felt the slender body stiffen in her arms.

"Tania?"

Tania pulled away, startled by the change in Cordelia's voice. Her sister was peering intently at her, all trace of lunacy gone from her face.

"Tania? Is it truly you?"

"Cordie—yes! Yes, it's me!"

"I thought you but another illusion sent to torture me."

"No. No. I'm real! I promise!"

Cordelia's finger stabbed toward Jade. "And who is she?"

"A friend," said Tania. "A Mortal." She frowned, confused. "You're not . . ."

"Out of my wits?" Cordelia said, wiping straying locks of hair off her face. "I am not, sister—not now. Not for the past five days."

*Five days? Cordelia's madness must have passed when the plague was lifted from Faerie.*

Cordelia smiled bleakly. "But I have feigned madness still, sister," she said. "In order to keep him at bay.

I do not know what he might do if he knew I am whole again."

"Him?" Tania asked. "Who do you mean?"

"Do you not know the author of this chaos, Tania?" said Cordelia. "It is our father's older brother—Prince Lear."

"No. He's gone, Cordie. He *was* here—but I got rid of him."

Cordelia looked thoughtfully at her. "You are deceived, Tania," she said. "He is not gone. Lear is still the puppet-master in this realm—and all dance as he pulls the strings. All save me—and that only because I was lost in the madness that his plague brought down on me, and his Great Enchantment could not take hold in my mind." She nodded vehemently. "Had he but waited a brief time with his spell, I would have been caught up in it, too. But he unleashed the spell while the plague was still in my blood, and so I was spared."

Jade took a step forward. "I'm sorry—I need to get this straight in my head. Are you saying that this Lear guy has brainwashed everyone?"

Cordelia narrowed her eyes. "I do not know the word you use," she said. "But Lear has come here often and delights in telling the tale of his great evil." Her clear eyes turned from Tania to Jade as she spoke. "He told me how he came first into Faerie with deadly force, taking our family unawares as they strove in the Throne Room of Veraglad Palace to keep the Gildensleep intact. I was sick and under the power of the Gildensleep, but all others of our family he imprisoned in amber. He then brought us to this place, the better to savor his victory. Far from my wits I was then, and he did not seal me up in an amber prison, because it amused him to toy with me and listen to my ravings. Most entertaining, he thought it. He comes betimes and taunts me still."

She nodded, her hands resting on Tania's shoulder. "I know what you did in the Throne Room. He laughed when he spoke of it. How he had fooled you into thinking you had defeated him. How he let loose the greatest sorcery the world has ever known—sorcery enough to fog the mind of every man, woman, and child in Faerie—even of the King himself and his most powerful ministers."

Horror and dread ran like ice water through Tania's body. "It was a trick?" She gasped. "He wasn't banished?"

After everything she'd done—Faerie was still not free?

*When will this ever end?*

"He was not," said Cordelia. "Behind the masks he rules in Faerie." She gave a slow smile. "When my sanity returned, I was wise enough to keep the fact from him. He still thinks me raving and witless, my mind ruined beyond repair by his plague, and so he has not sought to bring me under his spell."

"But why's he doing all this?" asked Jade. "It doesn't make any sense. If he can play mind games like you say, why aren't Tania and I affected?"

"You are not of Faerie, mistress," Cordelia said,

turning to Jade. "And Tania's mind is only half Faerie. His sorcery cannot get a tight hold on minds not wholly of this realm. You, Mortal, are immune to his spells, and Tania can be only partially controlled. But he had the power to put false memories into her mind and to hide certain truths from her."

"Like the truth about this tower," said Tania.

"Indeed," said Cordelia. "And I think it amused him to see you jump through his hoops, Tania, while he prepared you for the Darkling Tide."

"I don't know what that means," said Tania, a chill running through her.

Cordelia lifted her head and sniffed. "'Tis almost dawn," she said. "You should not tarry—oft times he comes at sunrise to bring meager food and water and to mock me with his achievements."

Tania remembered the footsteps she had heard the last time they had been in the courtyard.

"Where is he hiding?" Tania asked.

Cordelia laughed softly. "Hiding in plain sight, sister," she said. "Have you not guessed it yet?" Her eyes darkened. "Do you not know that your memories of Master Cariotis are not real? There is no such man as Raphael Cariotis—there never has been such a man. Under his spell Lear caused Eden to plant false memories of him in your mind."

Yes! Tania remembered how Eden had touched a finger to her head in the Great Hall and how her memories of Cariotis had followed.

She heard Jade swing around behind her. "Cariotis!"

Jade's voice was a frightened gasp.

"Well met, human child," said a gentle, soft voice. "Well met, my pretty nieces. And what coil do we have here, Cordelia? Have you been fooling your fond uncle these past days?"

Tania turned, anger blazing in her.

Raphael Cariotis stood in the open doorway, a jug and a cloth bag in his hand, a smile on his face.

Jade leaped at him, her leg rising for a high kick.

Cariotis dropped the bag and jug, and with a swift but seemingly casual gesture he sent Jade crashing headlong into the wall.

Tania flung herself at him, but his hand rose again, and she froze, hanging helpless in the air, unable to move, the blood pounding in her head like the galloping of ten thousand horses.

From the corner of her eye she saw Cordelia lift the chair to hurl it at Raphael. But his eyes flashed red, and with a shout of pain Cordelia dropped the chair and fell back two paces before becoming as immobile as Tania.

"'Tis a pity indeed that my devices should be laid bare so soon before all subterfuge becomes unnecessary," said Raphael, walking slowly around Tania.

Her skin prickled painfully, her every joint and muscle and sinew locked, only her eyes able to follow him as he circled her. She managed to form words through her gritted teeth. "Why are you doing this?"

He tilted his head. "Ah, you mean why are you not already dead, my child?" he said smoothly, no trace of emotion in his voice. "That is simple, Tania—I need you alive and alert if my great endeavor is to be fulfilled." He smiled, reaching toward her and brushing a lock of hair off her cheek. "In all of Faerie only you have the power to move between the worlds without the aid of enchantments. For all my mastery of the ancient sorceries of Ynis Borealis, I cannot pierce that strange veil." A cold smile grew on his face. "And yet I would be king of both worlds, Tania, my most cherished and beloved niece. And with your help I shall conquer both Faerie and the Mortal World."

Tania forced the words out between her lips. "Never! I'll never help you do that!"

"Oh, you misunderstand, Tania." He smiled. "I do not need your cooperation—I merely need to harness your gift." His eyes burned red. "In a certain place at a certain time shall all my plans come to full bloom. And you will be there, Tania. And when you stand with your back to the Quellstone Spire as the sun dims on the noontide of the Pure Eclipse—so shall I lead my armies into the Mortal World, and so shall you perish in fire and smoke!"

He gave a gesture and Tania was suddenly surrounded by a ring of cold, red flame. She could hear Jade, sprawled on the floor, groaning.

*I should never have brought her here!*

She managed a few painful words between aching jaws. "They have Isenmort . . . in the Mortal World. . . . They will destroy you if you . . . go there. . . ."

Raphael Cariotis laughed softly. "Do you think

I have been idle in my ten thousand years of exile, child?" he asked. His voice snapped. "I have not! Over the slow millennia I learned all the ancient sorceries of Ynis Borealis. I learned to wield powers far older than the Mystic Arts of Faerie. Older and mightier by far! I became the lord of the strange men that lived on that bleak northern island. I had them build me a great dark castle—the castle of Gralach Hern!"

*So Gralach Hern is not even part of Faerie! And the knights of Gralach Hern come from Ynis Borealis—they're not Faerie folk at all!*

Cariotis began to circle Tania again, and by the power of his eyes she was compelled to spin to follow his slow pacing, her whole body wracked with pain. She saw Cordelia standing frozen—Jade crumpled unmoving by the wall.

"Great spells I brewed in the high towers of Gralach Hern," Cariotis intoned. "One spell to make us immune from the bite of Isenmort, and another to allow me to enter and control the minds of others." He smiled like a wolf as he looked up at her. "So, dear niece, seventh child of my dear brother, I do not fear Isenmort, and neither do my warriors. We have drunk the dark brew of the Isenkur Goblet—nothing of metal can harm us!"

He began to laugh softly. "And as for your part, child? There I deceived you, Tania. When you touch the Quellstone Spire, it will not be to hold back the blending of the two worlds. As the stars align and the moon crosses the face of the sun in the time of the Pure Eclipse, I shall use your gift of moving between the realms to make the blending of the worlds last for all time." His voice rose. "Faerie and the Mortal World will be as one forever—and I shall rule in both realms, using the power of the ancient sorceries to keep all Mortals and Faerie folk under my sway! And you are to be the instrument of my utter victory! Without you my triumph would have been impossible!" He lifted his hand and a bloom of red fire flared out toward her from his palm. "Know that, and forfeit all hope, Tania Aurealis! You are the doom of both worlds!"

The ball of fire struck her forehead and her brain erupted into screaming agony.

# XXVIII

Tania came to her senses again, hanging paralyzed in a wheel of scarlet fire. She tried to shake the fog from her mind. She had the sensation that time had passed, but she did not know how much time.

She was still in that dark room in the Dolorous Tower, but Raphael Cariotis was gone and the door was closed.

*Not Raphael Cariotis! There never was anyone called Raphael Cariotis. Everything I remembered about him was put into my head by Eden under Lear's spell!*

Despair burned in her, hotter than the flames.

Some grainy light was filtering into the room through cracks in the shuttered windows. It was enough for her to see that Cordelia was missing and that Jade hung close by, her head lolling, her body caught in a ring of flames.

Lear's dreadful words came back to her. *"The doom of both worlds!"*

She groaned, trying desperately to move in her flaming prison.

*"I learned all the ancient sorceries of Ynis Borealis."*

If he was telling the truth, Lear had powers far greater than those of Oberon and Eden and all the mystic lore-masters of Faerie. He had an army. And he had the weapon he needed to rip open the barriers between the worlds.

He had *her.*

Dreadful images crowded in her mind. Pictures of those dark knights of Gralach Hern galloping through the streets of London, trampling people under their hooves, their red swords cleaving flesh and taking heads from shoulders.

Her own mum and dad would suffer under Lear's tyranny. Jade's family would be caught up in the horror. Connor and his parents—the lives of everyone she had ever known would be ruined.

What could all the armies of Earth do against sorcery?

Suddenly it was as if Lear had planted visions in her head to torment her. She saw soldiers trying to hold back the Red Knights—and she saw their weapons turn to ash in their hands. The Mortal World's armies would be cut down in the rattle and rush of a deadly cavalry charge. She saw tanks rumbling, saw them falter and halt and turn to stone. Missiles curved across the sky in her mind's eye, dissolving into smoke as they neared their targets. Bombs became chaff as they rained down. And all the while swords rose and fell, and she saw blood spraying and bodies crashing to the blood-soaked earth.

And she saw at last, in a vast castle founded upon a crag, King Lear of the Entwined Realms seated upon a throne that seemed to be formed of blood and bones, while the leaders of the two shattered worlds sprawled to do homage at his feet.

And she saw herself—most terrible of all—seated at his side, as Rathina had once sat helplessly at the side of the Sorcerer King of Lyonesse. Seated at his side and forced to witness the horror and anguish that she had helped him to create.

She heard Titania's voice. *"It's your especial gift that will allow you to do this."*

And her Mortal father speaking softly to her as she had taken the first step on the road to this nightmare. *"I'm more proud of you than I can ever say."*

*No! Don't say that! You don't know! You don't know what I'm going to do! You don't know the damage I'm going to cause.*

She would have wept, but the flames scorched her tears away before they could be shed. She wished she could faint—to return to oblivion—but her mind would not allow it. She struggled, sweating in the ring of red flames, but this time there was no blue fire to contest the red—no white light to give her strength. Her other selves had returned to their own destinies. Edric was far away in the north—if he was even still alive! She was utterly alone and helpless.

"Ugh! My head!" Tania swiveled her eyes at the sound of Jade's voice. "What the heck did that guy do to me? I hurt all over!"

"Jade?"

Her friend's head lifted, her eyes glassy for a moment but then clearing as she caught sight of Tania in the feeble light. The ring of fire held Jade in the air like a fist, but she was not paralyzed by it. Perhaps Lear did not think a Mortal girl needed to be held rigid, and so she was able to move a little.

"Oh, great!" she groaned. "I hoped it was all a bad dream."

"It is—but not the kind you wake up from."

Jade looked around the room. "Where's Cordelia?" she asked.

"Cariotis must have taken her."

Jade looked at Tania. "What are we going to do? How do we get out of this?"

"I don't know that we do," Tania said.

"I'm still alive," Jade said. "That's a plus, I guess." She frowned. "I remember that Cariotis guy turning up—then wham! Nothing." She narrowed her eyes as though in pain. "What did I miss?"

Slowly Tania told Jade what had happened after Lear had knocked her unconscious.

There was a long silence afterward, then: "Do you think he can be stopped?"

Tania shook her head.

Jade's eyes were suddenly full of alarm. "Can he really take control of both worlds?"

"I think he can."

"I wish . . ." Jade's voice trailed away.

"What do you wish?"

"I wish I didn't know about this," said Jade, her voice cracking with fear. "We're only sixteen, Tania— only *sixteen*—and we're going to die. It's wrong. It's all wrong. That's not how stuff is supposed to happen. I don't want it to be true!" Tears choked in her voice. "I want this all to stop now! I don't like it anymore. Make it stop!"

"I will make it stop," Tania said. "Listen to me, Jade! I've *done* things, you know? Amazing things! I've grown wings and flown in the sky. I've ridden a unicorn. I've walked between worlds. And I've already killed one sorcerer who was so full of himself that he thought he could come swaggering in and be like, 'I'm the total king of everyone! Bow down and worship me!' I *killed* him, Jade." She tried to ignore the stiffness in her jaw as she forced the words from her mouth. "Look at me, Jade. Look in my eyes. Trust me! I will find a way to deal with Lear. I will!"

A bleak smile crossed Jade's face. "Way to go, Tania!" she said. "That was almost convincing."

The sound of the door swinging open took their attention.

Raphael Cariotis stood in the doorway, the amber jewel glimmering at his chest, his features ruddy in the light of the flames that held Tania and Jade.

*Not Cariotis—Lear!* But although Tania knew the true face of the man confronting her, she could still not pierce the mask of his deception. He still looked like Raphael Cariotis—and her head was still full of counterfeit memories of her father's honored counselor.

"Ah, you are awake, Tania," he said, walking into the room. "That is good. I would not have you miss the most momentous event of your short life." He smiled and gestured so that she floated to the floor. "Noon approaches, my most cherished niece—it is time for your tryst with the Pure Eclipse."

"What about me?" Jade shouted, all trace of fear hidden now. "What do you plan on doing with me, mister? How do I fit into your loony plans?"

Lear turned and looked at her as though surprised at the sound of her defiant voice. "Indeed, what should I do with you?" he mused. "I had given no thought to it, Mortal child. I imagine you will remain here, locked in this place till you perish of hunger and thirst." He smiled coldly. "Or would you wish a speedier end, child? I can give you the gift of instant death." He raised his hand, his fingers curled. "Would you wish that?"

"Not really!" Jade said. "Thanks, all the same." She nodded to Tania. "I want to stay with her."

"You'd share her fate?"

"I guess so."

"Your wish is granted, child," said Lear. "It can do no harm. You shall ride together in the carriage. And I shall have the pleasure of seeing the terror in your eyes when the moment of her doom approaches."

"Thanks a bunch!" muttered Jade.

"What carriage?" asked Tania, her heart going out to Jade for her courage and friendship.

"Did you think I would make you walk all the way to the cave on the high downs?" Lear said. "Fie! I would not do you such discourtesy." He moved his fingers in the air, and although the red flames slowly died away, Tania found that she was still unable to move.

"You shall ride in comfort and style to the Cavern of Heartsdelving," Lear continued. "Accompanied by my most chivalrous and trusted knights, and applauded all the way by the glad and loyal subject of your father, the King." He snapped his fingers and suddenly Tania felt life and mobility return to her limbs. "Come," Lear said, turning and walking from the room. "The noontide approaches. We must be gone!"

Although she could move, Tania realized that she had no control over her body. At Lear's command she walked stiffly across the floor, and with Jade by her side they followed him down the spiraling staircase of Eden's dark tower toward their fate.

The festival of the Pure Eclipse was in full swing as the horse-drawn carriage made its way out of the palace and up through the crowded parklands. The sky was clear blue, and a fresh breeze sent the banners and flags and pennants of Faerie flying. A cheering throng lined the route that the carriage took up toward the heathered downs. Some threw flowers till the floor of the carriage was awash with roses and fuchsias and marigolds and violets and a score of other flowers besides.

There were even pink lilies in Tania's lap and rose petals in her hair. Jade sat stiff at her side, festooned in chrysanthemum and gerbera petals, her eyes haunted, her jaw set.

The man with the face of Raphael Cariotis sat opposite them, smiling and waving occasionally to the crowds of cheering onlookers.

"Can't they see we're his prisoners?" hissed Jade between clenched teeth. "Can't they see it from our faces?"

Lear leaned forward. "They see what I wish them to see," he said. "Two merry maids on their way to save the worlds!" He spun his fingers, and as Jade's arm rose to wave, so Tania found herself unable to prevent her own arm from lifting to the passing people. "You see?" Lear said. "You wave and smile and all is well."

Tania scanned the cheering crowds, searching desperately for Edric's face in among them—wishing with all her heart that he might have returned in time to save them. But there was no sign of him. The crowds cheered and music played and tumblers and jugglers and acrobats performed their arts while knights jousted and cooks prepared sumptuous food-stuffs and the high white sun climbed slowly to the apex of the sky.

In Tania's head, louder even than the roar of the crowds, was the constant drumming of hoofbeats. Hammering, hammering away in her skull—louder still and louder until her whole body ached with the pounding of it and she would have screamed for pain if she had been able to.

Jade had been right in guessing that the hoof-beats were connected to the Pure Eclipse. It had to be so—why else would the noise be growing as noon approached?

Tania glanced up at the sky. The innocent, powder blue sky and the sun a white flare too bright to look at. And no sign of the doom that was coming.

Jade let out a moan at her side.

Voices called to Tania.

"Bless you, Princess Tania!"

"The good spirits keep you eternally for your deeds this day!"

# XXIX

Tania had known of the cave on the downs all of her life. A small insignificant-seeming crack in the side of the hill, half hidden by heather and gorse, but which led to one of the most sacred places in all the land. She had even been through the low stony mouth once—on an expedition led by seventeen-year-old Eden, lighting their way with a mystical flame as she and Rathina and Zara followed. Tania had been nine, and her folded wings had chafed under her clothes.

A steep, narrow, winding shaft had led down and down to a sudden wide tunnel with a curved roof. There they discovered the course of the River Elfleet running swift and dark between rocky banks, noisy and icy cold when the spray hit bare skin. They had walked in file along the bank until they came to the awesome Cavern of Heartsdelving . . . years ago, when she still had wings, and before any shadow had fallen upon Faerie.

The carriage left the crowds behind and ascended

the last hill before the cave. Tania stared in shock and dismay. The cave was no longer a small mouth in the hill; it had been dug out and excavated until it was a gaping hole, surrounded by piles of raw earth and mounds of broken stone. Many of the Red Knights of Gralach Hern stood around the gouged chasm, their brooding presence sinister as they silently watched the approaching carriage.

Lear called for the carriage to halt before the ugly wound in the hills. "'Twas the best that could be worked in the time," he said, stepping out of the carriage and gesturing toward the great hole in the hillside. "When I am King of both worlds, machines of Isenmort will be brought into this land to perform such tasks with more efficiency. Ah, but they will bite into the backbone of this realm—they will gnaw at its very heart."

Tania was again tormented by visions. She saw the massive jaws of excavators gouging into the green hills of Faerie—and she saw smoke-spewing bulldozers, their blades hacking down the forest trees, their rumbling and clanking caterpillar tracks churning the ground to mud. Wrecking balls crashing into the walls of the Royal Palace. She saw flames leaping, A pall of filthy smoke hanging over Faerie like a funeral shroud.

She looked into Lear's eyes, knowing that it was his will that put these nightmares in her head and that he enjoyed the pain they gave her.

She fought back, filling her mind instead with pictures of her family: her Mortal mother and father, her sisters, the King and Queen, her beloved Edric.

Lear scowled.

"Would that you were pure Faerie," he growled as he curled his hands and forced her to step out of the carriage. "I'd play such games in your mind, child, that you'd never know peace nor love again!"

She glared at him. "But I am not pure Faerie," she spat. "I'll fight you every step." She forced her head to turn toward him. "Why don't you show your true face, uncle?" she asked.

"I shall, when the time is right."

She glowered at him. *Think! Come on, you can do it! Get control back. Don't let him make you do these things.*

Lear raised his hand and drew Jade down from the carriage.

"Let me go, you pig!" snarled Jade.

"Be silent, Mortal," he responded. "You are here by your own choice." He sneered. "Enjoy your fate."

While he was distracted for that moment, Tania was able to summon the determination to lift her right arm and swing it through the air.

Her open palm slapped hard against the side of his face. He stepped back, his expression startled and outraged.

She laughed, but her laughter was stopped with a violent suddenness. His fist closed in the air and she felt a hand in her chest, squeezing her heart. She shouted in pain, and for a second she thought he would kill her.

*Yes! Yes—kill me now. Then I won't be able to be used by you!*

But the pain subsided, and she was left gasping and shaking.

"You'll not best me, child," he said, rubbing his cheek. "And you'll not die until the moment I have already chosen." He smiled grimly, in control again. "Come, the time is almost nigh, and we have a little ways to go yet."

He turned, his willpower pulling Tania and Jade along behind him. The Red Knights watched impassively as the three of them entered the cave and began to walk down the steep slope.

"Way to go with the smack!" Jade managed to whisper to Tania. "Got any more where that came from?"

Tania shook her head. It had taken almost all of her reserves of strength to make that one futile movement. She knew she would not be given the chance to catch Lear off guard again.

The galloping hooves were still in her head like a migraine. It was getting so that she could hardly think for the thundering in her brain. But despite her pain the sight that met her eyes at the end of the winding slope came as a jolt.

Where there had been reverberating noise and racing water in the deep tunnel in the past, there was now only an eerie silence. The dark waters of the Elfleet were immobile, black as ebony, shining in the light of the red torches that lined the river's course. The waters had not frozen like ice would freeze—rather they seemed to have been turned to black stone in the midst of their flood and rush, so that the

surface was rippled and wrinkled and broken by pet-
rified waves.

"Be wary of your footing, children," said Lear as
he stepped out onto the congealed river. "It is a little
slippery underfoot—but I needed a wider pathway for
the use of my knights, as you shall see."

Tania and Jade stepped down onto the river's
uneven surface and followed along the torchlit pas-
sageway.

They came to a place where the river was split by a
sharp edge of stone. The main body of the black river
continued into a dark tunnel, but a small stream broke
off and led to an immense cavern.

The Cavern of Heartsdelving. Tania had seen it
only once before, its vast vaulted roof and its striated
walls lit only dimly by Eden's mystic flame. But now
the great cavern was revealed in its entirety by the
naked torches held up by the mounted Red Knights of
Gralach Hern. The pocked and fissured walls soared
up to a curved roof of rust-colored stone, from which
blue-white crystals jutted down like swords and spears,
glittering and flashing in the torchlight.

Tania guessed there must be close to a hundred
of the dour knights gathered there, circling the huge
round cavern, facing inward and as still and seemingly
lifeless as the waters of the narrow stream that lay like
a black tongue along the cavern's floor.

When it had been alive, the river had fed into a
calm lake, a heart-shaped body of water that Tania
remembered as a dark mirror, reflecting the faces and

forms of the princesses as they had gazed spellbound into its inky depths.

But now it was dead and smooth like black stone, and it reflected nothing.

At the lake's center a small bare island of rock rose to a white crystal stalagmite, its huge finger pointing to the high roof of the cavern. Tania knew the gravity and substance of that pillar of white crystal. It was the Quellstone Spire—the quintessence and focus of the mystic power that flowed through every aspect of Faerie. Like blood flowing through the heart of a body, so the power of the spirits flowed through this place, constantly refreshing and renewing itself before spreading out through stone and tree and river and beast and flower and soil, bringing every fiber of Faerie alive and fueling all the Arts called upon by Oberon and Eden and Valentyne and all other loremasters of the realm.

The cavern had been silent and reverent and still the last time Tania had been here—but now the heart-shaped lake was surrounded by people.

People who cheered and applauded as Cariotis led the two girls forward and up to the lip of the frozen lake.

Oberon and Titania were there, seated upon the thrones taken from the Great Hall. Tania's soul ached to see them. The Royal Family was gathered around the King and Queen: Eden and Valentyne, Hopie and Lord Brython, Sancha, Rathina . . . and Cordelia, too. And under Lear's spell the Royal Family seemed to have forgotten that Cordelia was meant to be dead. She stood with them, no longer filthy and dressed in rags but wearing a gown of leaf green. She was smiling and clapping. Tania knew at a glance that she remembered nothing of what had happened in the Dolorous Tower. Poor Cordelia was now as deeply under Lear's spell as all the others.

The earl marshall Cornelius was also in attendance, with his wife, Lucina, and their two sons, Titus and Corin. And there were other lords and ladies, too, representatives of many an earldom—all smiling as they looked toward Tania, all clapping, all glad to see her.

And Edric? Where was he? Hundreds of miles away, lost in the Earldom of Weir.

The only thing louder than the acclaim of the noble congregation was the crashing of hooves in Tania's head.

Lear stepped to one side, his arms reaching out toward Tania as the cheering rose to a wild climax. Only the knights of Gralach Hern did not join in the celebration. They sat on their black horses with their red swords at their hips and with red helmets upon their heads and red armor covering their limbs. And finally, and far too late, Tania realized what had so disturbed her about these horsemen—the thing that had twisted her stomach into knots whenever she had approached them. It was so horribly obvious now! Their swords and their armor were of metal—dark red metal.

Lear lifted his arms and the applause died slowly away to an excited, watching hush.

"Welcome, one and all," he called, his voice ringing down from the domed roof. "Welcome, indeed, to this most auspicious place at this most auspicious time!" He pointed to the very top of the roof. "Let us shed some light on what is soon to come," he called. "Let us bear witness to the greatest event of the age!"

Streams of fire ran from his fingers, up and up to the top of the cavern. And where the flames boiled against the stone, so the roof seemed to melt away, leaving a wide cavity through which the noonday sun came streaming down, filling the cavern with golden light.

There was a gasp and a murmur of awe as the sunlight poured over the gathered people of Faerie and illuminated the Quellstone Spire as if it were a rod of solid white light. Even the black waters of the lake shone now, and the torches of the knights of Gralach Hern were all but quenched in the deluge of daylight.

"Come forth, those who have been chosen as attendants to Princess Tania," Lear called. "Come forth and lead her to her destiny!"

Tania watched in dismay as Cordelia and Rathina and Titus stepped out onto the lake and walked slowly and smilingly toward her.

"Would you be with her still, Mortal child?" Lear asked Jade.

"You bet!" said Jade, and although her voice shook with fear, Tania saw a fierce courage in her face. Jade turned to the three approaching people. "Hey! Stop smiling. You have to snap out of it, guys. This is all fake! This is all so bad!"

But they didn't hear her—or perhaps Lear's will changed her words to a happy greeting in their charmed ears? Their eyes full of joy and their mouths stretched in unnatural, fixed smiles, Rathina and Titus took Tania by the hands. Smiling also, Cordelia walked in front, Jade forced to follow as the five of them set off toward the island in the black lake.

Hooves. Galloping. Hurting so bad. Beating at her brain.

All hope gone.

They came to the island and climbed the gentle slope to the crystal pillar. Tania was too far gone now to struggle. She felt defeated—tortured by the relentless thudding of the hooves.

Titus and Rathina led her up to the Spire, turning her so that her back was to the lambent crystal. Through her agony Tania was aware of a sudden creeping coldness filling the cavern. She forced her head up, staring into the small ring of the sky with the white sun at its heart.

The pain was boiling cold in her eyes. Fire and ice. The heat of the world's core and the deadly cold of the void between the stars, flooding her veins at one and the same time.

And still the crashing hooves! Louder and louder.

*Make them stop! Please, god, make them stop!*

The cavern was silent now. Watching. Waiting. As

Rathina and Titus pressed her against the Quellstone Spire, Tania could feel its power running through her like electricity, or like something more ancient and more visceral than electricity—like charmed and mystic blood in her veins.

Cordelia was smiling. Jade looked anguished and helpless, and there were tears running down her cheeks.

Hooves. Hooves. Hooves.

Slowly a strange darkness stole across the sky. In the Mortal World to look into the sun would have burned her eyes out, but here in Faerie Tania found she could stare into the sun and not be blinded.

She saw a thieving darkness biting into the sun's disk.

Her whole body vibrated with the galloping horses. So close now—so close she could almost smell their sweat and see the flames in their eyes.

The pirate moon glided over the sun's face, plundering its light and heat, moving at a stealthy pace, exchanging day for unnatural night, light for darkness, warmth for cold.

There was a final desperate flare of white light, as though the sun itself was fighting for its life. The light guttered a moment, and then all that remained was a thin ring of white in the sudden gloaming. The red torches of Gralach Hern burned with a hectic bloom.

Lear strode across the lake toward Tania, and as he came for her, so his shape and appearance changed, melting and morphing until he no longer wore the image of Raphael Cariotis. Now it was Lear himself who stood in front of her.

Prince Lear—his face so like the King's and yet so broken and warped by wickedness and hatred.

The crowds were hushed, even Oberon and Titania sat silent in their thrones as they watched Lear reach out his hand toward Tania.

"It is time," he said, his words only just audible over the horses in her head. "Time for the twining of the worlds. Time for me to come into my own!"

Tania felt the power of the Quellstone Spire flowing into her body, saturating her.

She needed no subtle side step now to breach the worlds. She felt the power bursting out of her, blazing from her every pore, convulsing her as it roared through the cavern.

She saw a second image superimposed over the cavern.

A London sky darkened at noon. A curving concrete walkway and a tree hanging over a canal lock. A stretch of calm gray-blue water contained by concrete banks. Redbrick buildings with slate roofs and white windows. A long wall colored with abstract patterns of blue and yellow. A gray concrete rampart rising at the end of the canal. Wooden lock gates. Flags hanging, windless. The tricolored flag of Great Britain folded in on themselves like gaudy wings.

A small group of young people were sitting in a patch of grass by the canal.

As Tania saw them, they stared around themselves

and scrambled to their feet, huddling together in sudden terror as the sights of the Cavern of Heartsdelving were revealed to them under their own Mortal sky.

She heard Lear laughing.

She was seeing Camden Lock—part of the Regent's Canal that wound itself through North London. The flags flew over the market where she and Jade and their friends often went shopping. She lived only a few streets away from here.

If she were able to run, she could be with her Mortal parents in a matter of minutes. But she could not run.

She turned her head.

There was a long, low white building alongside the canal. A plain white bridge with black railings and traffic moving slowly along a tarmac road. Three young women staring at her with eyes full of fear. They were all wearing jeans. A backpack hung from the shoulder of one of them. Another had her blond hair tied back with a colored band. Three ordinary young Mortal women who were seeing impossible things under the longest solar eclipse of the twenty-first century.

"To me, knights of Gralach Hern!" shouted Lear, his face exultant as he turned with outstretched arms to embrace his new dominion.

The Red Knights rode slowly forward through the people of Faerie, and as they crossed the lake the hooves of their horses clanged as if they were hundreds of hammers beating on sheets of iron.

Their swords drew with a hiss as they circled the

island, lifting their weapons high in honor to their tyrant King.

Tania saw the three young women turn and run in terror. She saw a sword rise and fall. The blond woman fell with a cry.

The first blow of the conquest of the two worlds.

The first Mortal blood on Tania's hands.

"Father!" Tania did not know where she found the strength to cry out to the King. "Father—don't let this happen!"

But King Oberon and Queen Titania and all the others of Faerie were gazing around themselves, their faces full of wonder and pleasure as the two worlds blended and melted together. All thoughts of the deadly effects of this dark entwining had been wiped from their minds. Lear controlled them utterly.

Rathina's face swam in front of Tania's eyes. "How marvelous it is!" she cried, her eyes glowing. "Did you ever think to live to see such a wondrous thing, Tania?"

Lear laughed, and for the first time the knights of Gralach Hern lifted their voices in a deadly chorus.

"Death!" they howled. Their horses rose up, hooves beating the air. "Death to the Mortal filth! Death to them all!"

# XXX

Tania watched, crushed by her own impotence, as the Red Knights of Gralach Hern wheeled their steeds around and went galloping along the towpath of the canal, cutting down everyone who stood in their way.

Galloping hooves.

Horses on the streets of London racing under a choked and smothered sun.

Horses in Tania's mind. The stallions of the darkling moon beating at her brain. Beating at her heart. Beating at her soul.

Beyond even the furthermost shred of hope, Tania hung between Rathina and Titus. She felt a fire kindle in her chest—a malignant fire she knew would grow swift and fierce to burn her body to ash.

She saw an image of Mary Palmer, her face sad, her voice regretful. *"If only you'd made up your mind to stay with us, Anita."*

"I'm so sorry. . . ."

Titania, now, her face next to Mary Palmer's. *"If*

*not for that first foolish side step on the eve of your birthday,*
*Tania, all would have been well. . . . That is what began it*
*all. . . ."*

"Is this all my fault?"

The voices of her two mothers in unison. *"It is . . .*
*all . . . your fault. . . ."*

Tania lifted her head, anger smoldering in her
as she stared into Lear's exultant face. "They *don't*
think that," she snarled. "You're lying to me again!"
The anger ignited and took hold. "Is that all you can
do? Tell lies to make people do what you want?" She
bridled her head back and spat full in Lear's face.
"You're pathetic! Without your tricks you wouldn't get
a stray dog to follow you!"

"Way to go, Tania!" said Jade.

Lear stepped closer to her, so she could feel his
breath on her face, so she could see the ugly fire in his
eyes.

"I was going to let the flames of the Quellstone
Spire consume you, child," he snarled. "But I have
changed my mind." His hands closed around her
throat. "Your work is done here, seventh daughter of
a seventh daughter—the ways between the worlds are
open and they shall remain open for all eternity. It is
time for you to die."

The cruel hands tightened around her throat.
Titus and Rathina held her arms, Cordelia smiled on
as if witnessing no more than a fond embrace.

Jade writhed impotently, tears flooding her cheeks.
"Murderer! You filthy murderer!"

A voice spoke in the black bedlam of Tania's mind, like a shaft of light through thunderclouds.

*"Hold on! Keep it together for a few more seconds. I'm almost there!"*

*Edric?*

No. That was impossible. It was a final cruelty inflicted on her by Lear. Edric's voice at the moment of death—Edric's voice to remind her of what she was going to lose . . .

Galloping hooves, as loud in her head as the colliding of planets.

And then, high in the wall, she thought she saw a bright point of light.

She thought she heard the rumbling of falling stone.

The cavern trembled. The point of light widened and sent out threads across the cavern's wall. Great hulks of rock slid and fell. Blasts of stone sprayed out like shrapnel. Smoke belched. The world shook.

And away beyond Lear Tania saw the wall of the cavern come bursting in, showering rock, revealing a world of shining blue light. A man appeared riding a great black stallion. It was Edric, one hand raised, blue fire leaping from his fingers.

Lear turned, snarling. The blue fire came roaring through the air like a meteor. Lear fell back, lifting a hand and blocking the sapphire flames with his own red fire.

What was this? More illusions at life's end? More of Lear's tricks?

*"Tania, fight back!"* Edric's voice was in her head. *"Use your mind to close the ways between the worlds! Quickly now! Before it's too late!"*

Not an illusion. This was real. This was happening!

The hooves were gone from her brain, and she could think clearly again. There was a white light behind her eyes.

Edric came galloping across the black lake, spraying his blue fire at Lear, the Dark Arts of Faerie competing with the ancient sorceries of Gralach Hern, and for the moment, driving Lear back.

There was chaos and uproar in the cavern as the people of Faerie scattered from the spewing gush of rock and stone. Not even Lear's deceptions could blind them to the devastating power of Edric's arrival. Tania saw that he was not alone—at his back were a hundred knights, all dressed in the black livery of the Earldom of Weir. All armed with swords and spears and axes.

Tania wrenched herself free of Titus and Rathina. They didn't try to restrain her—they were staring at the horsemen in alarm and disbelief.

She saw the tumbling rocks of the Cavern of Heartsdelving splashing into the Regent's Canal, sending up flukes of water as the people fled, Mortals mingling with Faerie folk as they fought to save themselves. Several of the Red Knights were caught by the rocks, twisting and falling and disappearing under the avalanche. Horses screamed in terror, their hooves kicking at the air. Glass splintered in windows all along the canal. Cars came to a slewing halt on the road bridge, the passengers stunned with fear as rocks rained down on them, clanging on roofs and hoods, smashing through windshields. Pedestrians scrambled over one another in panic, cowering in doorways or stumbling in headlong flight along the pavements.

"Tania!" It was Jade's voice. "Shut it down! For god's sake, shut it down!"

Cordelia stood close by, staring around herself, her face blank with disbelief. Titus had drawn his crystal sword. A dreadful light of understanding was growing in Rathina's eyes.

Tania glanced over to where she had last seen Oberon and Titania and Eden—but there was too much chaos for her to spot them now in the pandemonium of the rushing crowds and the rolling pall of smoke that rose above the bouncing and tumbling rocks.

Edric's wild charge had been brought to a shuddering halt. Lear was fighting back, a fist of red fire beating now upon Edric's blue light, making him rock in the saddle, making the hooves of his horse slip and slither on the black lake so that horse and rider were close to going down.

The other riders of Weir were scattering, pursuing the Red Knights, swords whirling, spears flashing in the dark air.

Tania turned, pressing her open hands to the Quellstone Spire. And now that her bare flesh was in contact with the power of the Spire and her mind was clear, the full force of the spirits of Faerie flowed into her and became part of her.

She forced her mind to find a calm place in all the riot. A small empty spot where her thoughts could form in peace.

She concentrated in the special, impossible way that her gift allowed.

*Focus on London. Think of walking between the worlds. Think of stepping out of Faerie and into the Mortal World. Leave Faerie behind! Think! Think hard!*

Reality distorted and twisted around her. The sounds and sights of Faerie sloughed away. The Quellstone Spire was still hard and smooth under her hands, but the ground beneath her feet hardened into concrete. The crashing of rocks was muted—the shouting and calling of Faerie voices drifted off.

The Quellstone Spire had traveled with her through the realms, but the Cavern of Heartsdelving was gone, and Tania stood panting and shaking under the London sky, darkened at noon by the Pure Eclipse.

But not all things of Faerie had been shed. She had closed the ways between the worlds, but not before mayhem had been let loose on the streets of Camden Town. The air was filled with shouting and screaming and the blare of car horns—by the sound of hooves on tarmac, the slash of swords, the cries of warfare.

Rocks and boulders scattered the ground. Smoke drifted. On the patch of grass where the picnickers had sat, Lear and Edric continued their deadly struggle, the red and the blue fires crackling and flaring—the two protagonists half hidden in contesting flames. Edric was being slowly beaten back as Lear's leaping fires rained down on him.

But they were not the only fugitives from Faerie. Tania could see the knights of Gralach Hern galloping along the towpath and forcing their steeds up the stone stairway to the road-bridge—the horses stamping among the snarled traffic as terrified Mortals fled and were cut down. A man in a business suit stumbled and fell under the hooves. A girl in a summer dress screamed as a sword pierced her. Two teens in T-shirts tried to shelter an elderly man. A woman snatched her child from a stroller and cowered in a doorway as the horsemen cantered past.

But it was not only Lear's horsemen that had come through with Tania—many knights of Weir were also on the bridge and towpath, riding the red devils down, crystal swords striking sparks from the swords of red iron.

Jade was there, too, gasping for breath. And Titus and Rathina and Cordelia, all of them dragged through in Tania's wake.

Rathina was the first to act. "All lies! It was all deception and lies!" she cried. Snarling with rage, she leaped over the strewn boulders to where one of the Red Knights lay crushed by the rockfall. She ripped his iron sword from his hand, spinning, seeking an enemy.

Cordelia staggered, her face blanched. "Tania! I forgot . . . I was not strong enough to resist. . . ."

"That doesn't matter now!" shouted Jade. "What

matters is getting rid of these murderers!" She stared at Tania. "Can you *think* them out of here?"

"No. It doesn't work like that," Tania cried.

"Okay." Jade's voice was determined. "We've gotta find some weapons." She pointed to the stone stairway that led up onto the bridge. "You guys coming?" she called, leaping up the steps.

Cordelia and Titus chased after her, Titus brandishing his sword.

Tania ran as well but in the opposite direction—toward her embattled Edric.

Lear was pouring his fire over Edric, and despite all that he could do to defend himself, Edric was being beaten back, his cries filled with pain and rage. His horse reared, neighing in terror, its hooves at the very edge of the canal. Blue light still struggled in the deluge of red flame, but Tania could see from Edric's stricken face that his reserves of power were fading fast.

Even as she came close, Lear let loose a final, devastating explosion of fire. It detonated in the air, sending fireballs streaking across the sky, inundating Edric and his horse in a cataract of flame. If not for the protective powers of the Dark Arts, he would have been burned alive.

Tania reeled, blasted off her feet by the concussion. She heard Edric's horse scream. Edric arched from the saddle. She heard Lear howling with laughter.

Tania skidded along the concrete, her body seared by flame and battered by hot air. She hit against a wall, gasping and choking, the breath beaten out of her.

Fireballs were raining down on either side of the canal, crashing through roofs, bursting through windows, filling the world with flame.

Lear stood over Edric with his arms raised, his fingers on fire.

"Little boy!" Tania heard his voice over the crackle of the fires. "Little boy with his little box of tricks!" He gestured toward the sprawled body of the dead horse. A kind of lifeless animation twitched through the fallen animal. On broken legs and with bones protruding bloody through its hide, the horse rose to its hooves, its eyes on fire, its mane a trail of red flame.

Lear swung himself up into the saddle. "Now we shall ride!" he shouted. "The child may have thwarted the greatest of my ambitions for the moment, but I shall be lord of this realm, come what may!"

Lear urged the dead horse onward, to gallop along the towpath toward the stairs onto the bridge, a flame jutting from his fist like a sword of red fire.

Tania shrank into herself as the hooves clattered past her, but Lear did not see her—or he chose to ignore her as he urged the undead horse on to join up with the rest of his knights.

She lifted herself up, half blinded by fire and smoke, half deafened by the noise of the leaping flames.

Edric lay at the edge of the canal. All around him the concrete was scorched black and riven with deep, smoking cracks.

"Oh god—no!" Tania scrambled through the burning debris, crawling on all fours. She leaned over Edric, looking down at his face, grimed and scarred by the conflict. His eyes were wide open, staring at nothing, the silver reflecting the flames.

She held his face between trembling hands. "No!" She bent over, kissing him, her tears falling on his skin. "No! My love! Not dead! I won't let you be dead!"

But there was no breath in his body, no flicker in his unseeing eyes.

She cradled his head in her arms, her face to the dark sky.

"Help me! Please!" she shouted, not even knowing who or what she was calling to. "He can't die!"

A faint white glow vied with the ruddy flames. So wispy and insubstantial that she could hardly see it. But she knew it was there; she could feel it as much as see it. A white mist curling protectively around her—and in the mist she saw many faces. Some she recognized; some she knew only in her heart. Ann was there, and so were Georgina and Flora and Gracie and Marjorie—and with them were a host of others—the solemn faces of everyone she had ever been, their sad eyes filled with light, their souls singing. And among them was the girl with her own face: the floating, brilliant spirit of Princess Tania.

The princess reached down out of the white mist, and her hand pressed against Edric's chest. His chest rose, and he gave a choking cry as life returned and the air was drawn into his lungs.

"This is the last." Tania heard the princess's voice as if from a million miles away and across a gulf of centuries. "We may never meet again. . . . Farewell. Do great deeds and do not weep for our father—he will make his choice willingly. . . ."

"What do you mean?" called Tania. "I don't under-stand—what choice?"

But the white mist was gone. All along the canal side Lear's fires were raging. But Edric was coughing and gasping in her arms. He was alive.

# XXXI

Edric jerked up, staring wildly around himself. "Lear!" he spat. "Where is Lear?"

"You're not strong enough to fight him on your own," Tania said. "He almost killed you! He *did* kill you . . . if not for . . ."

Edric scrambled to his feet. "He has to be stopped, Tania! I haven't ridden the length of Faerie to see him victorious." He caught hold of her, pulling her to her feet, his eyes blazing silver. "I need to know what has happened," he said. "Forgive me. I need to know exactly what Lear has done." He pressed the flat of his hand to her temple.

Tania felt a dizzying sensation, as though their two minds were fusing. She saw a kaleidoscope of images in Edric's mind.

Arriving at the borders of Weir. Unable to enter. Using the Dark Arts to make a blue fire that slowly burned its way into the mystical barrier that Aldritch had set up. Knights of Weir confronting him, swords drawn.

"I would speak with your lord! Take my sword. Lead me to him, I beg you!"

And once within the barrier the shackles of Lear's enchantment falling away from his mind. Realizing with dread and horror that Lear was not banished—that he was manipulating the minds of everyone in Faerie—everyone save for those within Aldritch's mystic barrier. The urge to turn and speed back to the Royal Palace, to warn them—to save Tania. But no! That would never work. Lear's sorcery was too powerful.

The only option: go to Aldritch and seek his aid, ask to approach the place from which the age-old magicks of Weir had been drawn, use them to weave a spell to use against Lear.

The gallop to Caer Liel on its mountain crag. In the Obsidian Chamber thrown upon his face in front of the Lord of Weir. Understanding now that there was no army being gathered in Weir—realizing that Aldritch wished only to protect his people.

*"Good, my lord, I come to beg your aid! Do you not know the power that threatens all of Faerie, lord?"*

Aldritch's harsh voice: *"I know nothing of events beyond my borders, nor do I care. Why come you here, Master Chanticleer, treacherous lover of this realm's greatest enemy?"*

*"Tania is not your enemy! A greater threat has arisen! Will you not listen to me, my lord, and then make your judgment? I fear you do not know the truth—and nor do*

*you know of the peril that will engulf you and all the people of the Earldom of Weir."*

*"Speak—your life hangs in the balance!"*

Telling Aldritch of Lear and of his dreams of conquest. Aldritch realizing that Weir would not be immune—not once all of Faerie and the Mortal Realm were conquered. Realizing that even within their barrier they would not survive once the whole of Lear's might and venom was focused on them.

*"For the good of Weir we must ally ourselves with the lesser enemy to defeat the greater! What would you have me do?"*

*"I would draw on the old powers of this realm."*

*"So be it."*

Aldritch taking him to the dungeon chamber where the ancient Spellstone of Weir lay hidden. Edric touching his sword to the stone and drawing from its potency.

Gathering a hundred knights of Weir and leading them south. Galloping like the wind, his soul full to the brim with alchemy.

The galloping hooves louder and louder in Tania's head—the horses of Weir were coming to do battle with Prince Lear and his Red Knights.

And now Tania understood why the hooves had been so incessant in her mind—why they had tormented her.

Edric had poured the Dark Arts through her mind and body to bring her from the Mortal World—he had amplified the strength of the Seven Who Are One with the blue fire of his sinister Arts. Tania still had the shadow of those Dark Arts within her. They were a part of her now, and the crashing of the hooves in her brain was the price she had to pay for allowing herself to be tainted by those Arts.

Even as all this was revealed in flashing images in Tania's mind, so she knew that a similar transfer of memories was being disclosed to Edric.

They stood facing each other, gasping for breath, eyes locked. As though on a single impulse they lurched together, kissing, but only for the briefest of moments.

Edric's eyes shimmered with silver light. "Together!" he breathed.

"Together!" she replied.

The exchange of memories had taken mere seconds. Smoke and fire still belched from the houses all along the canal, the red flames throwing sinister reflections down into the water, the foul-smelling smoke crawling across the concrete. The trees were also ablaze, crackling leaves cascading down as the branches blossomed fire. Cries and screams still echoed from the road-bridge. The Red Knights of Gralach Hern could be seen fighting grimly with Edric's black-clad warriors. Riderless horses galloped, foam flying from their lips. Horses lost their footing along the canal and plunged into the water. A knight of Weir hurtled from the bridge with a red sword in his heart. A red rider roared his triumph from the parapet but was caught in the middle of his victory cry, arching back as a sword pierced him through. He slumped from the saddle, and Rathina leaped up to take his place, swinging her bloodied sword above her head and shouting, "Aurealis! Aurealis for Faerie!" The horse reared and went cantering across the bridge.

Tania's heart leaped at her sister's courage.

"My knights will deal with Lear's horsemen," said Edric, catching hold of Tania's hand. "We have to find Lear!"

Together they ran for the steps onto the bridge. A terrible sight met their eyes. Under the unnaturally dark noonday sky, the road was clogged with crashed and abandoned cars and vans. And riding this way and that through the vehicles were the embattled horsemen, hacking at one another with swords, their steeds rising with flailing hooves as they wheeled and cut and wheeled again.

Terrified people were still to be seen, fleeing the battlefield or huddling together with shock and disbelief in their faces. Ordinary people: teenagers on Rollerblades, shopkeepers, tourists with cameras dangling around their necks. And the flames were spreading, taking hold and howling into the air, as wild as forest fires, bathing everything with a ghastly red luster.

Through the rising smoke the white corona of the sun could be seen glowing behind the wheel of the black moon. But already the full eclipse was almost done, and as Tania stared upward, she saw a flash like a sparkling diamond as the sun began to emerge again.

They leaped the black rail that lined the roadway. Edric sprang onto the roof of a car. "I see him!" he shouted, pointing along the road. "I see Lear!" A Red Knight urged his horse toward Edric, his sword a crimson whir. Edric ducked the sweeping blow and snatched at the man's arm as he thundered past, wrenching him from the saddle.

In a swift, liquid movement Edric took the man's place in the saddle, quickly catching up the reins and bringing the horse to a curving halt. Tania ran forward, taking hold of Edric's down-stretched arm, bounding up to sit behind him.

Edric dug his heels into the horse's flanks, and they lurched forward, weaving through the debris and the skewed cars—following Lear.

Tania saw Cordelia on the other side of the road. She had found herself a crystal sword and was battling fiercely with an unhorsed Red Knight. Titus was up on the dented roof of a white van in the middle of the road, swinging a long spear, holding off several riders. He must have vaulted to the top of the van without making skin contact with the metal—but all the same, the proximity of so much Isenmort must be a torment to him. Jade was with him, and she was wielding one of the red iron swords with a deadly, terrified fury.

Rathina was also close by, her horse rearing as she struck down hard on the neck of one of the Red Knights surrounding the van.

"What are we going to do when we reach Lear?" Tania shouted into Edric's ear. "How do we beat him?"

"You will be the sword; I will be the shield," Edric called back, his words almost ripped from his mouth by their speed.

"I don't know what that means!"

Their horse leaped the body of a dead knight of Weir. Edric made a grasping gesture with his hand. The dead knight's crystal sword jerked up from the tarmac, twirling through the air.

Tania didn't need to be told—she snatched the sword out of the air, her fingers tight on the hilt.

Edric's voice came to her again on the wind. "I'm going to try and contain his witchcrafts," he called. "You have to kill him, Tania! You have to kill him with the sword—you'll only have a few seconds. You mustn't hesitate."

From the depths of her soul a voice rang out. *No! I can't do that! I can't kill him! How can you ask me to do such a thing?*

"Tania?" There was a desperate edge to Edric's voice. "Do you get what you need to do?"

"Yes! I understand!"

"Don't be heroic! Take him by surprise."

"Yes."

They were galloping now alongside the concrete and glass walls of a supermarket, the flames of burning buildings reflected darkly in the rows of windows. They were galloping past shops and offices and side streets that Tania had known all of her Mortal life. They were galloping along Kentish Town Road on a Faerie horse—and the fires and the deaths and the chaos that surrounded them were all her fault.

A desperate determination clenched inside her like a stone fist closing about her heart.

Lear must die.

They were coming close now to the confluence of several streets—to Britannia Junction, where Chalk Farm Road and Kentish Town Road and Camden Road and Camden High Street and Parkway all met. Camden Town tube station was there. On an ordinary day a hundred buses crisscrossed the busy streets.

They crossed Buck Street. There was no one on the pavements now. A few desperate people cowered in the shops, unable to grasp what was happening. Tania saw two bodies lying in blood. Innocent Mortals caught up and destroyed in Lear's madness.

Edric pulled the horse up about fifty yards before the junction. Three or four double-decker buses were stalled at the crossroads—one of them on fire. The battle between the knights of Weir and the deadly horsemen of Gralach Hern was still raging, and it was impossible to see who was getting the upper hand as the horses darted to and fro through the empty cars that littered the streets with doors hanging wide and drivers gone.

Tania could make out the dark shape of Prince Lear rising in the stirrups at the crossroads, hurling bolts of fire from his fingertips as though he wanted to set all the world aflame.

"He mustn't see me," said Edric, twisting in the saddle. "He thinks I'm dead—we have to keep it that way." He slid from the horse's back. "I'll try and drain his power. If he doesn't realize it's me, he won't know where to strike back."

Tania stared down at him. "What should I do?"

"Give me a few moments to get into position, then get to him as quickly as you can. When you see his fire failing—strike quick and strike hard. You'll only have a few seconds."

"Yes. Yes, I understand."

Edric reached his hand up, and Tania took it for a moment.

"You and me for always!" he said.

"Yes. You and me!"

He broke the grip and went running across the road, keeping low, hugging the shop-fronts as he headed for the junction.

For a split second Tania thought the hooves had come back into her head—but then she realized it was her own heartbeat that she was hearing.

Fighting was going on all around her, flames were rising and smoke was blowing on the wind—but for a brief time Tania sat in the saddle and waited.

Edric slipped out of sight. She paused, glancing over her shoulder. Titus and Jade had jumped down from the white van and were fighting their way toward Cordelia. There were only a handful of Red Knights near them now—and even as Tania watched, Rathina's sword stabbed and another went cartwheeling from the saddle.

Tania turned toward the junction again. It was time.

She dug her heels into her horse's flanks, leaning forward, snapping the reins as the voices of courage and fear contended inside her head.

*Are you afraid?*

*Yes.*

*How afraid?*

*I think I'm going to die.*

*And yet . . . ?*

*I'll die with Edric. We'll die together if that's our fate. Together!*

*Or Lear might die.*

*Yes, Lear might die.*

*Do not hesitate. Strike swift and sure.*

*Yes. Yes!*

Lear was facing away from her, but she could hear his laughter as he flung his fireballs into the shops and offices and pubs and banks that lined the confluence of the five streets. A fist of flame crashed into the entrance of the tube station, sending the windows bursting outward. Tania prayed that no one had taken shelter in there.

All around him cars were burning. The smoke was thick and caustic in her nose and throat. It smarted in her eyes and stung in her chest.

She was close now—close enough to see something so ordinary and so astonishing that she could hardly take it in. Something she had known of all her life but which had never held any significance for her before.

Across the wide junction, beyond an open-backed blue van abandoned and in flames, beyond everyday traffic lights and black rails, beyond a pedestrian crossing, was a pub with a dark red fascia and open brown-wood doors. And above the doors, picked out in gold, were words she had seen a thousand times before.

The pub was called The World's End.

# XXXII

Lear rose in the saddle of the dead Faerie horse and threw a ball of fire in through the open doors of the pub. A moment later the whole of the front erupted in a rolling pall of oily, fiery black smoke.

The World's End.

Laughing still, Lear loosed another ball of flame, this time into the tall white stone face of the bank on the far side of the junction. But the fire sputtered and failed, breaking up in mid-flight and cascading down in a rain of dying sparks.

Lear reeled in the saddle as though some invisible force had struck him.

Edric!

Again Tania urged her horse forward, eating up the yards between them, her sword ready in her fist.

Lear crashed down in the saddle, all laughter quenched as he rolled groaning from side-to-side. The flames that surrounded them began to falter, as though their fires were fueled by Lear—as though they would fail if he failed.

*Don't hesitate! Strike hard and swift!* Edric's voice in her head.

Lear's head was turning as though he was trying to seek out the source of his power loss. He gave a shout, his arm stretched out, his fingers pointing.

Edric was there—crouching in a doorway, blue fire flickering at his fingertips.

"Not dead, boy?" Lear cried. "Then die now, and be rid of you!"

Lear roared with anger, red flames licking along his outstretched arm.

Tania was almost upon him.

At last, he became aware of her. He spun around, snarling, his eyes blazing with anger.

She lifted her sword, but as she brought her arm down, the vicious features changed and she saw Oberon's face under her blade.

"Wouldst you strike me down, daughter?"

With a choking cry Tania managed to deflect her blow.

A fist of fire burst from Lear's fingers, punching into her chest, driving her backward out of the saddle as her horse galloped on. She went crashing down onto the roadway with bone-breaking force, knowing she had failed—knowing Oberon's face had been no more than a trick to make her hesitate. . . .

The sword rang on the road, jarred from her fingers.

She heard Edric's voice calling. "Tania!"

She saw crimson fire arc through the air. She saw

Edric smashed to the ground, his blue fire smothered. The fires leaped up again all around them. She heard Lear roaring with laughter.

He turned his horse and walked it slowly toward where she lay, her whole body hurting, her soul in torment. He dismounted and stood over her.

*I've failed.*

"You would kill your uncle, child?" he asked. "'Tis most naughty of you! I must find a punishment to fit so heinous a crime!" He held out his hand, and Tania saw a small amber ball on his palm. "I shall not end you, Tania. No, indeed. You will be with me for all eternity." He smiled. "You will outlive the stars, Tania—trapped forever in amber."

The amber ball lifted from his palm and floated down toward her.

But before it reached her, she heard a strange, growing, rushing sound. A darkness like a huge black arrowhead moved into the corner of her eye. She heard a shrill chattering noise.

A flock of starlings hurtled between her and Lear, smashing the amber ball aside, so that it cracked and burst on the tarmac. Lear bridled back from the rush of birds, his face livid. But more birds came: pigeons mobbing him, pecking him and beating at him with their wings.

Tania scrambled away, struggling to master the agony in her body, fighting to get to her feet.

Lear's arms burst through the birds, sending many

of them spinning through the air or crumpling to the ground.

He turned his head, glaring past Tania to where Cordelia stood calling in a strange, high-pitched voice.

"Birds of the air you'd set upon me, child?" Lear raged. "Fool! All shall burn!"

Tania tottered to her feet, seeking her fallen sword. But the ground all around her was alive and moving. Rats were swarming from all corners, rats in the thousands, running forward like a flood of black oil, making for Lear.

He shouted in anger as the multitude of rats swarmed over his feet and clawed their way up his legs.

And even as he stumbled and fell back under the assault, Rathina and Titus and Jade came running forward with swords raised.

"Be gone!" howled Lear, standing firm, his body wreathed in red fire. The rats were blasted away from him, many screaming and in flames. The birds sped up into the sky, crying out and screeching as they fled the rising fires.

Rathina launched herself on him, sword whirling. A thrust of his hand sent a wall of fire at her, taking her off her feet and throwing her back.

"Rathina!" Titus shouted as she struck hard against the side of a car and slid to the ground. He snarled, eyes blazing as he threw himself at Lear. "You shall die for that!"

Jade was with him, moving with a silken grace as

she bounded forward, her sword poised at shoulder height, its point at Lear's throat.

She lunged at him, but his arm came up with deadly speed, striking the sword from her hand. She swiveled on one leg, her foot raised for a kick. He snatched at her ankle, pulling her off balance, tossing her to the ground.

A scream was torn from Tania's throat. "Jade!"

Titus struck next, but his blade kindled to flame and spun away from him as Lear's fires poured down over him and drove him to his knees.

An eerie trilling sound was coming from Cordelia's lips. The sky had begun to brighten at the end of the eclipse, but it darkened again now as fast-moving clouds of small flying creatures came pouring down over the rooftops. Tania felt herself battered and beaten as the insects careened past her. She saw bees and wasps and flies in the throng, beetles and butterflies and moths and dragonflies—all moving with a single purpose, all congregating on Lear.

The air was rank with the stench of scorched feathers and burning fur, but for the moment Lear's fires were being swamped by the deluge of insects that Cordelia had called down upon him.

Tania was aware of other fights still being waged around them as the Red Knights battled savagely with the men of Weir. But it was not the horsemen of Gralach Hern who wielded the true power here. It was Lear who had to be beaten.

She could hear distant police sirens. More people

coming to be killed by Lear—more fuel for his hellish fires.

Tania heard a sharp bark behind her. She turned. A fox stood staring at her. Lying by its feet was her lost sword.

"Thank you," she said, gasping and grabbing the sword up.

The fox stared into her eyes for a moment, then loped off to join the attack on Lear. More foxes were streaking along the roads—and there were cats with them, too, and running dogs, their jaws gaping and tongues lolling. It was as though every animal within a mile of this place had heeded Cordelia's desperate call.

*"Now, Tania! Do it now!"* Edric's voice in her head. Weak but alive!

"Yes!"

She ran forward into the swarming insects.

Lear was at the heart of the storm of fizzing and droning wings, his arms flailing, his fingers clawing insects out of his eyes.

He turned, seeing Tania—seeing her sword slicing toward him.

His face morphed once more and became the gentle, kindly face of Clive Palmer.

"Please, sweetheart—don't do it!"

"No!" Tania shouted. "Enough of your tricks! *Enough!*"

Using all her strength and all her willpower, she plunged the sword into his chest.

He fell without a sound, but all around her she heard wailing and screaming as the knights of Gralach Hern burst into living flames and were consumed and turned to smoke and ash.

The armies of insects drew off and the clamor of the other animals ceased. Tania stared around herself in a daze. Lear lay dead at her feet, his face old and gray and twisted with evil, blood oozing from his chest, staining his dark clothes. His fires shrank. A breeze blew the smoke away over the rooftops.

Above her the sun was already more than half free of the moon's dark embrace.

The Pure Eclipse was done, and a great and powerful evil had been destroyed.

Titus helped Rathina to her feet. Cordelia was knee-deep in dogs and cats and foxes and rats, her shoulders and arms covered in birds, insects in her hair and more of them perching on her fingers with wings buzzing.

Jade was sitting up, her eyes glassy but her face split by a wide grin as she looked up at Tania.

"You beat him!" she said. "But that was awful! Fighting for real is nothing like tai chi class!"

"I don't imagine it is." Tania helped her to her feet.

From across the junction, Edric came, limping and battered, but with a bright light in his wide brown eyes.

Tania dropped her sword and ran into his arms.

"You did it!" He gasped as they embraced.

"We did it!" she said, clinging tight. "We all did it!"

* * *

Tania and Edric stood hand-in-hand by the Quellstone Spire. All the riders of Weir were with them on the canal towpath, the wounded tended by their comrades, the dead lying over the saddles of their horses. Cordelia was there also, and Titus and Rathina.

Jade stood in front of Tania. "Will you be safe?" she asked.

"I think so," said Tania. She smiled tiredly. "I'm sure we will. I'm going to use the Spire to give me enough power to get us all back to Faerie. As to what happens after that . . . I really don't know."

Jade looked at Edric. "You look after her, okay?" she said. "Or you'll have me to answer to."

"We'll look after each other," said Edric.

The sound of sirens was growing louder.

"You'd better get out of here before the cops arrive," Jade said. She smiled at Tania. "I'll go straight to your place, right? I'll let your folks know what's happened, and that you're okay."

"And tell them I'll find a way to get back to them," Tania added. "I don't know how right now, but I will find a way!"

Rathina rested her hand on Jade's shoulder. "You are most welcome to come with us and dwell in Faerie, Mistress Jade," she said solemnly. "Songs shall be sung of your warrior's heart."

Jade smiled. "Trust me, I'm tempted. It'd save having to explain to my folks where I've been for the past week! But I can't come—sorry. There's no way I can live without my iPod and my computer and my mobile phone." She stepped back. "But you guys are welcome to visit anytime you like. Just try not to land in my mum's pond next time, all right?"

"We shall come if fate allows," said Cordelia. She turned to Tania. "Let's be gone, sister—I'd know how things fare in our homeland now that Lear is dead."

"Yes." Tania looked fondly at Jade. "I'll be seeing you, okay?"

"You bet!"

A burst of emotion sent Tania surging forward, and the two friends hugged tightly. After a few precious moments Jade backed off and made for the stone steps up to the bridge.

Tania swallowed hard, turning to Edric. "I wish people hadn't died. . . ." she said.

"Every death is a fearsome loss," said Rathina. "But without you the toll could have been very much higher."

"Sister?" said Cordelia. "Quickly now!"

Tania pressed her palm against the Quellstone Spire. She felt the power flowing. She concentrated.

The world rippled around her, and the ways between the worlds opened.

# Epilogue

Evening was falling over Faerie. The evening of the day of the Pure Eclipse. The sky in the west was bathed in a red so deep that it seemed the heavens were drenched in newly spilled blood. The sun was gone, and in the east the first stars were twinkling.

A gathering of Faerie folk stood on a grassy ridge above Fortrenn Quay. A winding stairway of split logs led down to the quay itself, where the *Cloud Scudder* lay at anchor, shining in the growing night like something that might have been fashioned by a jeweler.

As the sun yielded the sky to the night, so lights began to spring up all along the stairway—and more glowed bright in the quay and aboard the ship. All along the almost immeasurable length of the Royal Palace, torches ignited in windows and on battlements and upon the roofs of high towers and spires, like a linked chain of jewels winding away beyond sight.

Tania and others of the Royal Household were standing in a ring on the grass, facing inward, their heads bowed. They had formed the circle as the sun had touched the horizon, and they had neither moved nor spoken till the sun was gone.

They were mourning the dead. The dead not only of Faerie; they grieved for everyone who had fallen victim to Prince Lear's insane ambitions. They grieved most especially for the knights of Weir who had lost their lives in the final battle and for the innocent Mortals who had died in a struggle they would never comprehend.

Tania's hand was in Edric's hand. He held hands with Cordelia, and she with Hopie. Brython was there also, and Sancha and Earl Valentyne and Eden. The King and Queen. The earl marshall and Lady Lucina with their two sons. Titus held hands with Rathina, and Rathina with Tania, thus closing the circle.

At last the King raised his head. "In silence we have remembered them," he said. "And in the silent moments of our lives may we ever remember those who are gone, both friend and stranger alike." His eyes flashed in the dying day. "May we never forget the name of Lear Aurealis, my brother, whose broken spirit caused such destruction and disharmony. And by remembering, make it so that such a thing may never happen again." He released Earl Valentyne's hand. "And now we must enact the final part of this tragedy and pluck for ourselves some measure of joy for the times that are to come." He stepped out of the circle of people, taking the Queen by the arm. "Let us to the *Cloud Scudder*," he said. "Let us to Tirnanog!"

The ring broke up, and the Faerie folk wended

their slow and solemn way down to the waiting galleon. Tania held on tightly to Edric's hand, buoyed by his presence at her side. She couldn't help notice that Titus walked with Rathina and that they seemed to be speaking softly together.

As they all walked up the gangplank, Tania heard Admiral Belial calling orders to his crew. Ropes snaked loose. Mariners hung in the rigging. White sails were unrolled to shine like moonlight under the starry sky. And at the stern the standards of Faerie were unfurled, the yellow sun of the King and the pure white moon of the Queen flying in the growing wind.

When all were aboard, the gangplank was drawn up and the shining galleon slipped smoothly away from the quay and glided out into the estuary of the River Tamesis.

Tania stood at the prow, hand-in-hand with Edric, gazing out over the wide waters.

"I wish . . ." Her voice faded.

Edric smiled feelingly at her. "You wish someone else could have killed Lear?"

"Yes." She sighed. "I keep seeing it in my mind—every time I close my eyes. I see Lear with my father's face—and the sword—and everything. It's a horrible thing to have in my head."

"The pain of it will fade in time," Edric said.

"I hope so. . . ."

They stood together in silence for a while, the wind whipping Tania's hair, the fine sea spray tingling on her skin.

Two voices began to chant in a melodic chorus. Tania and Edric turned. Oberon and Eden were standing in the center of the deck, side-by-side, their faces lifted, their blue eyes shining.

A shiver of wonder and delight ran down Tania's back at the sound of her father and her sister calling in unison. They were singing for the spirits to come together and raise the great white galleon from the waves.

As they chanted, Oberon and Eden lifted their arms, hands palm-upward, fingers spread. No one upon the decks of the galleon moved. All eyes were on the two singers.

"Do you hear that?" Tania whispered.

Edric leaned close. "What?"

"A flute—I swear I can hear a flute."

"I don't hear anything."

Tania tilted her head, trying to get a fix on the faint melody. "No! It's gone." She let out a sad breath. "Maybe I imagined it."

The deck began to tilt under her, and she and Edric caught hold of the bow rail to save themselves from slipping.

And as Oberon and Eden sang, the *Cloud Scudder* rose from the sea, and the horizon fell away as they sailed up into the star-filled night.

Night-dark forests and rolling hills and glimmering rivers and sleepy hamlets fled away below the *Cloud*

*Scudder* as she sailed the skies of Faerie, heading arrow-swift into the far west. Tania stood at the rail, alone now, lost in thoughts.

A banquet was being arranged, and Edric had been called away to help.

The moon was so huge and close that she felt she could almost have reached out and touched its shining face.

She heard soft footsteps and turned her head to see Titania step up to the rail at her side. "All is in readiness for the meal," she said. "Will you come now?"

"Yes, of course." Tania looked into her mother's eyes. "Why do I feel sorrier for the people of the Mortal World who died?" she asked. "So many of us died here, but I feel worse about the people in London. Why is that?"

"Perhaps because they were the more innocent. Lear was of our world, not theirs." She sighed softly. "They surely have evils enough of their own without the escapes of Faerie bringing fresh destruction to them."

"How are they going to cope with what happened?"

"Mortals are very resilient, Tania—you know that," said Titania, resting her arm across Tania's shoulders. "They will say it was an act of terrorism or perhaps a gas main blowing up—and they will mourn and grieve. And then they will remake the broken buildings and mend the cracked roadways, and they will perhaps erect a monument to those who died. And the families will remember their loved ones for always, and others will remember what happened on occasion, and the Mortal World will turn, and old folk will die, and babes will be born, and life will continue." She smiled. "Mortals are a resilient breed, Tania."

"Jade will tell my folks what happened," Tania said. "And I *will* find a way to get through to them, even if Aldritch never allows the barriers to be lifted." She frowned. "But there's something I forgot—something I wish I'd asked Jade to do."

"What is that?"

"Connor," said Tania. "I should have asked her to go find Connor and make sure he's okay. He was pretty freaked the last time I saw him. I'd hate to think that his whole life was wrecked because of what happened. I mean, it's not like it was his fault."

Titania smiled gently. "Come with me. I think perhaps I can help ease your mind."

Puzzled, Tania followed her mother belowdecks. They came to a cabin fitted out with white furnishings. To one side was a small table, and in the middle of the table stood a bowl of clear crystal, brimming with water.

Tania dipped her fingers into the water. Ripples spread.

"When the water becomes still, think of Connor and see what is revealed," said Titania.

Tania leaned over the bowl, almost holding her breath as she stared into the wrinkled water. Gradually the ripples died away. Tania could not have said that there was a moment when she was looking into clear water and another moment when she was seeing something else.

But in the mirror of Titania's will Tania found herself gazing into a modern hospital ward, as though seeing the scene through a roving camera lens. People in green scrubs were running to and fro. Other people lay on beds divided by curtains. There was a sense of controlled chaos.

"It's an ER," Tania murmured.

Swing doors burst inward. A man lay on a gurney that came thrusting between the doors, pushed at speed by running paramedics. An urgent voice called, "Automobile accident. Victim has multiple fractures and suspected pneumothorax. BP 134 over 78. Pulse 108."

"Bring him over here," said a voice that Tania recognized.

A calm, steady voice.

"Nurse—we need to intubate this man, stat!" called Connor as the man was wheeled into a bay. He leaned over the victim. "We're going to get you stabilized," he said, his voice firm and reassuring. "Do you have any medical conditions we ought to know about . . . ?"

The vision vanished as though a white curtain had been drawn between Tania and the world within the bowl. She stepped back, blinking.

"Was that real?" she asked, gazing at her mother, feeling a little giddy.

"It was real," Titania answered.

Tania grinned. "He's going to be all right."

"I think you need not fear for Connor Estabrook," said the Queen. "His life is set fair. He will do great and good things, and the lost two weeks will not weigh overmuch upon him."

"I knew he wasn't really a bad person," Tania said. "The stuff he had to try and deal with here—it would have sent anyone a bit screwy." She let out a long, relieved breath. "I'm glad for him—I felt so guilty."

"Then let guilt be gone!" said Titania. "Banish all care, Tania. Come—the King awaits. We shall have one final meal together. . . ."

Tania hesitated. "What do you mean?" she asked. "Why final . . . ?"

The Queen smiled. "I meant a final meal ere we reach Tirnanog. Nothing more, child. Come—all your sisters are there at table; let us not keep them waiting!"

All Tania's sisters and all the other members of the Royal Family were gathered at the long oval table. There was much laughter between the dinner guests, and talk of old times past—of childhood days and of adventures and festivities and birthday surprises, of games of wing-tag along the corridors of the Royal Palace, of swimming in the Tamesis by moonlight. Of voyages to the outlying islands, and of trysts with the strange and secretive merfolk. Of feasts and balls and of the skies bright and noisy with firiencraft—and there was nothing that Tania did not remember now! Nothing that did not come alive in her mind as it was recalled.

But after a while a lieutenant of Admiral Belial's crew came to the door of the cabin.

"We are here, sire," he said.

Cordelia was the first to jump up and run from the room, her face shining with sudden joy.

"Where are we?" asked Tania.

"You shall see," said Hopie.

They all quit the cabin and went up on deck. They had come to a halt over a dark, hilly landscape. A boat was being readied. Cordelia was already aboard.

Tania leaned over the rail. She guessed they must be a hundred yards or so above the hills. She saw a patch of water. A lake. And close by its bank, she saw a small campfire.

"Where are we?" she asked.

"In the north of Sinadon," said Eden. "Close to the borders of Weir. We have paused in our journey to pick up the one family member who is missing."

Tania frowned, confused for a moment. A missing family member? "But . . ." And then it struck her. "Bryn!"

"Bryn, indeed!" said Oberon, coming to her side. "His sad exile is over—he shall learn that his wife is alive and well."

"Oh, that's so great!" said Tania breathlessly.

The small boat spiraled down into the darkness.

It was hard to tell exactly what was going on down there, but Tania thought she saw a dark figure by the fire—and also some larger shapes. Unicorns, probably, she guessed. In his grief at the loss of his new bride, it would be likely that Bryn Lightfoot would console himself with the animals that he loved.

The boat rose again, and Cordelia and Bryn stepped out onto the deck of the *Cloud Scudder*, their faces filled with perfect delight.

It was dawn. The sky was white behind the fanged mountains of Hy Brassail, etching them black and sharp in the high airs. The *Cloud Scudder* lay at anchor in the wide bay with the rocky shoreline that Tania and Edric and Rathina had last seen at the end of their long land-bound quest for the Divine Harper. The beaches of heaped, coral-colored pebbles led up to green foothills. Tania could even see the mouth of the very cave where they had been tied up and dumped by Lord Balor.

The Limitless Ocean stretched away to the western horizon, its restless surface glittering in the growing light. Towering clouds glided across the sky, shape-shifting, endlessly transformed by the sculpting wind.

The sails of the Royal Galleon were furled. Almost everyone was on deck, everyone save the King and Queen and Princess Eden. There was a sense of watchfulness and anticipation. For the time being the land in the sky was hidden from them, and without some guidance no one knew how they might find Tirnanog. Tania assumed Oberon and Titania and their oldest daughter must be belowdecks considering their options.

A voice called from high on the mainmast. "Something comes! Look yonder!"

Tania strained up and saw an arm pointing land-ward. She ran to the rail along with many others. A sinuous white shape was undulating its way down the beach.

"'Tis a dragon, be most sure!" someone called. "To arms, lest it attack!"

"No!" Edric sprang onto the ship's rail. "I know this beast. It will not do us any harm."

"The Great Salamander," Tania said breathlessly as the long, low creature came to the water's edge and slithered into the foaming surf. The last time she had encountered this uncanny beast, it had used its claws to rip her back open and release her wings. Then it had shown her the way to Tirnanog. "It is a friend!" she called.

The white shape glided through the water and came climbing easily up the side of the hull. People backed away as it rose above the rail. Its tongue flick-ered and its bulging yellow eyes stared this way and that.

Lithely it came sliding onto the deck, its white scales gleaming, its long wedge-shaped head turning from side to side. From its blunt muzzle to the end of its wide, ridged tail it was at least three yards long; it was no surprise that almost all the Faerie folk drew away from it in alarm.

Cordelia did not shrink back. She stood gazing at the salamander in wonder and delight. "Hail and well met, sirrah," she said, bowing to the creature. "My name is Cordelia Aurealis. I would know you better."

"Who summoned me?" hissed the salamander, and many gasped and stared to hear the animal using human speech.

"I did," said a voice from behind the crowd. The people parted, and Eden stepped forward. "And are you the door-warden of Tirnanog?"

The gimlet eyes of the beast turned to Tania. "Ask her," it hissed. "She knows the pain and the peril of knocking upon that door!" The tongue flickered again, and Tania almost felt that the creature was smiling a sinister smile.

"Will you show us the way to the Divine Harper's land?" Tania asked.

The salamander raised a foreleg, and the long curved claws glinted like scimitars. "Would you go there again, Alios Foltaigg?" it asked. "Would you revisit the agony and the ecstasy?"

"Nay, good beast," said Oberon, moving through the throng. "My daughter's trials are done for the moment. It is I who would speak with the Harper. I have old pledges to renew."

The Salamander looked long and hard at him. "And do you know the price of your petition?"

"I do."

"And you'll pay it willingly?"

"I will."

There was a pause. "So be it," said the Salamander.

It glided across the deck, and everyone fell back to let it pass. At the far rail it lifted its long head and roared. A gush of golden fire issued from its mouth, streaming up into the sky.

The flames condensed and hardened and resolved into golden steps that led a long winding course into the clouds. And Tania saw that one of the clouds hung immobile in the upper airs and that it shone with a blinding light, as though a sun was trapped in its towering dome.

Titania came to the King's side, and for a long moment they stood together, gazing into each other's eyes without speaking. Then Oberon turned and gazed over all the people gathered there.

Tania felt a sudden unease. She grabbed her father's hands. "What's wrong?" she asked.

He smiled and rested his hand warmly against her cheek. "Nothing is wrong. All will be put into balance, child. Have no fear. The folk of Faerie will be Immortal once more. All will be made well."

She swallowed hard. "And you'll be okay?"

"I will." He leaned forward and kissed her forehead.

"It is time!" hissed the Salamander. "The path is clear, but it will fade quickly. Go! Go, lord of Faerie!"

With a final lingering look at his daughters and at the Queen, Oberon turned and began to walk with slow grace up the burning golden stairway. And as he rose from step to step, so the stair burned away and vanished behind him.

Everyone watched in silence as Oberon climbed into the blue sky, until at last he was just a black shape against the burning whiteness of the cloud. Then he seemed to step over some shining threshold, and the blazing whiteness closed in on itself like an iris and the stairway was gone.

Tania turned to where the Salamander had been standing, but the beast was gone.

"What are your orders, your grace?" Admiral Belial asked the Queen.

She started as though his voice had shaken her out of deep thoughts. She turned, her eyes shining. "We shall wait," she said. "Word will come betimes. Be most sure—when it is done, we shall know."

Tania found Edric standing at the prow of the ship, gazing out over the ocean.

"I was wondering something," he said as she snuggled against him.

"Like what?"

"I was wondering what price the Harper will make the King pay for renewing the covenant."

"We'll know soon enough—one way or the other," she said.

They stood together looking at the sunlit ocean for a quiet moment as it rippled away and away into forever.

"Edric?"

"Yes?"

"Ask me." She looked into his brown eyes, her voice husky with emotion. "Ask me again."

He turned, taking her in his arms. "Ask you what?"

"You know." She traced the contours of his cheeks

and eyebrows with her fingertips. "You *know*."

"Are you sure?" he asked, his voice trembling.

"I am."

He hesitated, as though summoning all his courage. "Tania Aurealis, Princess of Faerie—Anita Palmer, daughter of Mortal parents—will you marry me?"

A gladness like leaping flames filled her. "Yes," she said, lifting her face to kiss him. "Yes, I will."